Mark of Ancients

Kay C. Rice

Trigger Warning

This book contains content that may be triggering. Contains explicit language, physical violence, death, anxiety representation, murder, and fade to black sexual content.

To: My younger self.

We did it!

To all those who believed in me, thank you.

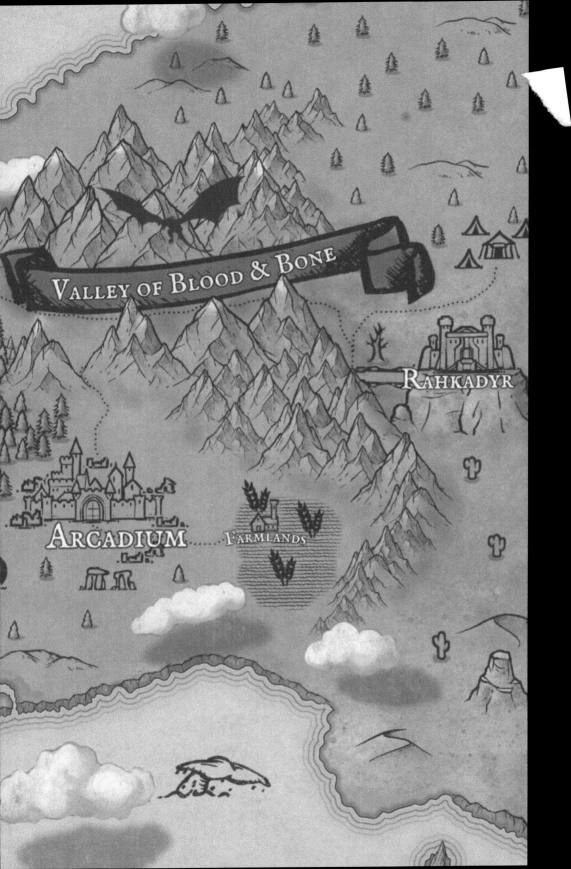

Before

Death only comes for us once, *usually* . . .

The smell of war is pungent. Death and decay surround me and the ever-present cries of pain hang in the air. We lost.

Death calls to me, tugging at the corners of my mind.

Not yet.

My ears ring and the throbbing in my skull makes my head swim. I stifle a scream as I struggle to sit up, biting down on the inside of my lip hard enough for the copper taste of blood to fill my mouth. The sharp pain shakes my body, as a steady flow of deep crimson pours from a gaping hole in my side.

Breathe, I remind myself.

I scan my surroundings, the once beautiful meadow now covered in bodies. The purple flowers litter the ground, now stained red. I manage to get to my feet, despite the nauseating pain throughout my body. Even though no life remains in the meadow, I pray to the Ancients he isn't among the lost.

I fall into a slain beast, the blue scales glistening in the afternoon sun.

"Find her!" A man's voice pierces through my thoughts.

Peeking around the large tail, three men come into view. The sword of a fallen soldier lays at my feet, still clutched in his hands. Tears sting my eyes. My second, Sam. A dozen of our enemies lay around him, showcasing his battle till the brutal end. I say a quick prayer for his soul to peacefully pass from this world to the next. "Until we meet again, my friend," I whisper.

"Ravina?" I hear the name echo through my mind. Relief washes over me like the rain, but dread follows closely behind.

"Ciena?" I let the reality hang between us. The threat is still real and she needs to stay hidden, no matter the cost. I rip my shirt and tie it around my waist, hissing as I pull the fabric tighter.

A bow sits not far from me, the few scattered arrows around me will have to do. I start to gather as many arrows as I can without being spotted. A thick bead of sweat rolls down my temple.

"Is she . . ." I hold my breath, not able to finish the thought.

The heavy footsteps of the men get closer.

"She is safe, playing at my feet," she assures me.

The relief feels like a boulder lifted from my chest. *"Thank you."*

I pull an arrow from my quiver and let it rest in my fingers. A deep breath fills my lungs; *One, two . . .* I pull the string taut, ignoring the dizziness. . . *three.* The arrow whistles through the air, landing with a thunk.

I duck behind my hiding place and listen.

"You are hurt, I can feel it." She says, her worry rattling through my bones.

"I'm fine." I draw my bow, muscle memory guiding the string back. I creep around the far side of the animal and exhale, letting the arrow loose. A beastly cry comes from the man left standing as he watches the arrow collide with his friend's neck. Surprise and terror etched on both their faces.

"You are a stubborn woman," she hisses.

"Stubbornness is one of my better qualities, don't you think?" A wide grin spreads over my lips and a chuckle escapes.

"I'm coming!" she insists.

"You are not!" I snap. *"All of this death would have been for nothing."* My head swims and my vision blurs. I place my hand on temple and wait for the world to stop spinning.

I feel her in the back of my mind struggling with the decision, but she knows what will happen if she's caught. She has lived through the nightmare already.

"Let me lend you my power," she urges.

"Not yet," I insist. "It's too soon." I creep forward, the last man disappearing from my view. My heart pumps hard in my chest but it feels too slow. My vision blurs around the corners and I fight to keep the darkness at bay. If I take her help now and her power wears off before this is over, I am as good as dead.

"You cannot die here," I say between gritted teeth.

Sweat drips down my head, mixing with dried blood and falling into my lashes. I wipe my brow and wince as I fall into the beast, its rough scales nicking my skin.

I drop the bow, unable to pull the string any longer, and slide a short sword from my belt just as another sword slices through the air. The zing of our blades echoes through the field and my side screams in agony, my makeshift bandage threatening to tear.

A savage, beastly sound rips from my attacker's throat. "You killed my brother!" He snarls. His eyes glaze over in fury, his assault coming down again and again. I drop down and drag my blade across his thigh, aiming for the artery. His fist connects with my eye, blood spewing on the ground at the blow.

I stumble, falling to the ground.

"I see fear in your eyes, Your Majesty." He stalks forward. "The King wants you alive, but I will enjoy watching the life drain from your eyes." He grabs my shirt, lifting me so my toes just scrape the ground.

I give a bloody smile, feral and unhinged. "Striverrah."

The ancient word is just a whisper on my lips. I can feel my body changing, the power dangerously intoxicating. A gentle gasp fills my lungs as my wounds stitch themselves back together. He lowers me, horror spreading across his face.

"The King didn't warn you?" I taunt. "Pity, but not surprising. Your death will mean nothing."

I pull a dagger from my belt, shoving it deep into his heart. His eyes bulge as he stumbles backward, dropping me in the process. His hands wrap around the hilt as he falls to his knees. His eyebrows draw together and he slowly shakes his head in disbelief.

"Tell your brother I said hello," I mock.

I grab my dagger and kick him in the chest, removing the blade in the process.

"That was a little dramatic." Ciena's calming voice drifts through my mind.

"Possibly." I shrug. *"But I have seen you eat a man whole, so . . ."*

I near the edge of the forest and take one last look at the meadow I used to play in as a little girl. My home ruined, most of my people dead, and the rest in hiding. I remember the days before power tried to sink its ugly teeth into our nation.

"I'm coming ho . . ." The hair on my neck stands on end and a deep feeling of dread settles in my stomach. I slow my breathing and listen. The bugs scurry across the ground, the birds wings flutter in the sky, and the gentle breeze whispers as it passes through the trees.

"Run!" Ciena yells through our link.

I don't hesitate. Pushing through the trees, my feet pound hard and fast. Ciena's borrowed magic pulses through my body. Each step propels me faster, but the human body isn't meant to carry such power and the price is heavy. I cover miles in minutes but it won't be enough.

Blood starts to seep from my nose, a sign of reaching my limit.

"Keep her safe." I push my thoughts to her, exhaustion taking over.

Then, I see it. Large wings create a menacing shadow over the earth. There is nowhere to hide.

"We never stood a chance," I say breathlessly.

"Just keep running, Ravina."

"We prepared for this, Ciena. Break the link." I bite out. My mind races as I try to reassure myself, but the pit in my stomach remains.

The dragon thunders to the earth as it lands. His legs like giant tree trunks ending in fearsome talons. The gust of wind from his powerful wings blow my loose strands of hair around my face. Dark scales like chips of obsidian glint in the light, his eyes seemingly too bright, too orange, to look natural. Two long horns adorn his head, and teeth like razor blades litter his mouth.

He watches me, waiting. If the King wanted me dead, this dragon would have already killed me. I look into his eyes and shout, "Why do you stay, when he slays your kind?" I do not expect an answer, nor do I receive one. I square my shoulders. "Take me to him."

His giant claws wrap around my belly. My insides drop as we swoop into the air. From up here, the death below is a haunting mass grave. A single tear slides down my cheek as memories I will never get to make come rushing at me. Giggles I won't cause, love I won't give, first words and tantrums I will never calm.

Was it worth it? I only let the thought linger a short moment.

A hoard of men become visible over the horizon. We glide seamlessly through the air and too soon I'm released to stand in front of a regiment of soldiers who spew profanities in my direction. I can feel the fury roll off them in waves.

My thoughts drift to Sam and the wife he will never see again. To the son who will never know him, and my daughter.

Oh, my daughter.

My body aches with grief.

I shake violently as the last of the Ancients' power drains from my body, dropping me to my knees.

"Your body betrays you, my dear." The Dark King approaches, his hands held behind his back. "It doesn't have to be like this, Ravina." He squats, offering his hand.

It almost seems like he cares.

Almost.

But I know who lies underneath his smooth demeanor.

"I was wondering if you were going to show, or if your men would have to do your dirty work for you?" I say and he sighs, his knees creaking as he stands and faces his men.

"You know why I am here, Ravina." He places his hands at the small of his back, "Where is the Ancient?"

I look around, "You know as much as I do."

He turns and rips me off the ground, his nostrils flare and his jaw clenches. He wasn't always this way . . . so hungry for power that he would slaughter innocent people; however, dragon's blood does more than make you strong . . . it eats away at your humanity.

He draws me close to his lips. "We could build an empire together." The words are a whisper for only me to hear, "I will forgive your treachery."

He sets me on the ground, pleading with me, trying to manipulate feelings that died many years ago. I could never forgive him; he has taken away the only thing that matters to me. Flashes of my husband holding our daughter spring into my mind, but I quickly lock them away.

"Zekiah." I place my palm against his chest, something I had done a million times when we were younger. "You are right, it doesn't have to be like this."

His eyes bore into mine, some of the softness from years past linger there. For just a moment, I think . . . I think I glimpse my old friend.

When his eyes harden again though, I know it was a mirage. A ghost of the friend I knew.

"I am the Dark King!" he bellows. "You mistake my grace for weakness, but I am growing impatient, Ravina. Bring her here, or you will die."

I made peace with dying before I ever stepped onto this field.

"Ciena, it is time."

"This could kill you," she says with desperation.

I hear the pain in her thoughts. I feel her struggle against it, but she also knows this is the only way. *"I am dead anyway, my friend."*

Another tear slips down my cheek, the last one I will let fall. *"Tell her I loved her always."* I swallow the lump forming in my throat.

The King's men gather around me and someone grabs my arm, but I grab his blade. I turn swiftly and thrust it into his neck, then plunge it into the stomach of another. The shock lasts only a second before I am relieved of my weapon, injuring three more men in the process.

"Enough, Ravina!" The Dark King bites.

"Until we meet again, my friend," I choke out.

"Until we meet again."

Then, she is gone.

Pain pierces through my body and I scream in agony. The blood running through my veins like acid as our bond breaks and my soul shatters. I am empty and utterly alone.

The Dark King's face turns red with fury, knowing what has just taken place. "I have no use for you without your bond."

I smile through gritted teeth, the pain threatening to swallow me whole. "How does it feel to know you have failed, Zekiah?"

He removes his sword, the sharp blade landing at my throat.

Death taunts me.

"Are you scared to die, Ravina?" The sword knicks my throat and blood slowly trickles down my chest.

Death extends his hand with a gruesome grin . . .

I take it, with my own defiant smile to match.

"No."

CHAPTER 1

We never know which moments will alter the course of our lives, and I was blissfully unaware of how mine was about to change.

My father used to tell me stories of an Ancient, a dragon god named Azule, who roamed the ocean. Her blue scales blended with the water, a perfect camouflage to hide amongst the waves.

Beneath me, the ocean thrashes violently against the cliff, rolling like thunder.

Then, it is silent.

Ready.

I soar through the sky, the wind caressing my wild curly hair, the sun kissing my cheeks; every worry disappears in those milliseconds. I plummet toward the water, its mouth open, ready to devour me, begging to pull me into the deepest darkest parts of itself.

I welcome the sting of the water across my pale skin as I break through the shimmering surface. Tiny bubbles dance around my curves, encasing my body in a watery embrace. The sun catches my necklace as I descend to the bottom, fish darting away from me as I drop deeper and deeper.

I allow my body into the cool darkness, the sun rays trying to reach me, coaxing me toward the surface. I wonder if the Ancient of the sea felt this free? I pull the water around me, dropping to the ocean floor. A tiny cloud of sand balloons at my feet as I touch the sea bed.

A familiar tug pulls at my body, excitement starting to creep in. This is the best part. The water is where I feel the calmest, my truest self. I have spent years training my lungs to stay under, but I know I will have to surface soon. Effortlessly, I glide along the ocean floor, pushing and pulling the water. My white hair bounces around me, like seaweed tossed by the waves.

A muffled splash comes from above me. A dark figure descends; arms stretched toward me. The ocean becomes violent and my lungs begin to burn. Panic sets in. *I was careful,*

I tell myself. A large arm wraps around my waist and pulls me up. We break through the surface, each gasping for breath like it could be our last.

The clouds have turned dark and the waves roar with life, each higher and stronger than the last. "I don't know why you jumped, but . . ." He pushes the hair from his face.

I slip through his grasp and leave him bobbing in the water, sentence unfinished, desperate to put space between us.

"Hey!" I hear him struggle against the water as he swims toward me, but then the splashing stops.

It's not your problem.

The cliffs tower over me, and reluctantly I glance behind me. He struggles, his breath becoming more labored.

You need to leave; this is not safe.

The thoughts in the back of my mind whisper truth, but I also can't leave him to die.

"I better not regret this!" I suck in a deep breath and dive back into the dark depths, the water welcoming me back like an old friend.

The current violently tosses him back and forth. His efforts to fight the watery beast are useless, the ocean unforgiving. The thought of leaving him, allowing the ocean to take one more innocent victim creeps into my mind.

I quickly shake it away, but my father's words quickly surface. *No one can know about your abilities, Fraya. It's too dangerous.*

The stranger stops moving and begins to drift with the ocean. I quiet the internal alarms pulsing frantically in warning and the panic churning in my stomach, then call to the ocean. The water stirs, ready to obey my commands. I sweep my hand toward me, beckoning the water, and within seconds I am pulling him toward land.

"Ugh." I grunt and drag his soaked body from the water. "You are not making this easy."

His lips have a slight blue tint. I consider coaxing the water from his lungs, but decide against it. Using my power again is too dangerous. I press my palms against his ribs, pushing until my arms burn. He shoots up, emptying the salty water from his lungs in wet splutters.

"Thank the Ancients." I fall back, allowing my worn body a moment of relief.

He reaches out and grabs my wrist.

I jerk my hand from his. "Excuse me?" I rub the place where his hand touched.

He motions out to the endless sky. The storm will be here soon.

"What happened out there?" He eyes me skeptically.

His breathing comes out uneven but his eyes are sharp and focused, staring straight through me. I fight the urge to squirm under his gaze.

I stand, wiping the sand and rocks from my skin. I leave him there, his question still hanging on his lips.

My father has spent my whole life hiding who I am; avoiding anyone too curious.

"Wait!" I hear him struggle to his feet behind me. "What happened?"

I whirl around to face him. "It seems as though you can't swim," I say dryly. "Now, I really must go before the storm gets here." I head back the way I came.

"No." He shakes his head and follows behind me. "No one can stay underwater that long."

His words make my heart race.

I turn to face him, and jab my finger into his hard chest. "Not that it's any of your business, but I have spent my whole life on the water training, fishing, and swimming. It may be impossible for you, but don't loop others into your inability to do something." My breathing becomes erratic. "A simple *thank you* for saving your life would be nice."

Why am I still talking to this man? I need to leave. Scolding myself internally, I turn away from him.

I hike up the mountain, the sand between my thighs chafe and my calves burn from the steep incline. I twist my long, curly white hair until salt water drips off my elbows. My fair skin slightly pinkened from the sun's gentle touch. My wet clothes cling to my curvy figure and a gentle breeze sends a shiver through me.

The stranger steps in front of me with his hands out. "Look, I'm sorry." He lets out a deep sigh, running his hand down his patchy beard. I watch a battle rage behind his eyes, as he carefully chooses the words coming out of his mouth next. "I watched you dive and when you didn't come up for air, I panicked."

"You were watching me?" I cross my arms over my chest, leaning my weight to one side.

"That's not what I meant. I tried to save you." He pinches the bridge of his nose, a hint of frustration creeping at the edges of his voice.

"You assumed I needed saving." My tone is harsh. A tiny pang of guilt twists in my stomach, but this is how it needs to be. We aren't friends.

I let my eyes wander down his chest, silently appreciating the way his wet shirt clings to his chiseled frame.

Absolutely not, Fraya! I reprimand my body for betraying me.

A devilish grin spreads across his face and I know I've been caught. I stand tall, clenching my jaw.

His eyes dance across my face and down the curve of my neck. My cheeks warm, but then I realize what he is gawking at.

Without a word, I retrieve my dry clothes and slide them over my wet camisole, all the while aware his attention has not left me. I let my hair cascade down my back, covering most of the ghost-like mark that whispers across my bare skin.

I look out at the ocean, feeling its pull as a heavy breeze whips my wet hair across my face. The storm clouds have moved closer, and the sweet scent of rain hits my nose.

I wrap my fingers around the purple stone nestled between my collar bones. The night my father wrapped the delicate chain around my neck, he told me when my mother wore this necklace it kept her safe. He never really spoke of her, but when he did, I absorbed as much as I could; desperate to know even a small piece of her.

"I love you until forever." He said as he rubbed his scratchy beard against my cheek, pulling me into a big hug.

Tiny gold flecks sit inside the stone, like sparks on the verge of a flame. The gold vines trap the flame in place for all eternity. The thought is haunting.

I shake myself from the memory and find the stranger's eyes still on me, his head tilted to the side, studying me.

"Where are you headed?" he asks. "I could walk with you. The woods can be dangerous."

I don't bother turning around. "I can take care of myself."

"My name is Luca, by the way," he yells.

"I didn't ask," I shout back.

CHAPTER 2

With each step away from him my body relaxes. *I never have to see him again*, I remind myself, trying to settle the growing panic building up in my chest.

I was careful.

Even still, the thought lingers and I pick up my pace. The crickets start their evening song as the sun begins to cast shadows across the forest floor. A lonely owl hoots in the distance as I near Abahlum. Tiny glowing bugs light a path amongst thorny bushes. The closer I get to home the more the trees thin. A deep groan comes from the heavens followed by the clap of lightning.

The crunch of sticks pulls my attention from the sky, but I'm quickly slammed to the ground. My head meets the earth with a deafening crack.

"Aren't you a pretty little thing? Are you out here all alone?" The oily voice hovers over me, as a heavy black boot presses against my neck. He leans his weight into me, trapping the air in my lungs. "Didn't anyone ever teach you it's dangerous to travel alone?"

I struggle against him, but my head swims with each movement.

"You don't know how to speak, sweetheart?" he hisses. "Good, I like a girl who knows how to keep quiet." He leans a bit farther into me, but the pressure is enough to make me feel like my head will pop off.

I'm soon ripped from the ground by my hair, and blood drips from my head in a slow trickle.

"I messed up your pretty face. Pity," he pouts.

I take a good look at my attacker, realizing two more men hover close by. A man with skin draped over bones scans my body greedily. A hint of relief washes over me when I don't see the stranger from the ocean.

This is just happenstance.

"We could have some real fun with this one." He runs his boney hand against my arm; a shudder runs down my spine. He looks at the man holding me and smiles, his teeth rotted and broken. "I've never seen one with white hair before." He picks up a curly strand and gently tugs it. I pull away from his touch and his eyes hold a hint of excitement.

The third leans, unbothered, against a tree using the tip of a knife to clean out his fingernails. The man holding me snaps my head back, touching his cheek to mine ever so slightly. His stubble is sandpaper against my skin.

My heart hammers in my chest, "You are correct about one thing, it is definitely dangerous in these woods." I snap my head forward and then slam it backwards, sending it crashing into the nose of my captor. The crunch of his nose is satisfying to my ears.

He drops his hold on my hair, desperate to attend to his broken nose. He wails as his skeleton friend stands frozen. Shaking the shock from his face, he lunges toward me.

He trips on the root I cracked my skull on. My knee meets his face and I leave him broken on the ground. Preparing myself for man number three, I slide my hand to my trusted blade, but it isn't there. My heart sinks.

I was careless and distracted, and it's going to get me killed. The third man lifts his gaze with a sly grin, but has not moved since the altercation started.

The absence of my blade is terrifying.

A hand wraps around my ankle, sending me crashing into the dirt. I strike out, smashing my foot into his face until he loosens his hold.

"You stupid wench!" The first man bellows. "I will make you pay for that." His nose is crooked and his eyes are black.

Dirt fills my fingernails as I crawl to my feet. The fat man digs his claws into my skin. "I don't think so," he growls.

A loud crack breaking open the heavens takes his attention. My bruised knuckles smash into his neck, a hit my father would be proud of. I feel his bones give way as he gasps for precious air.

"You talk too much," I hiss.

Pain explodes through my chest. A cry pierces through the stormy night and bounces off the trees, swallowed by the darkness. It takes me a moment to realize the scream came from me.

I look down to see a knife lodged in my chest, the same one the man against the trees cleaned his nails with. I don't know which makes my stomach turn more, the pain or his grime inside my body.

He steps closer and I place my hand on the handle, "I wouldn't. It has a nasty hook at the end," he says with an unnatural calm.

My head rests against the tree and blood drips down my useless arm. My body will heal, but I must get out of here alive first.

"You almost . . . killed me," the fat one breathes.

"Almost?" I smile and he glares at me, his careful composure beginning to crack. "You have mere minutes," I say between gritted teeth.

His breath becomes labored and the blue tint to his lips has marked him for death. Fear replaces hatred as he crumbles to his knees, his panic speeding up the inevitable.

The first drop of the storm splashes on my cheek as the leader leans into me, gently pressing the butt of the blade, the knife digging deeper into me. The corners of my vision blur.

The tips of his fingers dig into my jaw as he jerks my face to his.

"Now I am down a man!" His fist wrecks the side of my face. He grabs my chin again, forcing me to focus on him. "For such a pretty thing you have quite the temper. I was enjoying the show."

His calloused thumb runs over my lips, causing my teeth to bite into my flesh. I spit in his face and his mouth curves into a gruesome smile, ready to devour me.

"Maybe . . ." He takes his hand and presses deeper into my shoulder. "I will keep you for myself."

"I would rather die." My voice doesn't come out as I intend, it's weaker and airy. I fight to stay awake. The rain is pouring, the water clinging to my skin, my hair slicked to my face.

His grin is wicked. "That can be arranged." Agony rips through me as he twists the knife inside my body. I bite my tongue trying to stifle a scream.

Rain pelts the ground, pools of water forming around me. A familiar tug pulls at my body. "You're going to die now."

A grin spreads across his lips. "Yeah. Sure I am, sweetheart."

I let the ball of water I created envelope his head, trapping the air in his lungs. His eyes widen, his hands scratch at his throat trying to remove the threat, but he can't. He rips the knife from my chest and my world blurs. The deadly bubble of water releases, spilling over his shoulders.

"Kill . . . Kill her!" He stutters. Trying to cough out the water from his lungs. I fall against the tree, its grooves denting my skin.

The world spins as the large tree cradles me to the ground. A whistle slices through the air; one, two whistles pierce through the storm.

Then, darkness.

CHAPTER 3

Stormy gray eyes look down at me while rough but gentle hands press me down. A deep groan vibrates through my chest and his hands still.

"Don't move," the gruff voice states. The overwhelming scent of freshly fallen rain ignites my senses.

When I look up in his eyes again, my vision blurs and tears burn as he pulls a stitch through, closing my wounds. I wish I could tell him it was futile, these injuries will only be a painful memory soon.

He draws back and stills over me. "You are going to be a problem, aren't you?" he whispers.

I want to ask who he is, but the words fall from my lips.

My eyes snap open, sucking in a stolen breath. Sweat drips from my temples as I steady my pounding heart.

"I would take it easy. You'll pop a stitch." The man from the ocean says.

What was his name? Luca?

Each breath is a struggle. "What happened?" I moan.

Images of a knife plunged into my chest cause my heart to pound. I rub my aching temples and try to put the pieces together.

"I was going to ask you the same thing." He stokes a crackling fire and it casts dancing shadows across his face.

"Wait! Where are they?" My attempt to stand is anything but graceful. He casually nods behind him. Two bodies, but where is the third?

Using the trees for support I stagger closer, praying to the Ancients the third man is among them, but he isn't. The hole in my chest throbs and worry starts to sink in. He saw.

"Where is the third guy? There were three people!" The words spill out of my mouth with urgency.

"I only found two," he says.

I could scream, but I don't have the energy.

Even now, my heart thunders in my ears and moving is becoming difficult. How much blood did I lose?

"I need to find him." I stumble and each movement takes immense effort.

"What are you doing?" His heavy steps move closer behind me. "I thought I said you need to take it easy," his words are soft, but a quiet curiosity lingers behind them.

I ignore him and try to focus on putting on foot in front of the other.

"Why do you need to find him so badly?" I feel his hand wrap around my elbow but I jerk from his touch sending another excruciating throb through my body.

I lean against a large tree, my body begging for rest. He stays close but doesn't touch me again. "I know what those men did to you was awful, but you aren't going to find him like this." He motions to my weakened state.

I'm not sure which bothers me more, the fact that he's right or that he's the one saying it.

"Looks like I busted your stitches." Black thread peeps out at me as my skin tries to break from its prison.

"I guess I have the opportunity to practice," he says. One side of his mouth creeps up as I slide down the tree, the wet earth soaking into my clothes.

The ringing of my thoughts is deafening. Who is this person and why does he keep showing up? His sandy blond hair is a mess around his handsome face as he assesses my injuries.

My eyelids feel like they weigh a thousand pounds as I rest my throbbing head against the trunk of the tree, staring up into the mass of branches. Two large yellow eyes stare down at me and soon the stars fade from view.

The savory smell of roasting meat drifts to my nose, creating loud hunger pains in the process.

"Your stomach betrays you," Luca says.

I let out a deep sigh. "It seems you are still here."

A large rabbit rotates over the fire on a makeshift spit. My mouth waters as the juices sizzle over the heat, sending up the succulent aromas.

"Hmm, seems that way." A deep dimple reveals itself when he glances up with a smirk. I have never been attracted to dimples before, but his . . . may change my mind.

The stars still light up the sky, but the creatures of the night have started to quiet which lets me know dawn will be approaching soon. The bodies have disappeared and I'm not sure if I am grateful or unnerved by it. "Where are the men?"

"Do you really want to know?" He lifts his brow; his question feels like a test I didn't study for.

"If I didn't want to know, I wouldn't ask," I argue.

"I disposed of them before they could draw unwanted attention from predators," he says as he rotates the roasting rabbit.

His answer leaves me with more questions. How does he know how to dispose of bodies and where did he dispose of them? I leave the thoughts to burn in the back of my mind. "Where is the bow?"

Luca reaches into his pack and pulls out an old wineskin lifting it to me. "Bow?"

The trees around me stir as the wind rustles through them. The night is beautiful, all things considered. "I thought . . . never mind."

"That was impressive." He takes back the drink, the alcohol stinging the back of my throat. "Who taught you to fight like that?"

Memories of my daily training session flicker through my mind. "My father."

"He trained you well." He looks toward the fire.

"Oh no." Guilt drops in my gut.

Luca stands, blade in hand. "What?"

"My father. He must be so worried." I struggle to my feet. I am getting stronger already, my body stitching itself back together. Soon, my body will forget this trauma but I'm afraid my mind never will.

"You shouldn't scare someone like that." He plops himself back on the ground, his arms slung over his raised knees.

"You don't understand. I need to get home."

"It is still dark. Wait until the sun comes up." He motions for me to sit back down but I ignore him. "Why are you so stubborn?" He says throwing his hands up.

His words cause me to stop in my tracks. "Excuse me?"

"Why won't you just let yourself heal?" He asks, irritation dripping from his words.

The irony of his statement is almost funny.

"Why do you care? I don't even know you." My temples throb, a headache setting behind my eyes.

"You really don't trust people, do you?" His eyebrow arches, scrutinizing me.

"Why would I?" I motion toward my body.

He runs his fingers through his short hair, making it stand on end. "You're right." He whistles and his horse trots up beside him. "Here," he says. "If you're going to go, you should have this back."

I take a close look at the blade he pulls from his pack. The muscles in my jaw tighten. "Where did you get that?"

"At the cliff." He spins the blade in his hand, waiting. I attempt to retrieve it but he pulls back slightly.

My cheeks redden with embarrassment. "I will take it back now," I hiss.

"First, a simple thank you." A sly grin emerges on his chiseled face and images of my fist flying into his square jaw dance through my mind.

"For what?" I scoff.

"If I was keeping track, this is the second time I have had to save you."

I swallow, trying to keep my rising anger at bay. "It seems we remember things a little differently."

"Okay," he says. "How about we meet in the middle? Tell me what this says." He gently brushes his finger over the etched smooth black surface.

"*Hemoiesa Loi Cyion.*" The Ancient words roll off my tongue with ease, like I am whispering a secret. Those words were the first my father ever taught me . . . *until forever.*

"But what does it mean?" he asks.

No one is supposed to know The Ancient language. The King forbade it before I was able to walk. "Your guess is as good as mine. Now hand it over."

"Where did you get it?" he asks.

I step close, my voice a whisper, "That was not the deal."

I snatch my blade from his hands before he can register it's gone. I tighten my hold on the dark brown leather grip, stained with the oil of many hands. I slide it into the sheath snug against my thigh.

That's when I hear him, his stride unmistakable.

CHAPTER 4

In the disappearing darkness I see a change settle over Luca. He shifts toward the sound of my father's footsteps, removing a large sword as he scans the tree line. His blue eyes searching for the threat.

An ax flies through the trees, rotating end over end until it lands with a thud behind a stunned Luca.

My father, a bear of a man, comes into view. His eyes find mine and relief floods his face but it's quickly replaced with a murderous rage at the sight of my injuries.

My father advances on Luca and their swords clash, Luca meeting each of my father's strikes, blow for blow. Of the little I know of my father's past life, I know he was a soldier. I see one as he fights in front of me, a soldier; protecting his daughter.

But who is Luca?

A normal man could never match my father on a good day, let alone when he is blinded by fear and anger.

"Father!" I yell, but he doesn't hear me. His focus on the threat in front of him. The sun bursts from the earth, chasing the shadows as stunning colors bleed across the sky.

A deadly blow knocks Luca to his knees.

"Enough!" I yell, stepping in front of Luca before my father lands the final blow. His eyes enlarge as his blade stops just before slicing into flesh.

"You can't kill him." I place my hands on his arms, forcing him to see me.

His face softens, but Luca is not out of the woods yet.

"I was so worried." He places his large head against mine. The dark circles and blood-shot eyes reveal his lack of sleep.

Luca stands tense behind me, neither man completely dropping their weapons.

"You can relax Luca; he isn't going to kill you."

My father's blue eyes reflect uncertainty as he glances back at Luca, then back to me. I have only ever seen my father cry once and the sun reveals a glimmer of unshed tears trapped in his eyes.

"Yet," my father says under his breath as he looks at me, concern etched in his forehead.

"I promise, I am okay." My father lets out a deep sigh, his chest expanding and settling again.

My father's pensive eyes glance toward Luca and back toward me. "I don't like it," he says through a clenched jaw.

I bury myself in his chest, his large arms wrapping around me with a gentle squeeze. "I just want to go home."

The jostle of the horse makes my muscles ache. "You didn't have to commandeer his horse, I could have walked," I tell my father.

"Sweet girl, you look like you were run over by a horse. Do your old man a favor and just stay up there, please?" My eyes roll but I nod to appease him.

It's only been us since I was a baby. When I was younger I was so angry I didn't have a normal life. I didn't understand why we never settled and why I couldn't just be a kid. It wasn't until I almost drowned that I understood why we couldn't stay in one place, and why I would never be normal.

I have grown accustomed to being the new girl with strange white hair who comes and goes with the passing sun.

"That was rude." I cross my arms over my chest, "and you still didn't have to take his horse."

He looks at me with mischief in his eyes. "Yes I did." He chuckles, a deep laugh that shakes his body and the creases around his eyes wrinkle. He winks at me, but grips his axe tighter when he looks back at the disgruntled man who follows behind his own horse.

"Thanks for coming for me." I let my voice drop, my words only for my father.

Seriousness etches into his brow. "I will always come for you, Fraya." He pats my leg as Abahlum comes into view.

CHAPTER 5

The sound of children squealing as they play can be heard across the field. Fresh bread and the salty scent of the ocean hit my nose. Two of my favorite smells. I don't think I will ever have a real home but if I could, this would be it.

Our village sits comfortably between two large mountains, each plunging into the ocean. Fishermen stand on large decks preparing for the day's catch, with large nets sprawled out between them as they check for holes and weak spots before setting off.

Of all the places we have traveled, this is my favorite. I think it may be my father's too, as we have been here for a few weeks longer than anywhere else. It's been refreshing sleeping in the same bed longer than a few days, but I know it can't last.

"It's beautiful here." Luca mutters in awe beside me.

Two soldiers pass and make crude comments about my appearance. Luca lowers his head, shrinking away from the men. Entirely different from the man who fought my father in the woods.

The soldiers have been appearing more, taking more food, and leaving less for the hungry villagers.

Men have been murdered in the streets for hiding food for their families.

I slide from the horse and hand the reins to Luca. "Sorry he stole your horse."

"No, you're not," he says playfully as his fingertips graze my palm.

I drop my hand, rubbing it on my pants. "You're right." He lifts the corner of his mouth, showing his dimple one last time.

He turns from his horse. "I never got your name."

"Because I didn't give it." I wave and follow closely behind my father.

Our small white cottage is just off the water away from the main village, the wood worn with age and salt deterioration. The shutters hang from the windows, banging in the gentle breeze.

The inside is quaint with few furnishings spread sporadically through the living area. We sit at the small table in the corner, the wooden chair groaning under my father's weight.

"Let's take a look at you." He carefully inspects my head, but when he gets down just below my collar bone the tears flow freely.

"I'm fine. I promise," I say as I remove the bloodied patch, trying not to flinch. The hole in my chest is smaller and less gnarly looking. "See? Fine."

"I have one job, Fraya. One. To keep you safe." Deep regret and sadness crease his forehead. He cups my face in his hands, like he's done a million times before.

"I am okay." I lean my head against his, a symbol of love and acknowledgment. "But there is something else."

Worry draws his brows together. "Someone saw me." Although I am technically an adult and we have been through this many times, I stare at my father waiting for his direction.

He gets to his feet, his shoulders tense. Each movement calculated but rushed. "It's time to go," he says.

A few extra clothes are thrown into premade bags. This is not the first time we have had to leave in haste and it won't be the last.

"Get the supplies from town and I will get the horses ready," he says.

Our familiar routine creeps into my movements as I throw a pack over my shoulder. "Fifteen?" I ask.

"Fifteen," he says and kisses my temple before giving me one last squeeze.

"Fraya?" his voice drops slightly. "It will be okay, hurry back." He gives me a slight smile but his forehead creases with worry.

Fifteen minutes is not a lot of time to grab the supplies, but it will have to do.

The center is busier than normal for this time of day. Keeping my head down, I fill my bag and quickly thank the merchant. I am almost done when I notice a faint bloody handprint staining the side of a building. My heart begins to thump loudly in my chest.

Ignore it.

I inch closer and spot droplets of blood leading around the building.

I have time. I tell myself.

The blood trail stops at an abandoned barn. Rotten wood planks leave just enough space to see inside.

My heart stops.

In the far corner, a man leans against the wall with an arrow in his side.

I knew it. I knew I heard arrows.

A crunch under my feet makes me still.

"Have you come to kill me off?" he yells, but it's breathy and forced.

I step into the old barn and the man who rammed a blade into my chest sits before me, his skin a pale gray, his forehead covered in sweat.

"It looks like I won't have to," I say as I step closer, getting a better look at the man who was confident he could end my life. He looks pitiful now, moments from death.

"He is coming for you." He chokes on a laugh. His greasy hair is slicked to his skin.

I squat next to him. "Who?"

"Alkazah." He spits the word out like it left a bitter taste on his tongue. "People like you are not supposed to exist, you are a curse." His words don't sting as he intends for them to. I know I'm not normal. But, the term he uses is foreign.

"Who is coming?" I take the broken arrow and put some weight against it. He recoils from the pain, a deep cry gargles in his chest. I can't help but feel a small moment of pleasure. Mere hours ago he was the one torturing me.

"You're a monster." He coughs and blood sputters from his mouth.

"Answer the question," I demand.

"He is already here." He grins and coughs again. He tries to make himself more comfortable but it is useless. He will die soon.

Dread sweeps over me. "When did you contact him?" He leans his head against the barn wall. "When?" I shout but it is useless, he is drifting from this world into the next. I feel hallow as I crash through the barn door.

My legs don't feel fast enough and the sick feeling sinks deeper into my stomach. *He can't already be here.* The closer I get to our meeting spot the more my heart shakes. *I have time.* I tell myself.

As I near our meet up spot the clashing of swords rattles my bones. "No," I say in disbelief.

My father fights a group of men, the edges of his axes sinking into flesh. I pull my throwing knife from my sheath and aim, throwing it into the back of an attacker. "Run, Fraya!" he yells.

I can't, I won't leave him here. This is all my fault. An arrow lodges into his shoulder and tears sting my eyes. Snapping the arrow, he shoves the broken piece through the neck of a soldier then he thrusts his blade into the gut of another man. They keep coming. Fear tears a hole through my chest. There are too many of them.

The dagger at my thigh feels heavy as I slip it from its home and send it sinking into the spine of a man. His cries fade into the distance as I fight to get closer to my father. A soldier flings himself at me but but he is sloppy and his life is ended quickly.

I grab a fallen blade readying it for battle when time slows and the chaos becomes muffled. I watch as my father lets out a war cry and brings his axe down.

His cry is cut short and I stumble forward. "No!" I scream.

"Don't kill her!" a man bellows. "He wants her alive."

My world shifts as I reach to catch my father before he falls to the earth.

"No, no, no," I plead. The blade through his chest is pulled out slowly. His attacker stands over him with a victorious smile, triumphing over slaying their beast. My stomach rolls.

"Grab her!" someone behind me shouts.

A hand grips my upper arm, tearing me away from my father. Something feral unlocks within me and pain tears through my body, ripping through every molecule, until flames pour out of me.

"No!" I scream. A ring of fire encircles us and men start screaming as the blaze finds them and silences their cries.

"Please, no. I'm sorry, daddy. I don't know how to help." I cry as I try to stop the bleeding.

His eyes flutter, fighting to stay present. He attempts to part his lips in a smile, trying to calm me, even now. I try to cover the gaping hole in his chest, but the bleeding doesn't slow.

"Find Ciena." His voice cracks and my heart shatters a little more.

"I don't know who that is." I try to hold back my tears but the sobs continue to escape.

"The Ancient . . ." He chokes before he can say more.

"I am so sorry. Please don't leave me." I put my head into his neck.

His hand moves to the side of my face and I look up into his blue eyes as a single tear trickles down his temple. "I love you sweet girl, until . . ."

His hand drops from my face and I choke on a sob.

"Until?" I grab his hand and place it back against my cheek, hoping to feel some life in it. "Please say it, daddy." But he closes his eyes for the last time.

Wave after wave of despair rolls over me, trapping me in this moment . . . forever.

"Until forever, daddy."

And then, the only good part of me dies . . . with him.

CHAPTER 6

"Fraya." A voice in the distance waivers. It seems worried, but I'm stuck.

"Get up." It's a man, his voice deep and urgent. Hands jerk me from my father's lifeless body. The only person I have . . . only person I had.

"Leave me here," I say while jerking back to my father.

"We really have to go," the man whispers.

"I said leave me here!" I yell, looking up into ocean-colored eyes.

"I can't do that." Suddenly, I'm lifted from the ground and thrown over his muscled shoulder. I smell the burnt flesh before I see it. The whole field is gone, swallowed by fire. *My fire.*

He hoists me on top of the same horse my father "borrowed" less than an hour ago. Had it only been an hour? An arm slips around my waist keeping me upright.

A half-burned man, struggling to stand, tries to escape into the woods. I grip the arm around my body and Luca tenses. My dagger, still coated in blood, is clenched in my hand. This is the last thing I have of my father. I slide off the horse. Luca doesn't try to stop me as I stalk toward my father's killer.

"You are a monster." His voice shakes, the words catching in his scorched throat. His skin is bubbled and blistered, and half the skin on his face is gone.

"Maybe." I shrug.

"He will kill you." He stops struggling now, confined to his fate.

"Not if I kill him first."

I end his life just as he ended my father's and I feel nothing. *Maybe I am a monster.*

I stalk off toward the woods and hear Luca come up behind me. He extends his hand and I look at it. "How did you know my name?" I eye him skeptically.

"I heard your father say it." His eyes soften and I put my hand in his.

"Stop," I tell Luca. We have been traveling for hours, the heat suffocating and blood now dried to my skin. "I need to get off." I am more urgent now as my stomach churns.

Luca stops but my legs won't budge. He dismounts the horse and pulls me to the ground, my legs shaking.

I rush to a nearby tree and empty my stomach. The tree bark bites into my skin and a small creature scurries away from me. When I turn around his brows are pulled up but he says nothing.

"I don't need your pity," I say, wiping my mouth.

My hands are stained red from blood, none of it mine. My stomach rolls again and I bend back over, heaving up the contents of my stomach.

Luca squats in front of me with a canteen of water.

"We have to stop meeting like this," I say.

"I guess we will have to make the rest of our story a better one." He wets a rag and hands it to me as something passes over his face.

Understanding? Grief? Regret? Maybe all of it.

He stands quickly and says, "I'm going to get you some clothes."

I nod and scrub my skin until it burns.

When he walks away, I realize he must have seen what happened. I rub my hands over my face, at a loss of what to do next, but a rage sits in my stomach and I know the King must pay for what he did.

How and why do I need to find the Ancient? The King has been searching for her for years and has gotten nowhere.

When Luca returns he holds a pair of pants and an off-white cotton shirt. His clothes hang unflattering on my body. It smells like him, a hint of earth and salt.

Another wave of despair washes over me and I try to piece together what I have left. The only way I can move forward is by locking away every memory of my father. I carefully construct a wall and slam the door shut on everything I was and instead force myself to focus on the one thing I know will keep me going . . . killing the Dark King.

"Would you take me to Pendshire?" I ask before I think too much of it. The trip will take four days. "I know it's a lot to ask," I quickly add.

"I tend to travel alone." He puts his finger to his chin. "But I guess I can make an exception," he agrees with a warm smile.

I walk over to the giant horse rubbing my hand down his neck. "Thank you."

I manage to get my stiff achy body back atop his horse who seems happy to be moving again, but the silence rings in my ears. The silence makes me think and I don't want to right now.

"Where are you from?" I ask as I pick at the intricate designs on the saddle.

"Everywhere and nowhere." His chest vibrates into my back. I'm tempted to relax against him. Everything hurts and I am exhausted.

"Sounds familiar." A silent painful pang stabs at my heart, but I push it down, smothering it.

"You aren't from Abahlum?" he asks.

"No." I leave it there, hanging.

"He seemed like a good man." The words are careful, tip toeing around my broken pieces.

"He was," I admit.

Was.

Past tense.

Lock it away, Fraya.

"On another note. Remind me to never get on your bad side," Luca says.

"Wow, how can you be kind in one sentence and an ass in the next?" I ask in disbelief.

"It's a talent, really." If we were on the ground this is where he would take a bow. Proud of his joke.

"Luca?" He hums in response. "Why were you there?"

"I was leaving when I saw the flames. I didn't know who it was until I got closer," he says. "When I saw you there. . . I just. I couldn't just leave you like that," he says. I hear him swallow hard behind me.

My heart speeds up in my chest. *He didn't see, he doesn't know.*

"Thanks," I say. The word is soft and careful.

"Anytime." The sun starts to set, performing a colorful dance before us. Hours pass before another word is spoken.

Just as my body begins to relax, Luca says, "We should set up camp." Luca stops the horse and wraps the reins around a nearby tree.

Camp is set up quickly and quietly.

I lay under the stars, the fire creating warmth against the cool summer breeze. The horse chomps the grass nearby and the crickets sing a beautiful night time melody. But the night only brings heartbreak, and a darkness I drown in. My nails dig into my palm, trying to feel anything other than the sinking despair that haunts me. The pain is the only thing keeping me going.

Luca's voice breaks the silence, "Do you want to talk about it?"

I try to respond, several times, but there is nothing. Talk about it? The fact that my very existence killed my father?

Lock it away, Fraya.

The silence drags until Luca speaks again, "I watched someone I love die once." The rawness of his words tells me he relives this moment often.

"Does it get easier?"

"It gets different," he says and turns his back to the fire. "Pain and suffering are meant to make you stronger." His voice is carried by the breeze.

"I think we tell ourselves that to make it hurt less," I say as a tear slides down my cheek and into the velvety grass.

The stars overtake the black abyss that is the night. A stunning masterpiece with every color shining across the sky.

Alkazah? What does it mean? I turn the foreign word over in my head a few times, but do not come up with anything.

"Get some sleep. Your dreams may be kinder to you." Luca says and covers his head, leaving me alone with my thoughts.

"Do you know how the stars were flung into the sky?"

"Of course, daddy. You have only told me a thousand times."

"I forgot."

A tiny giggle escapes my throat. "How did you forget?"

He sighs deep, his shoulders dramatically rising and falling. "The curse of being an old man."

"Okay, daddy." I point my tiny fingers to the sky. "Close your eyes." I peek over to make sure his eyes are squeezed shut. "Now imagine only darkness fills the night sky."

"*That* is *really dark.*"

"*I know! Well, three of the Ancients thought so too, so they decided to paint the night.*" I sweep my arm across the heavens. "*The Ancient, Azule, loved the ocean so she splattered blues of every shade.*"

"*But what about the other colors?*"

"*Daddy!*" I scold, "*I'm getting there.*"

He chuckles but lets me finish.

"*Hausa loved the land. He made sure the earth saw her reflection. Greens, oranges, pinks, and purples were added to the canvas.*"

"*This is my favorite part,*" he grins.

"*I thought you didn't remember?*" my tiny voice shrieks.

"*You always remember your favorite part.*" He says this like I should know it, like it is as plain as the beard on his face.

"*Last was the Ancient Noir. She was as dark as the night, darker even. She said without the dark you can't appreciate the light. Then, she created a beautiful backdrop allowing the stars to erupt with life.*"

I wake as the sounds of my father's voice slips from memory. Silent tears bleed into my hair; I can't escape this pain even in my dreams.

CHAPTER 7

For three days, we push through in silence. I've traveled this road before, and know the twists, turns, and valleys.

As the sun dips below the horizon on the fourth day, the city comes into view. Red bricks line the streets and buildings tower overhead, some two and three stories tall. Pendshire was one of the only towns the Dark King allowed *luxuries*. His men had access to women, food, and plenty of booze. This was one of the many places my father and I stopped for supplies but we never stayed long and I was rarely allowed in the city; too many eyes.

Merchant tents are still standing, full of fruits and vegetables. I draw my hood and move around the vendors, picking out an assortment of delicacies.

Luca stares at me. "We have food, you know."

I bite into the sweet green apple, the juices running down my face. "Yes, but vendors know and see everything," I say, falling in step with the tricks my father has drilled into me since I was a little girl.

Oil lamps create a warm honey glow on those walking by. A young boy with dark hair knocks into me. Luca reaches out grabbing the boy by his arm causing him to squeal in pain.

I drop my apple, reaching for his hand. "What are you doing?" I ask in shock.

"Give it back," he demands. The boy shrinks under his gaze, lifting two oranges from inside his shirt cautiously to me. Luca drops his hold and the child quickly scurries away from us.

"Was that necessary?" I snap.

He scratches his patchy beard and tilts his head. "He was stealing."

"He was hungry," I argue.

Luca's eyes hold nothing. "Stay here," I say.

The young boy slips behind a broken door. I grab more fruit and leave a few coins for the merchant before slipping behind the split wood. I blink, adjusting my eyes to the darkness. "The grumpy man is gone," I whisper. "I am just going to leave these here." I set the food on the turned over box and step back.

Three figures step around a makeshift tent, cautiously eyeing the fruit. The boy from before keeps his siblings at bay, but they never take their eyes off the bright colored food before them.

None wear shoes, their skin stained with dirt and their hair cut short against the scalp.

"Why?" He squares his shoulders and tilts his chin up.

"Why what?" I ask with a raised brow.

"I stole from you," he admits.

I smile gently. "At no point should a child ever have to worry about where their next meal is coming from. If I was in your shoes, I can't say I wouldn't have done the same thing."

He stares at me for a long moment. "Thank you." He motions for the younger kids and they quickly scoop up the food.

Heavy footsteps sound outside and I freeze. I know those steps. Soldiers.

"We don't like them either," the littlest one whispers.

"That noticeable, huh?" I smile back at her, despite the lack of oxygen going to my lungs.

She shrugs her tiny shoulders. My mouth goes dry and I try to swallow but the sound seems to bounce off the walls. She steps forward, careful to not make a sound. One of the men clears his throat and spits against the wall. I allow myself to relax and listen for any information but hear nothing.

"They're gone," she whispers.

"Thank you," I breathe in relief.

I rush back to the square, mindful of everyone around me.

I quickly spot Luca. He stands out in this crowd. His strong, lean frame catches the attention of many who pass by. A beautiful woman stands in front of him now. Her ruby red hair flows past her shoulders and a long finger nail runs up the middle of his abdomen. All eyes are on her as her light skin turns dewy under the warm glow of the lamps.

A smile creeps over his lips and although I wish I could look away, I can't. My stomach twists in an unfamiliar way as she leans in close to his ear, whispering a secret meant only for him.

A deep laugh erupts from Luca, and her porcelain face turns to stone but her eyes hold a fire. The slap that follows even stings my skin.

The grin remains as he flexes his jaw. When he finds me staring, his smile turns wicked making my insides squirm even more.

He saunters up to me, a lopsided grin fresh against a nasty raised handprint. My eyes spin in my head, "You can't go anywhere without causing problems, can you?"

"What can I say, I am drawn to trouble." He winks and I bite the inside of my lip, trying to ignore the somersaults in my belly.

What is wrong with me?

"She seemed eager to give you whatever *trouble* you are after."

"I don't pay for things freely given, darling." His eyes glitter with amusement.

"Call me *darling* again and I will rip your tongue from your throat."

He chuckles but seems unphased by my threat. "I found the inn by the way." He puffs his chest out.

"Great! Where are the rooms?" I say, my body worn and ready for a nice hot bath.

He smirks. "Room," he corrects and walks off. It takes only a moment to register what he means.

"Singular, as in only one?" I ask in disbelief.

"That is what *room* means, yes." He gently pulls on the reins of his horse and slides a key into my palm.

"There is only one room available. The stables are just up the road, if you need me that is where I will be." All jest is gone when he asks, "Will you be okay?"

I nod my head, not trusting words. If I am honest with myself, I don't know. This will be the first night I have ever truly been alone.

He points to the wall of doors. "Room three."

I breathe a heavy sigh, heavier than I meant to. Luca tilts his head to the side and leans against the building. "If you want me to stay, *darling*, just ask."

My neck heats up. "Don't flatter yourself, *darling,*" I mock.

CHAPTER 8

My tiny room is only big enough to hold a bed and a small chair in the corner.
I stand in front of a broken mirror in the bathroom and run my fingers over the new ghostly marks that whisper across my skin. They would be beautiful . . . if they weren't a constant reminder of the monster I am.

I was born with what I thought was a birthmark on the back of my neck. The day I almost died, I knew it was more.

The water sucked me under its deathly current, and my lungs burned with a fire I had never experienced. The fear was the worst part, worse than the dying. I just wanted it to stop; I begged for it to stop.

Then it did.

That first breath out of the water felt different, I was different. I could feel the water's energy; command it, manipulate it. That's when the mark grew.

I felt as each piece etched into my skin, every curve and line cascading down my spine.

The new marks rest around my collar bone, like a shackle, before dropping in between my breasts.

My hands find their way into my hair, and I begin to braid instinctively. My fingers weaving the hairs in and out, the way my father had done a thousand times before. He never took scissors to my head. *"Your mother would kill me,"* he had said. Instead, he learned how to braid and did it every day.

I take the pair of scissors resting on the sink and chop. Each strand falling to the ground feels both liberating and soul crushing.

A stranger stares back at me.

Her white hair hangs at her shoulders framing her round face. Her emerald-colored eyes lack life. They are empty.

I swallow the lump forming in my throat.

The steam rises from the bath, and I carefully step in, sliding under the water to trap my screams. I let the water go cold before I decide to get out.

A slight tap on the door stirs me from my thoughts. I realize I am gripping the sides of the tub hard enough to make my palms throb.

An intruder wouldn't knock.

I carefully open the door a few inches. Luca leans over and asks, "Why are you all drippy?"

I lower my eyelids and stare at him, "I took a dip in the river," I say sarcastically.

"So, you are naked behind that door?" he asks with a lifted brow.

I roll my eyes until they ache. "What do you want?" I say with a sigh.

"I have a proposition for you," he says.

"No," I say and attempt to shut the door, but he throws his hands out quickly and it bounces back.

I drop my head. "What?" I ask in defeat.

His eyes glitter with excitement. "Come out with me. Just for a little while."

I look back to my bed, my body longing for its comfort. The hard ground has given me new aches and pains, and I want nothing more than pillows and a fluffy blanket right now.

"You are kidding," I say.

"Not even a little," he admits.

He must see I am about to slam the door because his foot slides in the way. I press my lips together and give a tight-lipped smile.

"Move your foot," I demand.

He throws his hands in the air and says, "Listen, if you stay cooped up in this room your mind will attack you all night. You won't sleep because you will be consumed with thoughts of that day. Come dance with me. Forget the real world for an hour, wear yourself out, and then go to bed."

"You speak as if you have experience," I say. The cool air wafts into my room causing my skin to prickle.

"I am familiar with pain and the tricks it plays on the mind," he admits.

I hate that he's right. I've been trapped in an endless nightmare since it happened. We stare at each other, the moments ticking by. "Fine. Five minutes."

"Twenty," he replies.

"Ten," I counter.

"Fine," he reluctantly agrees.

I look down at the boot. "Move your foot."

"Would you like me to assist?" He wiggles his eyebrows at me.

His words send a flutter down my skin. I hate him. "Only if you move your foot." I let my voice hover above a whisper. His face stumbles, but then his handsome smile is back.

"As you wish." He steps back swinging his arms out in a dramatic gesture of compliance.

As his foot slides from the entry way I quickly slam the door and lock it. I hear him as he leans against the door. "That was a dirty trick you played, darling." His voice dips low on the last word for emphasis.

"I will hurt you." I yell through the door.

"I look forward to it," he chuckles.

"I like your hair," Luca says as I exit the room.

"Me too." I step around him. "Where are we going?"

A triumphant smile reveals his straight white teeth and he grabs my hand, pulling me after him.

I hear an enticing melody; the stomping and musical instruments vibrate the ground as we get closer.

"I don't think this is a good idea." I step away from the noise.

"I promise I won't let anything bad happen," he says.

"Ten minutes," I remind him and let him pull me through the crowd of people.

I have always loved the way music whisks me away and infuses my soul. I sway with the beat and my tense muscles begin to relax.

"You smile!" Luca says. He inches closer with a smile of his own.

"Only when there's a reason to," I say with a shrug.

"I am honored to bring such a beautiful smile to your lips." He grins causing his dimples to wink at me.

"You are not a bad dancer," I say.

"I will tell my teachers you think so," he says.

Teachers?

For a moment his smile falters but it's quickly replaced and he is spinning me in his arms once again.

Bodies move around us, people laughing with their loved ones, and my heart starts to hurt. As the music slows he wraps his arm around my waist, pulling me to him. He slides a loose curl from my face, his fingertips just grazing my skin.

I step back and disappointment settles on his shoulders. "It's been ten minutes."

CHAPTER 9

I let my feet guide me to the room.

I'm almost to my door when the smell of roasting meat seduces my nose and my stomach lets out a loud grumble. Letting my nose lead the way, I turn the corner to see a quaint pub nestled into a group of buildings. When the large door opens, the warm smell of freshly brewed ale and stew envelops me. I spot an empty stool at the bar and make my way to it.

A woman with raven black hair approaches. "I don't think I've seen you here before," she says as her eyes twinkle with curiosity.

"No, just stopped here for the night. The smell from your kitchen is what drew me in," I say and slide onto the wooden stool.

Her green eyes brighten, "We do have the best food around, but I will let you be the judge of that."

I run my hands over the aged wood, its grooves polished with oil to avoid splinters. "Then, I will have your favorite."

She smiles and slides a full glass of frothy drink toward me. "It will be out soon," she says and disappears into the kitchen. The door swings open and a dark-haired man walks in, his presence demanding as he strides up to the bar. Those closest to him quickly step out of his way and none meet his gaze.

A heavenly aroma fills my nostrils as the woman sets a plate full of roasted meats and potatoes in front of me. My stomach audibly thanks her with a loud growl. I stuff a whole baby potato in my mouth, savoring the buttery garlic flavor.

I let out a silent moan as the man sits a couple stools away.

"What can I get you, hun?" she asks the stranger.

"What she has looks good," he says in a deep sultry voice.

I don't look up as I answer. "It is good." I let my bread soak up the juices before plopping it in my mouth.

"The way you are stuffing your mouth convinced me," his words are curt.

I choke on the roll as I turn to scold him. My heart hammers in my chest, his cool eyes stopping my words. *I know those eyes.* They penetrate my soul. He is heart thumpingly handsome.

His hands clasp together as he leans against the bar, his sleeves scrunched up revealing black tattoos that crawl up his muscled arms.

I am grateful when a woman's voice cuts through my thoughts.

"Stop," she says in terror. "I said no."

A large man places his meaty hands around the hips of a young woman.

"No need to get feisty. We will have a good time," he purrs.

I turn my attention back to my food, the fork in my hand gripped tightly.

You need to stay out of it, Fraya. The reasonable part of me argues, but as I watch the fat man slide his hand over her butt, I am in the woods again. She pulls against him and as she struggles his grip only tightens, hands turning white.

I slide my stool back, the screeching drawing attention. The young woman's eyes find mine, pleading for help. *Why is no one helping her?*

"She said no," I growl.

He glances over lazily and smiles, "Well, hey there, kitty cat. You want to play too?" his voice slurs.

"Just let her go so I can return to the first real meal I have had in days." I walk over and place my body in front of hers.

He laughs, making his belly shake and I gag. He beckons me closer with his free hand. "It seems like we will have more fun anyway," he says and reaches toward me.

"I wouldn't," I warn. "If you want to keep that hand."

"Do you know who I am? What is a sweet kitten like you going to . . ."

His sentence is cut short by the blade at his neck.

So much for keeping a low profile.

I press the tip into his bubbled neck. "Let. Her. Go." A small trickle of blood escapes his skin and his eyes widen in fear.

"You are just like your mother." The thought echoes in my mind and I nearly drop my blade. I swallow my confusion and press harder.

He quickly sobers up enough to slowly remove his hands from both of us.

"I was just having a little bit of fun," he stammers.

I lean in close and whisper into his ear. "Next time, my *little bit of fun* won't leave you breathing."

I slide the blade back into its home and leave the pub, scolding myself for getting involved. I recall the strange whisper in the back of my mind and unease settles over me.

I turn down a dimly lit road. *Why did I get involved?* The sensation of being watched creeps over me, and soon my footsteps are echoed by the heavy thud of another. I turn away from the inn, worried my stalker will find me later.

I strain my ears and listen as the steps get closer and duck behind a wall. I slow my breathing and when they turn to me my blade is at their spleen.

"Why are you following me?" I push the tip of my blade a little farther. This is not the fat man from the bar.

"Are you sure you have a good grip on that blade?" he asks. Faster than a blink, my wrist is in his hands and my blade is clattering to the ground. Then, my hands are above my head and my back pressed against the rough wall before I can take another breath.

I struggle against his hold, bucking against him until I send my knee into his groin. He buckles and his grip tightens as he slides my wrists farther up the wall. *How?*

"You have a temper," his voice radiates in his chest, sending prickles down my spine.

He towers over me, and even in the dark his piercing eyes bore into mine. I find myself wanting to lean in, the smell of fresh rain wafting off his skin. My heart involuntary flutters in my chest, like a bird in an iron cage. *What is wrong with me?*

"So I have been told," I bite back. His eyes search mine, something hidden and dangerous looming behind them. "I know you," I say, trying to inch closer as he pulls deeper into the shadows.

"You don't." He drops me, my arms falling with a slap to my sides. My heart deflates when he steps away. A mask sliding over his handsome face.

Why does he feel so familiar? His dark curly hair hangs loose around his face and his beard is perfectly sculpted to his features.

"Go home." He turns his back to me and steps into the moonlight. He can't be much older than me and I would remember if I had ever run into him. His face isn't easily forgotten.

"You were at the tavern," I finally say.

"Go home," he orders.

"I don't have a home," I snap, but quickly suck in a breath, mortified by my confession.

"Well, you can't stay here," he argues.

How dare he. Who does he think he is?

"Who are you to tell me where I can and can't be?" I ask, stepping closer to him. I am inches from him now, the scent of freshly fallen rain rolling off him is intoxicating. He steps away and his hands clench into fists as he looks away from me.

Do I stink? I slightly lower my head but smell nothing.

Why do I care? I mentally roll my eyes.

Crossing my arms over my chest, I wait for an answer, but he leaves without speaking a word.

I stand in the middle of the road for a moment longer, replaying our altercation, and am only left with more questions.

If I'm honest, the fact he demanded I go back to my room makes me want to do the opposite.

I decide to walk the streets for a few minutes longer before returning to the inn for the evening. As I step into my room, the strange feeling of being watched makes my stomach turn. I stare out into the darkness unafraid.

CHAPTER 10

A loud banging rattles my door.

"Fraya!"

I throw my pillow over my face and let out a long groan. Reluctantly, gathering the covers around me, I get up and open the door. Luca stands there, disheveled. The smells seeping off him make me gag.

"You look awful and you smell worse." I hold my nose and step away from him.

"While you were in here sleeping like a princess, I was with the horses. It wasn't clean." Horror flashes over his face, I can only imagine what his night consisted of.

I stifle a laugh. "When will your room be ready?"

"It won't be. The current resident decided to stay a little longer." He shifts his weight from one foot to the other and itches his scraggly beard.

"You can't be serious," I say.

"I am as serious as the smell lingering on my skin." A small bag rests at his feet. "I need a bath."

Stepping back, I open the door further. "Come in, your smell is assaulting my nostrils." I giggle as he rolls his eyes.

I won't be staying anyway, so he can have the room.

Luca heads to the wash and I throw myself back on the bed. My thoughts drift to the mysterious stranger and a deep curiosity settles in my belly.

"Might as well get this started," I mumble.

"What?" Luca hollers.

"I am going to town," I reply.

He pops his head out, his chest glistening. "Get me something pretty." He winks.

I stare at him for a moment too long before turning toward the door. I hear his deep chuckle as he closes the door. "I've got a *pretty* shoe I can stick somewhere." I mumble.

The town is not as busy first thing in the morning, but I like it that way. I can get everything done and be on my way. The streets begin to crowd as the morning turns to afternoon. The clang of hammers and merchants yelling fills the air.

I stop at every shop stocking up on supplies for my trip to Rahkadyr.

Hands full and feeling accomplished, I round the corner and mash into something solid. My clothes spill to the ground, scattering around my feet.

I drop, quickly scooping everything together when a man squats, picking up the clothes closest to him. To my horror, underneath my riding pants is a new pair of undergarments. My face flushes red and when I look up the same stormy eyes from the bar stare back at me.

Heat crawls up my neck and out my ears.

He gently tucks my underclothes into the pants and folds them over, concealing my embarrassment.

"Thank you." I say quietly, taking the clothes from his hands. Our hands graze as he places the clothes into my pile. He quickly recoils as if I burned him.

"Yikes. I'm not contagious." I let out a slight chuckle.

Unwelcome images of his body leaning over mine will forever be burned in my mind. I clear my throat. "You're still following me then?"

"Maybe look where you are going next time," he says but his eyes don't meet mine.

"Wow, see you around DG." I grunt and tuck my clothes under my arm.

He pulls his eyebrows together; how does he look even more jaw dropping?

"DG?" His voice is flat with a tiny hint of curiosity.

"Dark and grumpy. I didn't know your name, so I gave you one." I shrug. "Do you like it?" I say with an innocent smile.

He says nothing and the name sticks. I watch as he swallows hard, the muscles in his jaw slightly flexing.

I nod, our exchange officially past awkward.

"Okay, well . . . I would say this has been great but that would be a lie," I say, catching a glimpse of a hidden grin before I turn away in search of the barn.

I smell the horses before I see them, the heat amplifying the stench. I spot Luca exiting the courier office. He glances my way and I feel caught as though I have been doing something I shouldn't. He doesn't seem to notice me, instead scanning the crowd. His eyebrows draw together tightly and when he doesn't find who or what he is looking for, he leaves, disappearing into a small crowd.

CHAPTER 11

I f I thought the smell coming from Luca was bad . . . this is something else. My eyes
water as I approach with my nose pinched closed. An older man shovels manure in
the corner.

"Excuse me." I say politely but he doesn't respond. He continues raking the shovel
across the ground.

"Hello?" I raise my voice slightly higher.

He jumps before turning around, his hand gripping his heart. He silver hair is thinning
and wiry gray hairs grow out of his nose.

"Sorry to startle you," I say. "I just need a horse."

He raises his hand to his ear and leans close.

"I need a horse," I yell. I feel slightly foolish speaking this loud.

In the last stall I see Luca's large horse. I look down, wanting to separate myself from
everything that reminds me of that night.

"I only have two available." He points to a beautiful chocolate colored mare and a gray
stallion. His coat shines with white spots against his dark smokey fur and his mane is as
white as the hair on my head. He is stunning.

"The chocolate one is a great horse." He slowly walks over to her stall.

"I want the gray one," I say matter of fact.

"He bites. I think you may be better off with the mare," he pushes.

"I will take my chances. Thank you." I stand my ground and although he looks weary,
he reluctantly agrees.

I hand over the payment and he slides it into his apron, then goes back to shoveling. I
stuff what little belongings I have into his saddle bags. "I will be back soon," I whisper.

The stallion chomps at my hair and I offer him an apple instead. "We will be friends,"
I say as I pat his large neck. The horse only huffs and crunches his apple.

On the way back to my room I contemplate the trip to Rahkadyr. It is a long one and I don't know how I will get into the castle and take his head, but I have plenty of nights to figure it out. The thought of the King opens a bleeding wound I smother with anger.

The sweet smell of bread and spices wafts to my nose. The heavy footsteps of soldiers pass by, making me pull my hood tighter. My eyes dance from one shop to the next, a window exhibits glass bottles glinting in the sunlight. I grab some herbs and move on to the next store.

A quaint shop called "The Bookstore" sits at the end of an alley.

Original. The thought kisses the back of my mind, not of my own making.

The ding of the bell above the door causes me to jump out of my skin. "Be there in a minute," a gentle voice floats through the air.

Dropping my hood, I run my finger across the spines, the leather smooth and cool against my skin. Rows of books line the walls from floor to ceiling. I could lose myself in these pages. A crash sounds behind me and I turn, pressing my body against the shelf.

"Fraya?" the woman's voice holds a slight quiver.

I draw my brows together. "Yes?"

I have never seen this woman before and no one here should know me. Her hair peppered with age sits in a tight bun on her head.

"I don't understand." She reaches toward me with shaky hands. "Why are you here?" her voice is soft as butter. Her honey brown eyes stare into my soul.

"I'm sorry, but do I know you?" I pull my hood over my head, trying to keep my hands busy and stepping away from her touch.

She gasps and a slight chuckle escapes her. "You must be . . .What? Nineteen now?" The whisper is just enough that my blood turns cold.

Who is this woman? I am torn between running and the innate need for answers. She couldn't know me, no one does. My father made sure of that.

"Who are you?" I ask.

The bell rattles and two figures walk through the door. I stare at the old woman, waiting for an answer to the question that hangs between us.

The men stare at each other, locked in conversation. Swords fall against each of their backs and leather armor rests over their chests and arms. My body stiffens as I pivot away from the soldiers.

"They say she is trapped between two worlds," a younger voice chimes.

"They are only stories, kid," says the older gentleman. His kind smile reveals perfect white teeth.

I clench my fists, my palms sweaty.

"Why else would he want her?" the young one persists.

The old woman clears her throat and turns her focus to the men. "Can I help you?" she asks while handing me a book and steering me toward the rear of the room, away from the threat.

"We are looking for a woman," they say in unison. I duck in between two bookshelves. An inch of dust coats the shelves and I resist the urge to run my fingers through it. Peering through the shelves, I pretend my attention is on the many books in front of me.

The kid rests his hands against his leather belt, his short blond hair lays perfectly atop his head.

"Ah." Her head tilts back and she places her fingers together, the whole motion uncharacteristically dramatic. "I see. Well, the brothel is two streets over."

I can feel the embarrassment seeping off each of them as they stumble over their words. "No ma'am," both men stammer. "I'm afraid you misunderstood. We are looking for a particular woman."

"Honey," she whispers. "I don't judge, but I don't think I can give you what you're after. I'm a bit out of practice."

A laugh rises to my lips and I don't know if I'll be able to contain it much longer.

"We are on orders from the King, ma'am. This woman is dangerous," the younger man sounds serious as he tries to reign in the conversation. "She has already attacked a man in a local pub."

"Oh dear," she says, covering her mouth with her wrinkled hand.

Feet shuffle closer to the door as the woman leads them out of her small shop. The bell rings once more. "She has white hair," the young soldier says. "Tell a soldier immediately if you see her." The older man has not said a word, but his cheeks have remained flushed.

"I will," she lies.

The door closes and I double over, unable to contain myself any longer. I can't remember the last time I laughed this hard. "Those poor souls. I think you scarred them for life." I wipe the tears that creep from the corners of my eyes and manage to catch my breath.

"They won't be back anytime soon that's for sure." She says with a slight chuckle. Her eyes twinkle with a loving kindness.

A seriousness comes over her and concern etches in her brow. "We can't talk here. It isn't safe."

I know she isn't wrong, but the thought of waiting one more second for answers, sits like a heavy stone in my stomach.

"Midnight. Meet me at the edge of town." She places her soft hands around mine. "I never thought I would see you again." She gently pats my hands.

"Alright, now go." She shoos me out the door. "Stay hidden and no more attacking people," she whispers sternly and shuts the door, but not before a hint of amusement in her face.

It takes me a minute longer to process what just happened. This woman knows me. Somehow, she knew me as a child. The King is still actively looking for me and the longer I stay, the more danger I am in.

One thing is for sure, I can't leave until I speak with her again.

Midnight.

CHAPTER 12

I reach for the door of my room and pause, my fingers just grazing the handle. I let all of my thoughts go before I open the door. I need to be ready if Luca asks any questions.

Why would he ask questions?

I shake my head and reach for the door again, but it is thrust open and a shirtless Luca stands in front of me. His face is clean shaven, his jaw strong, and his blond hair now tamed.

Bless the Ancients. My mouth falls open but I manage to quickly pick it up.

My eyes travel down his abdomen and I shake my head to refocus my thoughts.

"Like what you see?" The dimples in his cheeks make an appearance.

"Why are you naked?" I lean to one side and let out a sigh.

He looks at me with mock offense, "This is *not* naked. But if you want —"

"Enough." I put my hand up, stopping his next words.

He straightens his back and tilts his head to the side, "You were gone awhile."

His words are soft but I can hear the question in his statement. I take a deep breath in, steadying myself. "Are you just now getting out of the tub?"

"Would you have liked me to wait for you?" he asks with a raised brow.

"No, I just thought. Never mind." Letting him know I saw him in town feels like an invasion of privacy somehow.

"Is everything okay, can I help with anything?" He steps forward and his eyes bore into mine. I tell my legs to move but they remain. He doesn't touch me, doesn't have to. The heat from his body being this close makes my stomach flip.

Say something.

"I just need to relax." I push through the door and throw myself on the squeaky bed, his spell now broken.

"I have some errands I need to run." He pulls his shirt over his head and I watch as his perfectly chiseled body disappears.

I have a serious problem.

"Fraya?" Luca's words are careful. "If you need me here, I will stay."

My heart thumps in my ears and I sit up slowly. I stare into his soft blue eyes and see no hidden amusement or jest.

I give him a warm smile. "Thank you Luca, but I am okay. I promise."

"I will bring you back food, it makes everything better." The dimple in his cheek peeks out for me to see. "Don't miss me too much," he says. I fall back against a feathery pillow and let my arm drape across my eyes, a headache forming behind them.

"I won't, but I do want food." I yawn, cocooning myself in the covers, and allow myself to drift off.

I stretch, the muscles in my body reeling in pleasure, and then snuggle closer to the source of warmth surrounding me. An arm falls over my shoulders and pulls me closer while a warm breath tickles my hair.

My body goes rigid.

Why is this man's half naked body in my bed? I lift my lashes and a half smile peers down at me. *Even in his sleep he still wears that stupid smug look on his face.*

My legs curl up to my chest and then I kick them out as hard as I can, satisfied when a heavy *thunk* follows.

"Ow!" He coughs a few times and rubs his chest. "You seem disappointed to see me." He sits up, resting his back on the wall.

"Why are you in my bed? Anyone ever told you it is rude to enter a woman's bed without an invitation?"

He has the audacity to laugh at me. My blood boils.

"Getting into a woman's bed has never been the issue, darling. Getting out on the other hand." He smirks and runs his hands through his disheveled hair.

"I seemed to have little issue getting you out of my bed," I say defiantly.

"Ah yes, but you did indeed invite me."

"I did no such thing!" I recoil in shock.

He lifts his brow, his eyes darting across my face. I can feel my cheeks redden under his gaze.

"Then why were your arms wrapped around me?" I ask.

His grin is so large I think it will crack his face when he says, "That was all me."

I lift up and throw the pillow hard at his face, but he easily catches it in the air. Sitting with my legs crossed, I pull the covers around my chest suddenly feeling exposed.

He sits on the edge of the bed and pulls in his legs, letting his arms rest on his knees, suddenly serious. "When I got in, you were having a nightmare. I came over and you asked me to stay."

I vaguely remember the dream but I shove it away, not wanting to relive the memory of my father's cold dead eyes. "Sorry I kicked you in the chest. I wasn't expecting all of–." I motion toward his body. "That."

"Or . . . you didn't expect to like it." A boyish grin spreads across his beautiful thick lips. I close my eyes and the image of his arms draped over me makes my insides squirm; how his skin smells like the ocean and his chest rose and fell like the mountains. I hate that he's right.

"Hey, Luca?" I blink and when my eyes reopen I find his blue ones staring back at me. Losing track of my thoughts, unable to ask anything at all, I tuck a loose strand of hair behind my ear and his eyes darken, making a part deep inside me awaken.

"Yes," he says and looks up at me through his thick lashes.

The old woman comes to mind then and I am on my feet. "What time is it?" I rush to the door, the cool evening air rushing in.

Luca tilts his head, confusion etching his features. "Is that what you wanted to ask?"

The moon is disappearing from the sky, I don't have much time. "I need to go for a walk."

I swing the door closed expecting to hear a *click* but there isn't one. When I look back, Luca is standing in the door with his shirt still off and his pants loose around his hips. He looks lost.

"What's wrong?" his voice dips, concerned but also urgent as if he is waiting for a threat.

"I just need some fresh air," I stammer.

What am I supposed to say? I have to meet a strange lady that may know parts of my past I have longed to learn my whole life, and she may have known my mother? Also, I am willing to risk walking head first into a trap just for the slight chance of getting answers?

No, that's crazy.

He may look like a god but I don't know if I can really trust him.

"I just need to clear my head." It isn't a complete lie. Luca is becoming a distraction I can't have right now. Distractions get you killed.

I find my way to the edge of town and wait.

Sitting down with my legs crossed, I feel the earth's pull. The ground is littered with wild flowers that glow in the moonlight, and a gentle breeze plays with my hair. For a brief moment, as the chaotic world stops spinning, I feel like I can finally breathe.

"The Hausa Ancient loved the earth too." Her voice is soft as a whisper.

When I open my eyes, the old woman's deep, brown ones stare back at me. The wrinkles around her eyes soften her features and her warm smile puts me at ease.

"Hello, Fraya. I would sit with you, but I am afraid I may not be able to get back up." Her laugh is gentle as she extends her hand.

"I will give you the answers I have. Follow me."

CHAPTER 13

The hills leading to her home look like waves of rolling greenery lulled by the wind. Her home sits hidden in between two worlds; where the blossoming hills meet a foreboding wood. Smoke billows from the chimney, inviting me in. The inside is cozy, stuffed with fur rugs and old furniture.

I tug at my clothes as we sit, wishing she would end her silence and relieve the pressure in my chest. She places her palms against my fidgeting hands. "I never saw your mother happier than the day you were born."

Hot tears immediately sting the corners of my eyes. *She knew my mother.* The old woman leans back, placing her hands in her lap, as her mind drifts back to a different time.

"I was still a child when I was called to the castle for her birth, newly fifteen. Ravina screamed for hours after she entered this world. She had something to say and she was going to be heard." Her mouth quirks up at the memory. "I watched her grow up, become queen, and eventually, your mother," she finishes.

Blood runs through my ears, the heavy beating of my heart drowning out the rest of her words. *My mother was the queen?*

It takes me a moment to realize the old woman is saying my name.

"You didn't know?" she asks, her brows slightly together.

"That Queen Ravina was my mother? No." I try to keep my tone even, but the bite remains.

"I thought your father would have told you."

"He didn't," I snip. If she took offense to my tone, it doesn't show. The dagger rests heavy against my thigh. The last piece I have of him. Was it all a lie? I pull it from the comfort of its sheath and run my fingers over the steel.

"Where is your father now?" she asks.

I drop my stinging eyes to the dagger, flipping it over in my hands. I can't utter the words out loud. Every time I try, the words are choked off.

"Oh, honey." She stands and pulls me into her arms. Her warm hug pushes open a door to anguish that I am trying desperately to keep closed. Hot tears slide down my cheeks. I shove the door closed on my grief before it consumes me.

I pull back and wipe my tear-stained cheeks, pulling a blanket from the chair and draping it over my body like a protective shield.

"Would you like me to continue?" she asks softly.

I force my body to relax and tuck this information down for later. "I'm sorry. Yes, please continue."

The old woman nods. "What do you know about who you are, what you are?"

I hesitate before answering, "I know I am supposed to find Ciena . . . and I can do this." I lift the liquid from her tea cup and swirl it around before gently placing it back, not a single drop spilled. "I don't have as much control over fire, so I won't try that."

She nods, not seeming surprised at all by my unnatural abilities. "Also, I now know I am a princess." I shrug my shoulders as if it is no big deal, but it is in fact a big deal, much bigger than I could have anticipated.

"Your mother was bonded to Ciena. She is Moir, the Ancient of Ancients. You are known as Alkazah. The last Alkazah."

This is the second time I've heard that term, *Alkazah*. I feel foolish. I should know who I am, where I came from. Shame sneaks up when I realize I'm angry with my father for keeping this from me.

"Alkazah?" I ask.

"Only an Ancient can pass down its power to the offspring of its bonded," she says. "Ciena was bonded to your mother, when Ravina conceived the Ancients power passed to you." She pauses, waiting for the information to sink in.

"Why didn't he tell me?" I drop my gaze to my too short fingernails.

"I am sure he had his reasons, Fraya, all of which aimed to protect you," she reassures.

"Why didn't she stay?" The words come out in a whimper. I am embarrassed and feel like a child.

The old woman presses her lips and her brows draw together. "Your mother wanted to, but she and your father knew if she did the King would never stop hunting her. He would have found her and you."

"He found me anyway, so it looks like my parents died for nothing." I can't look at her. It hurts to breathe.

"Putting you in my arms was the hardest thing your parents ever did." She places her soft wrinkled hand in mine. "Don't minimize their love for you and the sacrifice they made because you are angry." Her soft rebuke is just that, soft and kind.

Hours pass like minutes until my stomach growls, breaking the heaviness that sits between us.

"Will you get the firewood from the back? Seems the night has gotten away from both of us and we need to eat," she says matter of fact.

I nod, grateful for the break. The sun starts to peak over the horizon and a cool brush of morning air sends prickles over my skin. The morning fog raises like a soft silvery veil across the earth and creeps into the dark forest that lays behind the old woman's home.

I have never seen trees so thick that the sun struggles to reach the ground.

I stare into the void and listen to the humming of noisy bugs as they wake from their slumber, and a lonely hoot owl cries from the darkness. A chill prickles down my spine and dread washes over me. A predator is watching. A twig snaps and my breathing stops.

I can't shake the feeling that someone or something is out there, waiting.

"Child, what in the name of the dragons has taken you so long?"

I nearly jump out of my skin when she rounds the corner. "I thought I heard something." I place my hand over my wildly beating heart.

The old woman stops, silently watching the darkness. Seconds feel like minutes as she listens to the songs of the forest. Her body tenses and when I am sure she is about to agree, she relaxes; dismissing my concern.

She waves a unconcerned hand toward the darkness. "The forest is noisy, child, it is nothing."

I scan the tree line, expecting someone to walk out of the darkness at any moment.

CHAPTER 14

With a belly full of eggs and roasted potatoes, I sit staring into a void as my mind reels at all I have learned. I am Alkazah; I am not one hundred percent sure what that means. My father lied to me my whole life, and to top it off; I am a princess. My mother was Queen Ravina of the Western Region.

I glance at the floor, counting the hairs of the fur rug laying at my feet. "Who was my dad, really? I know he wasn't King."

As the words fall from my mouth, I feel sick. The question has sat in the back of my mind all night. Was he really who I thought he was?

Her shaky hand finds my chin and lifts my face to hers. "He *was* your father, Fraya." She answers my unsaid question and relief washes over me. I feel ashamed for thinking otherwise.

"He fell madly in love the first time he saw your mother, although they both tried to ignore it, especially your mother. He was a soldier and she was a princess, a fiery one." She gives a light laugh at the memory.

"And Ciena?" I ask.

"Your grandparents died when your mother was still young. The burden of ruling an entire region fell on her shoulders. Your father would find her going for long walks in the forest. The large trees brought her comfort, she once told me they had been there long before her and will be there long after. It was the only constant thing she had at that time."

I spent my whole life wanting to know about my mother; who she was, her favorite food, what she looked like, and what type of person she was. Sitting here listening to these stories, she still feels so far away.

"When she found Ciena, hunters had already drugged her. Bleeders had trapped her, and your mother couldn't stand to see another dragon suffer that fate; she didn't know Ciena was an Ancient until later."

I remember my father telling me about the blood draining being why the dragons fled. Too many were slaughtered. Their blood amplifies strength and heightens senses, but it's short lived, highly addictive, and dangerous.

"When the Dark King found out about Ciena, he would stop at nothing to get her and obtain her power." She shakes her head and a deep sadness sits behind her eyes.

Everyone knows about the great war that took the queen.

Not only did the Dark King take my father, but he took my mother from me too. I clench my jaw to bite my temper. This is the last place I want to lose control.

"Your father told you to find the old dragon. I don't know where she is, but this may help." She pulls out an old map, its edges torn and ink faded.

She pauses for a moment. "Everything okay?" I ask.

She sits it down and smiles, but it doesn't reach her eyes. Something changed. She waits a few moments longer before grabbing a bag, stuffing a few items down to the bottom. "If I didn't know any better, I would say you are trying to get rid of me." I force a half laugh from my throat.

She waves a hand at me. "Nonsense."

Her attention is drawn back to the thin paper that sits before us. "The old city lies under these mountains." She circles the mountains to the north with her fingers. "You need to be careful, Fraya. Something dangerous lingers there."

"Besides a dragon god?" I jest, but there is no humor in her eyes.

Rahkadyr sits far to the East, past the trees that reach the heavens. The King hides behind his army but he can't hide from me.

Folding the map, she places it in the bag. "Make sure and go through the old trees." She holds my face in her soft wrinkled hands and says, "We have been waiting for you." Sliding the bag over my shoulders, she shoves me gently out the door.

"Who?" I ask in confusion.

"Your people." A pride I don't deserve swells in her eyes. I am not a savior.

"Stay safe, child." She lingers at the door. "I am so happy I got to see you one last time." She puts her fingers to her lips, her hands slightly shaking.

I pull her into a big hug that she happily returns, and I can't help but feel that there is something I am missing. "I will be back." I squeeze her cold wrinkled hands in mine. "I promise."

"Go, child. It's time."

CHAPTER 15

The stalls are empty, except for the horses. Looking at my horse, I realize he needs a name.

Thinking about the way he looks like smoke and ash, I ask him, "Do you like the name Ash?" I pet down his mane, setting the bag down to dig fresh clothes from his pack.

He flicks his ears and nibbles at the bag. "Okay, what about Smoke?" I suggest. He bobs his head up and down vigorously, obviously pleased with his new name. "I will take that as a yes."

I strip my clothes, the cool air pricking my skin.

A deep voice clears his throat. "I am all for riding naked, but maybe not in public?"

I press myself against Smoke, covering every exposed part of my body I can. Peeking at my intruder, I see DG's back turned to me. My heart slows, but my skin flushes as I tug my shirt over my head.

"I was changing," I hiss.

"Can I turn around now?" he asks.

"Mhmm," I say and finish packing my horse. "Why are you here?"

"I could ask you the same thing." He looks around. "In a hurry?"

"What makes you say that?" I turned to look him over. Still every bit as ruggedly handsome as the first time I saw him. It takes more effort than I want to admit to pull my eyes away from him.

"Because most people prefer to get dressed in privacy." His tone lacks mocking, just facts.

"Maybe, I'm not *most people*." I tilt my head and drop my weight to one side.

Leaning against the stall door, he crosses his arms over his wide chest, broadening his shoulders. The shirt he is wearing appears tailored, fitting his large frame perfectly. His gray eyes, sun kissed skin, and dark hair are suffocatingly attractive; his presence overtaking the small space.

"I am beginning to see that," he says, and I swear one side of his mouth tilts up.

I raise my brow. "Is that so?"

I keep my focus on him, unwilling to be the first to break eye contact. Then, I step closer to him, this stranger whose name I don't know but somehow feels so familiar. Who makes my pulse quicken with just a glance.

His body tenses with each step I take. *Interesting.*

I stop, just close enough that the heat from his body warms my skin. Our eyes tethered together; tension wrapped around us like a whip.

"Are you going to let me pass?" I drop my voice, just above a whisper.

Without a word, he takes his body weight off the stall, creating a space just big enough for me to pass through. "Thank you," I say as I snake through the small space. Sparks dance across my skin as I brush past him.

I rub the nose of Luca's horse, trying not to think about how the touch of his skin made me feel. Luca's horse snorts, his breath hot against my hand. Memories of my father forcing me to ride this horse sting, guilt stabs me in the stomach like a rusty knife. I grit my teeth to stop the tears, the familiar ache forming in my jaw.

"Beautiful horse. He yours?" Something hidden is laced in DG's words but I let my curiosity die.

I swing the stall door open and slap the horse on the rump. "Get," I say.

"He's plan B." I watch as the horse gallops into the darkness, clearing my throat before I turn back to DG. "See you around, DG."

"See you, Litchska," he says with a warm husky voice.

The simple word makes me pause. "Do I want to know what that means?"

"Probably not." A slight smirk etches across his beautiful face but is soon swallowed by stone.

"Maybe you will tell me one day." I say and lead Smoke toward the exit.

"We will see," an unexpected playfulness enters his tone.

I glance back to see DG has already disappeared into the night. I put my foot into the stirrup when I hear rustling. "Need another goodbye?" I ask.

Luca steps out of the shadows, something wicked hidden behind his eyes. "A first would be nice. Were you expecting someone else?"

Why do I feel like I've been caught doing something I shouldn't be doing? "No one in particular."

His long stride covers the space between us in seconds. "Did waking up in my arms spook you so much you couldn't even say goodbye?" His features soften and for a moment a pang of shame stabs me. I look over his shoulder checking for DG, not sure why I care if he overheard Luca's words.

"No, I wasn't thinking of that actually." The memory causes unwanted heart palpitations. "I just have somewhere I need to be. Thank you, really, but I must be going."

"I want to go with you," he says.

"No." I put force behind the single word, making my stance clear. He cannot go.

"I want to make sure you're safe," his voice holds a tenderness that wasn't there before.

"I need to do this on my own," I insist.

"What exactly?" he asks, skeptically.

This is the question I have been rolling around in my head since I left the old woman. The Dark King killed the only person I had in this world. He robbed me of my mother and I would like nothing more than to watch the life drain from his eyes.

But the last thing my father whispered before leaving this world was to find the Ancient. Why?

"I haven't decided yet," I answer truthfully.

"I have given you no reason not to trust me, Fraya." He closes the small gap between us. I step back, only slightly but I can see the disappointment in his eyes. "I don't think I could ever forgive myself if something bad happened to you."

A knot forms in the depth of my belly, "I don't need saving. I can take care of myself," I keep the words soft.

A scoff comes from the back of his throat causing me to take a large step, jerking my head back. "What was that?"

"Nothing. It's nothing," he pushes away my question.

My insides are hot, "Tell me," I demand.

"It's just . . . that's our thing. You fall into trouble and I rescue you." He shrugs his shoulders.

His words roll over me like a swarm of locusts. "Excuse me?"

"It's not a big deal, I enjoy it," he grins. "Really."

He lifts his hands to touch me. "Don't. I only needed *saving* when you came around. Why is it everything went to shit the moment I met you?"

"If I hadn't been there, you would still be in those woods or leaning over your father's dead body." His eyes widen, color fading from his skin, regret changing his features.

His words are a punch in the gut, and the air in my lungs dissipates. *How could he say that?* I need to get out of here.

"Fraya?" His hands wrap around mine.

"Don't." I jerk my hands from his and back away slowly, Smoke close beside me. Anger makes my skin hot.

"I didn't mean it," he begs. "I swear."

"From the moment I met you, death has followed . . . and you are the only common thread." My chest heaves.

He quickly closes the gap between us, cupping my face in his scratchy hands.

"I said don't touch me." I thrust my palm into his chest. I hear him hiss in pain and watch as he shrinks away from me. His shirt is singed and a perfect handprint burned into his skin. Disbelief, horror, and pain cross his face at the same time. Intrigue rests in his eyes as he looks at me and back to his burnt flesh.

My stomach churns, *I didn't mean to do that.*

CHAPTER 16

The sound of Smoke's hooves beating on the ground echo my racing heart. The look on Luca's face as I mounted my horse plays over and over in my head. As the morning turns to mid-day, sweat beads and rolls down my back. The unforgiving sun glares down on me, reddening my skin.

A rare breeze glides over the long grass, and the dandelions float through the sky like fairies dancing on the wind.

Only when the sun begins to dip below the horizon and the crickets sing, do I stop. My body trembles with exhaustion but my mind won't relent. I stare at my hands . . . hands I can't control.

Smoke walks up and chews my hair, comfortingly nudging me with his nose. I stroke him, burying my face in his fur. He dips his head into my bag and snatches my last apple.

"Rotten horse," I say and snatch my bag from him.

"Things will never be normal, will they?" I let out a heavy sigh. The revelation sinks like a heavy stone in my stomach. For the first time in my life, I am utterly alone. Warm, salty tears stream down my cheeks. "I'm alone and no one is coming for me."

I coax water from my canteen, the simple motion bringing me comfort. *"I have always wanted to see the world, would you like to see it with me, sweet girl?"* I remember the excitement in discovering new places and scenery, it wasn't until later I realized we weren't going on an adventure, we were running. Because of me. *Always because of me.*

I reach up to grip my necklace but only feel my skin. Both hands shoot to my throat, wildly scouring for my mother's necklace. *No.* I get to my feet, patting my body down, then dig through my bag hoping, pleading, and praying to the Ancients. *No. No. No.*

A deep ache settles in my chest and a cry vibrates through my lungs, bouncing through the hills. It could be anywhere. I let out a long deep breath and swallow my disappointment. Taking my map from the bag, I run my fingers over the creases of the worn paper, my tears staining the page. I can't think about it.

"It's just a necklace," I try to tell my self.

"Your mother's necklace," my thoughts rebel.

I must pass through the Valley of Blood and Bone if I am to reach the mountain the god resides in. My father made it a point to *never* travel through there. I always thought it was to respect the lives lost, but I now know it held memories too painful to revisit.

A small white paper flutters to the ground. The writing rushed and scribbled.

Fraya,
You will find what you are looking for,
or maybe it will find you.
Until we meet again . . .

The sun bleeds across the sky, the reds blending with yellows and golds. With no sleep and no clear direction, I set off east. Loneliness settles into my stomach, so vast the hurt echoes deep within my body.

Days pass and my meager supplies begin to dwindle. A quaint village comes into view and I push forward, pulling my hood over my head.

"Alright, Smoke. In and out." I take a deep breath and lead him forward. "No problem." I pat Smoke's large shoulder. *No problem.*

The streets are empty. *Strange.* Dust kicks up as we reach the center of town. The ground is cracked and dry, begging for a drop of rain. A woman scurries into her house, careful to keep her eyes glued to the ground.

I hear them before I see them, the stammering of hooves, and the grunting of men. Smoke's ears flicker. "We need to get out of here." I duck behind a house, the wood falling off the sides. An older man has his back toward me, leaning against part of the shed with one hand.

"What are all these men doing here?" I wonder.

"Looking for you," my mind replies.

My mouth goes dry and a long sigh comes from the man's lips followed by splattering of urine. I gag and slowly start to back away when Smoke whinnies.

"Hey!" He jumps, turning around. "What are you doing?" he asks while zipping his pants and I avert my eyes. "I'm talking to you," he says.

I hear his footsteps draw closer; a thousand scenarios run through my mind, including how long I will have to escape after I kill him. He grips my arm. "I'm talking to you," he says as he jostles me but I keep my head down, my hair covered.

"If I'm not mistaken, you just relieved yourself with that hand. It would serve you well to get it off me." I lift my eyes to meet his. I am done letting people run my life.

"Who do you think you are?" He tightens his grip, his ego bruised. Smoke bobs his head and stomps wildly.

"Harin!" a tiny voice shouts. "You found him!" a little girl with tight curls calls from the windows. I keep my face neutral, not to give away my confusion. Her sweet face remains calm, then she disappears from the window. Her tiny feet are heard stomping through the small cottage.

The door swings open and a child no older than seven steps out. The soldier still maintains his grip on my arm as the little girl takes Smoke by the reins and walks around the house.

"Are you coming?" She looks at me over her shoulder.

I nod as another soldier steps around the house. "Arny! There you are, man, we've been looking for you. It's time to head out."

He pulls me close and whispers, "Today seems to be your lucky day." He releases me and disappears behind his friend.

CHAPTER 17

"I'm Lucy." She stands in front of me smiling from ear to ear missing her two front teeth.

Her mother steps from the shadows. "Get inside, they may come back." She ushers her daughter through the leaning door. "You too, come on." She motions for me to follow.

I hesitate for a moment. "You are safer here than out there."

I relent, following behind Lucy. "I hope you like chicken," she says as she bounces into the adjoining room.

My stomach grumbles at the smell coming from the kitchen. "I love chicken, Lucy. Thank you."

It has been days since I ate anything other than apples and jerky.

"Sit, sit." Lucy tugs my arms until I am sitting at the table. Her enthusiasm is contagious.

"You were really brave out there. I'm Fraya by the way," I tell her.

She shrugs. "Those guys are not nice and you seemed like you needed help, so I helped."

Her mother turns and watches her daughter lovingly, her dark brown eyes beaming with pride.

I look up to the young girl's mother. "Thank you for your help, ma'am."

"I am not old enough or wise enough to get called ma'am. Maxine, please." I nod as she places a large plate in front of me. My senses take in the food before my mouth does. The fried chicken, potatoes, and gravy make my mouth salivate.

Lucy stands on her chair. "That's so pretty!" she screeches and points to my neck as I stuff a juicy piece of chicken into my mouth.

"I was born with it." I pull my shirt closer to my neck.

"Why is it white? It matches your hair," she notices.

"I'm not entirely sure, but my father used to tell me the Ancients painted it on my skin. However, I think it's just a birthmark. What about you?" I wrinkle my nose at her.

She sits and places her small hands under her chin, elbows firm against the table, kicking her legs, and choosing her next words carefully.

"I think if the Ancients chose to paint on you, then you must be really special." Her words hit me straight in the stomach. *Special.*

I look into her caramel-colored eyes. "I think if anyone here is special, it's you." Her face lights up as she looks at her mother, who nods lovingly.

She chimes in with another question but her mother quickly interjects. "Eat, Luce." Maxine sets the plate in front of her daughter.

"Why are there so many soldiers here?" I ask between bites.

Maxine's face contorts and pain flashes through her eyes. "It has been years since so many soldiers entered this village," her voice catches and my heart tugs. "The last time they were here they took everything, including . . ." her voice drops and Lucy takes a large bite of her potato. "My husband, Lucy's father."

"I am so sorry," I say. I know it is not enough. No apology could give her back what she has lost.

"It's not your fault, dear. The Dark King has taken something from all of us."

Maxine wipes the grease from Lucy's chin. The look she gives her daughter and the way she brushes the hair from her face, makes me long for something I thought I buried a long time ago.

"Why are you helping me? It is a big risk?" I ask.

Maxine looks at her daughter and then back at me. "There was never a question of *if* we were going to help you but rather *how*."

A loud banging sounds at the door. "I figured out who you are and I know you are in there. Come out or we will break it down," the soldier bellows.

All three of us jump to our feet. Lucy's eyes widen as she looks to her mother.

"The washroom window connects to the horse stall, hurry." Maxine urges.

"I will not just leave you here," I protest.

"You don't have a choice." She stands tall. "We both know the mark on your skin is no mere birthmark, child."

"I can't let you do this," I object.

"If you get caught, it was all for nothing. You're wasting time, now go." She shoves me toward the washroom as the door bursts open. "Go!" she yells.

Piercing pain shoots up my legs as I hit the ground. I peer around the side of the building; four men stand outside the door blocking anyone from leaving. "They're getting away!" a deep voice yells. I watch the four men scramble inside the house. Throwing myself over my horse I bolt out of the stall.

Just as I am about to hit the clearing, two men step out from behind a house with bows drawn. Smoke struggles to stop, his front legs raise in the air, throwing me to the ground.

Ow!

"What the hell, Smoke?" It doesn't take me long to find what spooked him. A third man appears fighting against a beast of an animal, he has got to be the largest dog I have ever seen, more wolf than anything.

"The whole platoon is looking for you, girl." Another man grabs me and tightens his grip. "How much do you think we will get for bringing her in?" The man with the dog licks his lips at the thought.

"You really don't want to do this," I insist.

"We do, actually," he hisses in my ear.

"I don't know, man. Maybe we should just . . . let her go." The second soldier shifts on his feet.

"Don't be a coward. She can't be that dangerous." The man holding me loosens his grip.

I slowly step away from the bickering men, but keep my ears open as the hand on me drops away.

"Her soul is divided between the heavens and the earth. She is not human." His words are full of fear but something lingers behind the fear.

"You're right, she is a curse." His attention turns back to me, a small vial in his hand and pops the top off. "We have to get rid of her."

A drop of shimmery red liquid stains his lips. *Is that. . . dragon's blood?* His lips curl up in a gruesome smile and the veins in his body bulge from his skin. His pupils enlarge and only a small sliver of white remains.

Dropping his weapons, he rolls his shoulders and cracks his neck. "Ready?" he asks then charges. The other soldiers stand, waiting.

I lower my body, pulling my blade from my side. The beast of a man jumps, the movements more animal than human. The sharp edge catches his flesh, and I watch as it stitches itself back together.

I can't even do that.

He quickly strikes again, sending his fist into my chest. I hear as my ribs crack under the pressure. I struggle to find my breath and stumble backward. Shock and pain vibrate through my body.

With each blow, he grows more wild, stronger, and faster.

"It's the blood, Fraya," the voice in the back of my mind says.

I focus my mind and pull water from a nearby trough. If I can no longer hide who I am, then I won't.

"Enough!" I slam the water into his chest repeatedly, sending him barreling backward. The others take a step back, eyes bulging from their heads.

"What are you doing?" he yells at his fellow soldiers. I look behind me, the men have disappeared. "Cowards!" the monster yells.

The trembling soldiers in front of me drop the weapons as I slide my knife into my belt loop. Flashes of my father spark a pain that sits in my soul, and I watch as a wild flame licks the ends of my fingertips. "Make a choice," I demand from the men.

A slit of silver slashes across the throat of the dog handler and he crumbles to the ground. The beast he controlled whines and takes off. The second man nods in my direction, his eyes wild with fear, and sprints in the opposite direction.

"Seems like you are all alone," I hiss.

"I didn't need them anyway." He empties another vial of dragon's blood into his mouth, moaning as the liquid spills into his stomach. A wave of nausea washes over me. "The King wanted you alive, but it seems like that isn't going to happen."

I thrust my hand out to attack, but the flames just crawl up my arms. I look at him and back at my arms, panic rising. He just laughs. "Seems like you are all bark and no bite."

He draws his sword, his muscles twitching rapidly. He steps toward me, his chest heaving, one knee drops to the ground. He growls, forcing himself back up, only to stumble in the process.

Blood slips from the corners of his mouth as he clutches his chest. A slight whimper comes from his throat, and then his life leaves his eyes as his body hits the ground, hard.

I stand there, staring at his lifeless form waiting for him to get back up, but he never does. I hear more soldiers approaching, but my eyes remain fixed on what is in front of me. Why would anyone do that to themselves?

"Are you going to just stand there!" My head snaps up, my eyes meeting Luca's. "Fraya, Go!"

I shake my head and grab Smoke's saddle, throwing my body over it as he flies through the field, toward the mountains that lay nestled behind the trees with Luca close behind.

CHAPTER 18

Adrenaline courses through my veins as we burst through the protection of the woods. My breath is labored and uneven as I stare at Luca in disbelief. *Where did he come from?*

Luca shuffles through his bag. "Why are you here?" I demand through uneven breaths.

Smoke's nostrils flare and he tosses his winter mane with impatience. "Your horse isn't well trained," Luca observes.

Smoke bites toward him, causing him to flinch away. I laugh and pat him on the neck. "Or, he just doesn't like you."

He ignores my comment, "Ah, here it is." He lifts my necklace, the gold flecks sparkle in the sunlight. "I know how important it is to you."

"How?" I cradle the stone in my hands before clasping it around my neck. The light pressure comforting and familiar.

"I found it in the stables." He lowers his gaze. "Look, I don't expect forgiveness."

"Good, because you aren't getting it," I snip.

"You shouldn't have to do this on your own, Fraya," he says. "But, if this is what you want, then I concede."

"I thought you preferred to travel alone," I counter.

His blue eyes find mine. "Yeah, well . . . it seems you are the exception to that rule." His smile reveals the dimples in his cheeks, and in any other moment his words and smile may have made my stomach swim. If I'm honest, a place deep inside me churns ever so slightly.

I clench my teeth and swallow the lump in my throat. "What you said was awful."

"I know, and I will turn around and go home right now if that is what you want," he says.

Home?

"I don't trust you," I say.

"And you shouldn't. Not right now." His words make me pause. "You are special and I want to be a part of it. That's the truth."

"You don't even know where I'm going," I say.

"I can guess," he says. His eyes slightly roll, like it is obvious. "If it was me, I would want to kill the man who took away my family."

Smoke digs his hooves into the ground. "I took the life of the man whose blade took my father's life."

He nods in agreement. "Yes, but not the man who ordered it."

I clench my jaw. We are deep enough into the forest the soldiers cannot find us, but still the possibility makes me uneasy. We need to move.

Maybe it would be better to keep him close. "I still don't trust you."

"Understood," he says.

"Lead the way." I motion my arm in front of me.

"I don't know where we are going," he challenges.

"That way." I motion my arm toward the woods.

He clicks his tongue and his horse moves forward, the brush crunching under his hooves. I spot a bright white feather nestled under his saddle and pluck it from its home as Luca saunters past.

"A white owl feather?" I say to myself. I run the velvet feather over my palm as the trees become denser. The sun struggles to break through their thick canopy. Foreign sounds taunt my ears; a bird shrieks above and the bugs hum in response. Even the trees seem to pulsate with power, the slight breeze swaying the high tree tops and cascading back to earth on a tidal wave of euphoria.

"What do you have there?" Luca asks.

"This?" I lift the feather so the hints of sunlight catch the sheerness of it. "It's pretty huh?"

"It is." He holds out his hand and I delicately place it in his hands for him to inspect. "This would make an excellent quill pen." He hands it back, the edges of his fingertips grazing mine.

"White owls aren't *typically* found in this region," I say.

Luca shrugs as a strong gust of wind comes from above, my hair flying around my face. Something large darts through the trees. A high pitched whiny comes from Smoke and I lock my thighs against the saddle, pulling my body close to my horse. *What the hell was that?*

"Shhh. It's okay," I whisper. I am not going to get thrown off this horse twice in one day.

The treetops shake again, a beast hidden among them. Luca keeps his eyes fixed on the heavens, muscles twitching and his sword clenched. Its presence rattles my bones and then it's gone. We both stay frozen for a few minutes longer. When I am finally able to move my muscles again, I pat Smoke's shoulder.

"Let's go big guy, nice and slow." The heaviness lessens with each step.

I relax my shoulders and take a deep breath. "What was that?"

"If I had to guess . . . a dragon," he answers.

"I thought . . ." My words trail off unfinished.

"Most were gone? Many people do, but they have just gotten better at hiding. How else would that soldier have gotten dragon's blood?" he shrugs.

"How could people do that? How can they drink their blood?" I shudder at the thought.

"There are people out there who would do anything for power, even risk dying." He pats his horse and says, "We should really get going." We don't want to be here when it comes back."

Evening approaches quickly and as I lay under the tree canopy my mind refuses to settle. My body involuntarily twitches, making rest hopeless.

"Your tossing and turning make it impossible to sleep," Luca mutters.

"It's no better over here." I take a deep breath and sit up, the fire's warmth almost uncomfortable.

A deep grunt comes from across the fire, "What's on your mind?"

"Can I see?" I ask, but as soon as the words leave my lips, I regret them. Of course, I don't need to see. He says nothing for a few minutes and I slowly succumb to my embarrassment.

"Okay," he says and slowly unbuttons his shirt, a white bandage coming into view. My heart squeezes as he unwraps the cloth revealing a blistered handprint, angry and charred. I scoot until I face him, knowing I'm not the only one who will remember that moment for the rest of my life.

"I am so sorry, there is no excuse for this." I glance up at him, my hand hovering over his chest. My fingers slightly graze his warm skin and his body tenses under my touch. I gently push his shirt to the side to get a better look and see just how angry his skin is.

"If you want to take my shirt off, all you have to do is ask." He grins causing my skin to flush.

Without thinking, I reach up and shove his chest. He withdraws in pain, his arms gripping my upper arms. I immediately drop my jaw and bring my hands to my mouth. "Oh shit."

"I'm beginning to think you *are* trying to kill me," he jokes.

He slowly releases his hold, his face no longer contorted in pain. Slowly sliding his rough hands down my forearms, my skin tingles under his touch. I don't move and I don't breathe as he glides his thumb across my knuckles.

"Fraya," his voice is husky, beckoning to look into his eyes. Eyes that could suck me in like the depths of the ocean. "I will never be able to take back what I did, but I will regret it for the rest of my life."

I don't trust you.

I pull away from him. "We should rest." I pretend not to see the disappointment on his face and return to my bedroll.

You don't trust him.

CHAPTER 19

I jolt awake to a heaviness pressing down on my body, a large hand snug against my mouth. My heart bangs against my chest and terror courses through my veins. I struggle against the person pinning me to the ground but he stays flat against me. I reach out, the handle of my dagger gripped in my palm.

"Shhh," Luca's whisper hardly registers in my brain. His face is only inches from mine and his weight makes breathing difficult. "Don't move." His lips brush my ear and a shiver runs down my spine.

The ground rumbles beneath me and a throaty growl comes from somewhere within the darkness. A large animal is stalking us. The creature steps closer, the embers of our fire creating an eerie glow against the three-inch talons attached to blue scales.

It's a dragon!

My heart feels like it's about to explode, while his keeps an even rhythm. How is he this calm? He was the same way the moment he met my father. The only hint of fear is the slight twitch in his jaw.

"Luca?" I whisper.

His chest vibrates against mine, the only indication he heard me. A harsh gust of wind whips my hair, the fire now just embers.

We are going to die.

"*Fraya, get up,*" a cool whisper floats through my mind.

"What?" I look at Luca who turns his attention to me.

"Shhh," his tone is stern.

"*Get up!*" it commands.

I squirm under Luca but he pins with his hips, his weight suffocating. "Get off me, Luca," I bite out through gritted teeth.

"Are you crazy?" he hisses.

Possibly.

"If you don't get off me right now, so help me." He tucks his shoulder and rolls off me, and the dragon shifts toward us. I stand, taking in the beast before me. It stands the height of two men. Its nostrils flare and its eyes are a tidal wave of blue with flares of purple.

This was a bad idea.

An Azule dragon. Why is it this far from the sea? Her face is sleek, and her body is long, perfect for maneuvering quickly through water.

The horses are nowhere to be seen and our weapons along with them. Luca stands with a flimsy belt knife in his hands. No match for what stands before us.

A long tail slithers toward us, a dozen or more spikes sprayed at the end.

"Tell her to stop," the calm voice floats through my mind.

"What?" I ask, feeling ridiculous.

"Tell her to stop!" it commands.

Luca hacks at the tail but quickly swings in the sky by his ankles. She opens her large mouth revealing rows of razor sharp teeth.

"Fraya!" His voice waivers, the first real admittance of fear.

"Stop!" I demand the dragon.

She doesn't look my way, instead fixed on the meal in front of her.

"Fraya, if there was ever a time to use your flame, it's now!" He swings wildly at the beast in front of him.

"I said stop!" I push into her mind until all her attention is on me. Her eyes narrow before tossing Luca to the ground, slithering to me with deadly speed. She tilts her large head, surveying me and it takes every ounce of will power not to step away from her. With her this close, I can see how each scale creates perfect armor. Large horns sprout from her temples and curve inward, pulling her face tight. What should be two smaller horns are tucked snug behind them, but one is missing. Small nubbed spikes adorn her slender cheek bones.

I contain the tremble deep in my bones, not wavering under her fierce gaze. I wait for further instruction but it never comes, the hushed voice in my mind is now silent. *Great.*

"How can you speak to my mind, human?" the dragon says. I can feel her now, pressing at the corners of my mind.

I straighten my shoulders, *"I am Alkazah, born of the Ancient Moir."*

Her slender face lowers, closing the short space between us. *"Impossible!"* she objects. The blue tint of her scales are painted every shade of the oceans. Teals, indigos, and sapphires blend together in a stunning masterpiece.

"You need to leave." The command feels foolish. Standing in front of a creature that could eat me whole, demanding it to do anything seems insane.

I can't help but wonder how my father and I never crossed paths with a dragon during our travels.

Luca holds his ribs as he struggles to his feet, a hunting knife clutched in one hand. I slowly shake my head.

"Humans hunt us, drain us, kill us!" Her pain hits me in waves. The heaviness of loss thick in her voice, her ache mirroring my own.

"Not this one," I tell her.

Two large wings spread from her shoulders, making herself larger. *"Humans are all the same. They took everything from me."*

"The King is who took everything from you." I take a deep breath, locking my heart up tight. *"He took everything from me as well."*

The beast lowers her wings, *"So, it is revenge you are after."*

I press my lips together. *"Among other things,"* I say.

She turns her attention to Luca, who still has his hunting blade drawn and crouched low to the ground waiting for a reason to strike. *"Trusting people will get you killed, Alkazah."*

She lifts into the sky, disappearing into the thick canopy of trees. I let out a deep breath, tension flooding from my muscles.

I just spoke with a dragon . . .

CHAPTER 20

Days bleed together and my body has grown numb and is mangled from bug bites. Sweat trickles down my spine, my hair clinging to my skin as we trudge deeper into the thick forest.

"Do you even know where we are going?" Luca huffs. He has tried to be a good sport as we walked endlessly day in and out with no clear direction.

"Do you have someplace else you would rather be?" I ask.

"Then this hot, sticky, death trap? I can think of a few." He kicks the sticks scattered on the forest floor. Although we have not had another run in with a dragon we both know it is only a matter of time.

"You look awful," I tease.

"You don't look so great yourself."

The unforgiving sun sits high in the sky, and the horses are still missing. "I need a distraction," I say.

Luca lifts his brow and gives me a devilish grin. "Not that kind of distraction, you brute. Tell me about your family."

"There isn't much to tell. I have a father who wants nothing to do with me, and a brother who can do no wrong." He strides past me.

"That sounds awful," I say.

He shrugs. "Maybe one day I will be good enough, but I won't hold my breath." He sighs deeply and says, "Besides, there are more fun things we can talk about."

I arch my brow, "Like what?"

"Like, how did you stop that youth dragon from killing us?"

Trusting people will get you killed. Her words ring in the back of my ears. A warning. I have managed to avoid this question but the longer we wonder through this hell hole, the more difficult it is becoming.

"Youth? How can you tell its age?" I ask.

"Overall size . . . but most importantly, the older the dragon, the larger its crown of horns are," he says.

"How do you know that?" I try not to sound skeptical, but dragons are not something lesser people have knowledge of. They have remained in hiding for decades. Their blood is precious, not only because of the power it gives but because they are hard to find.

"How about a trade?" he suggests.

"Hmmm. What do you have in mind?" I increase my pace to match his steps.

"An answer for an answer."

A large tree lay against the earth. I pull myself up and give my throbbing feet a much-needed break. "Okay," I say and remove my shoes, grimacing at my bloodied feet.

Luca seems excited. "Great. You can go first," he says and leans against the mossy tree.

"Why do you avoid talking about your family?" I ask

A sigh leaves his body, like he is forcing away bad memories. He glances down at my bare feet as I splash what little water I have left over them. "Because not everyone has a father like yours." He lifts his body from the log. "Give me those." I must look as confused as I feel because he points to my blistered feet.

"Absolutely not," I say and shake my head.

He crosses his arms at my protest. "You would rather risk infection?"

I reluctantly shake my head and he tears off a piece of his shirt. "My turn," he says. "Have you always had your abilities?"

"No." It isn't a lie but it isn't the whole truth.

"When did they start?" he asks.

"One question." I remind him and pick at the bark, the coarse edges rough against my skin. "Why do you travel alone?"

He wraps my feet gently, taking his time to answer. "I don't have to worry about anyone else." He shrugs.

"Seems kind of lonely," I say as I throw my freshly wrapped feet over the log and slide to the ground.

"It can be . . . but people tend to distract you from what's important," he says.

We trudge deeper into the never-ending forest. If I'm honest, I'm not sure we are heading in the right direction anymore, but I continue to put one foot in front of the other. *At some point it has to end, right?*

"Who taught you that?" I don't hide the disdain that lingers behind my words.

"It was instilled in me when I was a boy. Beaten into me really," he admits.

My heart squeezes at his confession, how could anyone hurt a child. "And what *is* important?" I ask.

"I will let you know when I find out," he says with a hint of sadness.

"What about your mother?" I ask, trying to change the subject.

"She died many years ago. Yours?" he asks hesitantly.

"Same." I nod and kick at the sticks that litter the forest floor.

"Aren't we just a sad bunch?" He jests and knocks his shoulder into mine.

I twirl my hair around my finger and ask, "Do you miss her?" I wrap my hand instinctively around my necklace, protecting the treasure.

"Only at night," he says. The rawness of his words hit deep in my soul.

"How are you doing?"

"I'm fine," I lie.

"How did you stop the dragon from killing us?" he asks again, this time softer.

I don't answer instead we walk in silence until the sun makes its way across the sky, our shadows walk ahead of us. A large snake sits like a rope over a thick branch, peering down. Its scales are a most vibrant shade of yellow, with red and white spots.

Luca steps up behind me, his chest inches from mine. The snake flicks its tongue wildly in our direction. Luca leans in and whispers, "The more beautiful it is, the more deadly they tend to be." His breath is warm against my skin and when he steps away my wildly beating heart starts to level out again.

I don't know if I should be offended or flattered by his comment, and I find myself a little of both.

"What about your scars?" He points at the mark that gracefully flows over my skin. The mark that expands as my powers do.

"What about them?" I ask.

His brow arches. "Are they in fact scars?"

"Honestly, I don't know what they are." I run my fingers down my collar bones, the raised skin smooth to the touch.

"Part of the answers you are looking for?" his voice turns up in question.

I nod slowly, "I suppose so."

My stomach grumbles. Along with our horses and most of the supplies, our food is gone as well. I can't help but think Smoke was eaten by the dragon, but I hold out hope that isn't the case.

"Are you hungry?" he asks.

"I am always hungry," I joke.

CHAPTER 21

By the thirteenth day, every step infuriates me. With each minute wasted, we are more likely to be caught and farther away from my goal. Time drags and my thoughts drift to dark places, memories I don't want to remember, images I don't wish to see.

"We should rest," Luca urges.

My stomach groans from hunger pains. In the last two days we have both had no more than a handful of berries.

"We are already behind," I say as I keep one foot in front of the other. The crunching of the leaves and branches under my blistered feet create a steady rhythm.

"Fraya." He jogs up to me. "Fraya, stop," he yells and gently tugs my arm.

A comforting lull tugs at my body.

"We should stop for the evening," Luca says.

I smile broadly, anticipating the cool water gliding over my skin. Luca slightly shakes his head, confused by my sudden mood change.

"There is water nearby," I tell him as I hurry forward, not waiting for him to follow. Soon the sound of rushing water floods my ears. We break through the foliage and a large body of water lay before us.

The water is calm where the spring feeds the river, then spills into a violent current just below. I sprint toward the water, removing my clothes as I do. The shock of the cold water takes my breath away. I pull the water around me, scrubbing my skin of the grime and filth of the forest.

"Are you just going to stand there?" I holler. I raise my hands gesturing for him to make his way into the water.

"Did you forget I nearly drowned not too long ago?" he reminds me.

My feet rub against the smooth stones at the bottom of the river bed. "It isn't that deep; besides, you stink." Tiny little fish dart around my legs feasting on my dead skin. "And if you happen to drown again, I will be right here to save you. I promise." I flash him my most genuine smile before splashing him with the cold river water.

Water runs down my arms and armpits. *Oh, how I've missed the water.* For a moment, sadness and grief slip into the back of my mind. The last time I felt this carefree, my whole world turned upside down.

Luca slowly unbuttons his shirt and removes his bandage. His burned skin is red around the edges and starting to peel. The cold of the water will feel nice against the angry burn.

His pants sit low, revealing a faint scar above his hip. "What happened there?"

"A sparring accident, nothing too serious." He waves off my concern with a flick of his wrist.

"Who trained you?" I ask curiously.

He sucks in a deep breath as he steps into the cold water. "I've had many teachers over the years." His attention snaps to me, his expression changing by the second. "Mostly learning through my travels." He spews out the words quickly before submerging himself under the water.

I watch as he scrubs his body, water sliding over his skin. His movements are rushed and he keeps his eyes down. "I am going to try and catch some dinner." His body glistens against the setting sun.

An owl hoots in the treetops and I find bright yellow eyes starring down on me.

We stare into the fire, its reflection bouncing in Luca's eyes. A mosquito buzzes next to my ear before I swat it away. My belly is full of the small hog he managed to catch and kill, the first real food we have had in days. Luca pulls his sleep sack from his bag and lets out a long sigh.

"What?" I ask.

He lifts the ripped sleep sack for me to see. The bugs are monstrous little demons, and without the sack his skin will be more mangled with bites than it already is.

I inspect mine and say, "We can share." The three words leave my mouth before I can truly think about them.

I peer up at Luca, whose flirtatious grin reveals his deep dimples. "Are you inviting me to bed, darling?"

"Would you rather sleep with the creepy crawlies?" I ask.

He dramatically shivers his body and replies, "No."

"Are you used to much finer accommodations?" I joke.

"Much," he says, but I can't tell if he's joking or not.

"Butt to butt?" I ask. *Butt to butt! Seriously. Kill. Me. Now.*

A deep chuckle comes from his chest. "How about you get in and I will work around you."

I can feel the blood running to my cheeks as I wiggle my body inside the sack. The bag shuffles and then his warmth fills the tiny space. In all of twenty-one seconds I realize this is the absolute worst idea. *But I couldn't just leave him to get eaten alive, could I?*

Both of us squirm until we are cocooned in darkness, listening to each other's breath. Something touches my foot and I shoot up, my head slamming directly into his jaw.

Absolutely the worst idea. I groan.

"Owe." I rub my throbbing head where his chin dug in. "Are you okay? I'm sorry."

I feel his arm reach up and rub his jaw. "Just be still," he says as he moves my hair to the side. His chest sits snug against my back and every time I try to relax, my muscles tighten back up.

"Are you happy?" I ask. The question meant to keep my mind distracted from the large man cradling my body.

"Right now?" he asks. I can hear the smile on his lips.

"In life," I mumble.

His body slightly shifts and I feel him gently exhale. "You ask hard questions, you know that?"

"So, you aren't happy?" I absently rub my feet together, waiting for his answer. The song of the night seems much louder suddenly. The crickets wail and the frogs groan wildly.

"I don't think I know what happiness feels like," he admits.

I sit with his heartbreaking answer for a few moments. Thinking of my father. Remembering him waking me up in the early morning by rubbing his scratchy beard against my little cheeks. When I couldn't sleep, we would count the stars until my eyelids were too heavy to remain open. When he found me during one of the scariest moments of my life. *"I will always come for you."* I choke at the memory of his words.

I was happy . . . but I don't know if I will ever be again.

I turn until my body is facing Luca. My eyes haven't adjusted to the darkness yet, but I sense him starring. He takes his free hand and gently rubs my cheek causing my gut to tighten. "You are trouble," he breathes. I am grateful for the darkness now, fully aware of the flush that has spread across my cheeks.

The noisy forest is suddenly silent as his fingers run down my neck and tilt my face up. Just before our lips meet, gray eyes fill my mind. Gray eyes . . . not blue. I pull back and Luca deflates.

What is wrong with me?

"Everything okay?" He drags out the words, just as confused as I am.

"Never better," another lie trickles from my lips. "I just . . . can't."

"Okay," he replies. It's short and to the point, leaving me with a strange heavy feeling. We both roll until our backs touch, each of us straight as a board.

What just happened? And why do I feel guilty?

I lay awake listening to Luca's deep rhythmic breaths. His back pressing against mine with each one. The longer I lay here, the more trapped I feel. My chest squeezes and breathing becomes more difficult with each passing second. My skin sticks together and my bladder is screaming at me.

I inch my way toward the opening at the top, leaving a sleeping Luca to sprawl onto his back.

I poke the embers of the fire, hoping there is still some life left to light the way. I gently remind myself to breathe, remembering the way my father used to force be to take exaggerated breaths when the world felt like it was crumbling.

I carefully empty my bladder, but start hurrying as intrusive thoughts run through my head regarding the yellow snake and my bare bottom.

I pick up sticks as I make my way back to the fire. Sitting opposite of the sleep sack, I absently toss the sticks one by one into the fire and watch as the tiny flames turn to large ones and back to small again.

Fireflies in the darkness cast momentary brightness throughout the forest, and frogs croak against the backsplash of the summertime evening chorus.

Luca's bag lay slightly open and a nagging curiosity tugs at the back of my mind. A twinkle of gold catches light in the fire and I peer closer, opening the bag further with a stick. Sliding my hands into the bag, I pull out a blood red envelope.

My stomach turns and I grab my heart as I see the King's golden seal. I take out the darkened paper and read.

I am growing impatient.
Bring the girl to me.

Rage boils inside of me, spilling out at the seams. I quickly find and open another.

If what you say is true, she could be of great use to us.
Make haste.

How could he? I re-read the letter, trying to make sense of it. "The white owl feather was from a messenger owl," I whisper.

"What are you doing?" Luca asks in a raised voice.

I stand swiftly, the other letters falling into the fire. "What are these?" I ask, not wanting to believe my eyes.

Luca is on his feet in an instant. "Why are you going through my things, Fraya?"

"Answer the question!" I demand. "These are letters from the King, Luca. They are talking about me, aren't they?" I throw the letter into his chest.

"It's not that simple, Fraya." His brows knit together as he reaches out to me.

"I wouldn't even think about it," I warn. Taking a step back, I raise my hands in defense.

He straightens his shoulders, drawing his back straight. "If you would just listen," his words are barely more than a hiss and his eyes turn cold, his face stone.

"What was your plan? Take me to the King and watch as he executes me?"

"You're being dramatic," he says.

His words are a slap in the face. "I suppose there *are* far worse things than death."

I feel the water hum behind him, wanting to bend to my will. "You are a liar."

Keeping my eyes on him, I lull the water back and forth behind the unsuspecting Luca.

"This doesn't have to be a fight." He slowly draws his hunting blade from his belt loop.

But it does. "I should have let you drown," I spit.

"Probably," he admits. "But you didn't."

"I won't make the same mistake twice."

His brows knit together in confusion at the same time he's submerged; his screams trapped by the wave that carries him downriver.

CHAPTER 22

I run until the burning passes and my legs go numb, then I run some more. Trying to put as much distance between Luca and I as possible. No matter how hard I race, the memories still catch up.

How could I have been so stupid!

I have made nothing but horrible choices, one after the other, ever since I've been on my own.

I break through the tree line and a valley lay before me. My legs are no longer able to support me, and I fall to the ground, the grass tickling my arms. My chest heaves, my lungs begging for oxygen.

Heavy footsteps crunch near me and someone clears their throat. I jump, grabbing the shirt of my attacker and wrap my legs around him as he falls to the ground. My blade snug against his throat before he can take another breath.

"Whoa. Easy, Litchska." I pull my hair to the side and stare into DG's gray eyes. My body rises and falls with each of his breaths. I don't release my hold on the blade.

"How are you here? Why are you here?" I ask in disbelief.

"I am on my way home. I would appreciate you removing your dagger from my throat." Something wild passes through his eyes. "I won't ask again," he warns.

In a flash, I am flat on my back, relieved of my weapon, and staring up into his stormy eyes. "There are a lot of things that can kill us out here, let's not add each other to the list." A darkness passes over him, but just as quickly it disappears.

He eyes me skeptically, waiting to see if I am going to behave.

"If I wanted you dead, you would be," I spit.

He gently releases me, a slight tug pulls at his lips. "Of that I have no doubt, Litchska." I grab the hand he extends.

"What are you running from?" He glances behind me.

"Bad choices." I dust my clothes off and when I look up what lay before me stops my breath. A graveyard of bones. Large skeletons, now a permanent part of the landscape. My breath escapes me as I survey the land, the pain and death still lingering.

"The Valley of Blood and Bone. It's..."

"Haunting," he fills in. "I know." His gaze still lingers at the edge of the forest.

Dozens of dragon remains scatter the valley, stretching further than the eye can see.

My eyes flicker between all the destruction. "I was told no one comes through here."

"Most don't," he says.

My feet lead me through the carnage, each part worse than the last. "Why do you?"

"So I don't forget," he says.

"You act like you were there." I run my hand along the ribs of a long past dragon. "How could anyone do this?" I whisper.

DG turns from me, his shoulders tight. "Why were you running from the forest like you were being chased by the dead?" he asks.

"Maybe I was." I straighten up, the sting of Luca's betrayal still fresh. Mere hours ago, my lips almost met his. *Thank the Ancients that didn't happen.*

We walk in silence, unable to form words even if I wanted to. I grip the bridge of my nose, the desire to scream at the top of my lungs, curl into a ball and cry, or become violent washes over me simultaneously.

Nature has begun to reclaim the land but evidence of the fallen are visible in every direction, frozen in time. No burials, no closures, no peace. All around me white and purple flowers push up through pieces of dull metal, now permanent pieces of the landscape.

A small pack and a bow rest up against a rock. "Are you hungry?" DG flips the flap over and reaches into his bag pulling out jerky before I can decline. We stand beside bones bleached white from decades of sun exposure.

This is where my mother drew her last breath. I wonder if any of these remnants belong to her. A sickening feeling washes over me and suddenly my growing stomach turns sour. I look out at the vast graveyard, a new sense of dread seeping into my bones.

"Are you okay?" DG asks.

I brush my fingertips over the ribs of a dragon. "I'm fine." I look up and I'm swallowed by his gaze.

He hesitates but steps closer. "Why don't I believe you?"

"You don't even know me." I try to smile but it doesn't reach my eyes.

He looks past me and clenches his jaw. "Are you expecting anyone?" he asks.

My gut drops. *How?*

A breath of relief escapes me when I turn and see Luca is not standing behind me. Only it's quickly replaced by terror as a group of raiders come barreling toward us, hoods drawn and weapons raised. Their curved blades gleaming in the afternoon sun.

The beating of hooves gets closer, drowning out any thoughts.

"We can't outrun them," I say.

"Then we fight." He grabs his bow and arrows. "You ready?"

"I have no other options," I say.

He looks at the dagger in my hand and shakes his head. "You are going to need more than that." He pulls out a small sword and hands it to me.

The muscles in his back twitch.

Without hesitation he tightens the bowstring and the arrow whistles across the valley, hitting his target in the stomach. We watch as he slides from his horse, trampled in the process.

He takes down three more before a woman stands firing arrows of her own. "We need her alive!" one snarls.

I am so tired of being hunted. I can feel the anger seeping from me. Taking a deep breath I tighten my hands on my weapon. I don't have enough control over my fire, yet. I could kill everyone here, including DG.

They stop just shy of us, their horses protesting the sudden change. "We only want the girl."

For a moment, I think he is going to hand me over to them. He has no allegiance to me. We are outnumbered and he owes me nothing. A single arrow hits between the breasts of the archer quicker than a flash of lightning.

After a moment of shock, we are consumed by chaos.

I slice through the calf of one man, then arch my dagger up through his thigh. He bleeds out in seconds. DG impales another with their own sword. We dance effortlessly around each other. His back toward me, we block blow after blow.

"We just want the girl," one man snarls.

DG moves with grace and ease, the man fighting beside me is ruthless.

My body starts to drag. The adrenaline coursing through my body wearing thin.

I don't know how much longer I can do this. My mind betrays me.

"Keep fighting Fraya." The cool whisper in the back of my mind gives me a boost of energy.

DG pulls a man off his horse, killing him with an old bone. A sharp pain slices through my body. I look down and see my thigh fileted open and my stomach turns. "He wants you alive, but he never said undamaged."

DG ends his life swiftly. "You're bleeding," he says, his breaths hard and uneven.

"So are you," I reply.

A large man with black marks across his face topples him. "DG!" I holler before throwing my dagger into his attacker's back. He shrieks in pain, failing to grab it out of his spine. Three men left.

Two more men attack DG as the last grabs my throat and repeatedly smashes me against the large bones. He kicks at my legs and an explosion of pain makes me see stars.

I shoot my arms up through his interlocked hands to try and pry them from my throat but his grip is too tight. I look over to DG, who is still in the heat of battle. Slowly, I am lifted from the ground. I thrash wildly in a desperate attempt to be free.

The corners of my vision fade to black, I reach for the man's wrists and watch as his face contorts in pain. His face reddens and veins bulge from his forehead as he struggles against the pain from my flame.

A beastly growl comes from behind him and then his hands go slack. My legs fail and the earth embraces me.

How?

DG stands over me, his expression wild and a bloodied blade clutched in his hand. The once white bones, now stained red.

I try to force myself to stand but my legs don't comply.

Bless the dragons this hurts. It is only temporary; I try to remind myself, but the pain is unbearable.

DG leaves me there. *Probably for the best.*

A piece of me can't help but feel disappointed though. I inhale a deep, deep breath, allowing the oxygen to fill my lungs and hoping it will somehow ease the pain. I spot a puddle of blood as it pools around my leg and the ground drinks it greedily.

"How much blood loss is too much?" I wonder aloud.

The earth moans in response, jostling my worn body.

CHAPTER 23

DG's heavy footsteps sound and I say, "I thought you left."

He kneels and wraps a tourniquet around my leg. My insides roll from the pain as he tightens it to staunch the bleeding. We shouldn't have survived the assault. Again the earth lets out a subtle moan.

He must sense the fear in my stiff body because he says, "The earth tremors here. It has done so since before I was a boy."

The tension in my body eases, "Why?"

"No one really knows, possibly unsettled spirits?" He gives a small shrug. "I'm going to pick you up now."

"No small talk?" I tease.

"Are you ready?" he asks.

"Do I have a choice?" I choke on a laugh but he doesn't smile, instead his eyes remain fixed on mine, his expression blank. "It seems I do not."

His hands gently wrap around me, heat exploding where his hands touch my body. He remains rigid but he is mindful not to jostle me too much as he stands. Despite his cool demeanor, his heart thuds like a stampede of wild horses.

"Where are we going?" I ask as my head falls against his chest.

"Out of view," his words are curt and sting more than I care to admit.

When the sky is slightly shrouded in treetops, he gently lowers me to the ground. The sudden emptiness I feel when his arms no longer wrap me in an embrace is startling.

His knife slides up my pants, cutting just enough to expose the gash. "This is going to hurt," he says.

I hiss as the alcohol hits my skin. "Ancients! I thought we were friends!"

He lathers ointment in his hand but hesitates. "What's wrong?" I ask.

He hands me a rag. "Bite down on this."

I look at him inquisitively and he says, "This will stop the pain in minutes, but it's going to hurt first." He looks down at my exposed leg, the flesh peeled open. "Can I continue?"

I nod, but I'm not fully prepared for the agony that follows. My fingers dig into the dirt as I scream through my clenched jaw. He coats my leg in seconds and sits back, waiting.

The rag drops from my mouth. "It was you, wasn't it?" I breathe.

He remains quiet and watches the goop intensely. Slowly, I begin to feel the cooling and I let my body relax.

"I remember you," I tell him. "That night, you were the one who saved me."

He gets to work sewing my flesh together. I feel nothing but a tug every now and again, remembering the way his hands worked the first time he stitched me up.

"Why didn't you stay?" I ask.

Still nothing, but he doesn't deny being there the night I was attacked.

"We have fought and bled together. Can I at least have your real name?"

"Klaus." He wraps my leg in a thick bandage.

"Well, Klaus. Thank you." I give a weak smile.

He looks up at me now, but says nothing.

"You said you were on your way home. Where is home?" I pry.

He sits down, his hands falling to his raised knees. "Rahkadyr."

I jerk slightly. What are the chances he lives in the King's city?

"Don't move," he demands. "You will rip your stitches."

There aren't many other towns out this way, Fraya. Where else would he live?

I look over to him and see cuts and bruises mark his skin. A large slash on his forearm looks worrisome.

He carried me all that way, wounded.

"Do you have a name?" he asks.

"Fraya . . . but I happen to like Litchska."

He nods, but something dances behind his eyes, a wild expression momentarily crosses his face.

"You're bleeding," I say.

He looks at his arms and shrugs.

"Give me the needle and thread." I reach my hand out, waiting.

His brows draw together but he hands me what I asked for. "Don't move your leg," he demands.

I fight the urge to mock him like a child, but instead wait for him to edge closer. He hands me his knife without speaking a word, his attention toward the valley. I reach over and grab the numbing cream, gently rubbing it over the area. He doesn't flinch but his muscles remain tight.

"I will do my best, but I am afraid this will leave an ugly scar on your tattoos."

"I have plenty of scars." He turns his attention to me. "But this may be the most memorable."

His look sends a flutter deep into my stomach and I put my head down, trying to focus on each stitch instead of the way his voice makes my palms sweat.

"You did well back there," he says.

"Surprised?" I lift my brow, waiting for his answer.

"No," he says in all seriousness.

"You can thank my father." The words spill out fast but the pain creeps in like a heavy fog; slow and blinding.

My breathing slows and my chest aches. *When will this pain stop? I should have been there. His death is my fault.* Each thought slams into me, breaking me down a little more each time.

"Litchska?" I feel rough fingers hesitantly touch my face. "where did you just go?"

My vision clears and I bite back the hot tears threatening to spill over. The needle dangles from his arm. "I'm fine." I grab the needle and blink hard a few times before continuing.

"Why are you out this way?" He turns his attention back to the forest.

It is my turn to stay quiet.

"You are either running away from something or running toward it." He sounds like he maybe doing a bit of the same.

"Can't it be a bit of both?" I tie off the last stitch and wrap his arm. "Good as new . . . ish."

He stands. "I will get us some food."

"I can't stay here," I say quickly.

"And you can't leave." He points to my leg. He's right, I can't support any weight right now.

"You saw." It isn't a question, there is no way he could ignore the burn marks around my attacker's hands.

"I didn't see anything you didn't want me to see, Fraya." He doesn't look at me when he says it.

"Klaus?"

"Hm?" his deep voice vibrates in his chest.

"Thank you," I say.

He stops and turns his full attention to me and my insides squirm. "You do not ever need to thank me for making sure you are okay."

CHAPTER 24

I wake as my head rolls forward, the jerk straining my neck. The stars illuminate the sky and when I look down a blanket is draped over my body. Klaus rests with his head leaned against the large tree with his arms crossed over his chest; his arms rising and falling with each breath. His legs stretched out and locked at the ankles.

I reluctantly lift my head from his shoulder and test my leg before I consider standing, bending my knee slightly as I look up to the sky. I take in a large breath and slowly release it realizing this is the first moment since it all started where I feel at peace.

The moon peeks through the trees, lighting a small path. Dozens of stars fall from the dark sky, an omen of good luck. A small smile breaks through my lips as I remember the first time I watched the stars fall.

"Daddy, look," I shout from the top of his shoulders. I pull his forehead to gaze at the bright streaks that fly across the sky.

"Why are the stars crying?" Concern leaks from my tiny voice, but my father only chuckles.

"They aren't crying, sweet girl."

"Then what are they doing?" I look down at him, my big eyes full of questions. He takes me off his shoulders and sits me on the ground beside him. Laying back, we both stare into the vast sky.

"The legend says that each fallen star is a dragon egg falling to earth."

"A dragon egg!" I say with excitement.

"Yup, and maybe one day . . ." he says as he boops my nose. "You will be lucky enough to find one."

I giggle with excitement.

I wipe the silent tears that slide down my cheeks and stand, the physical pain a welcome one. I glance back at a sleeping Klaus, his handsome face in a scowl. *You can't trust him.* I cover him with the blanket and stop. I reach into my pocket, my fingers cradling a smooth stone.

The mermaid tear is almost transparent with hints of greens and blues, flattened by years of tumbling in the harsh ocean. It is beautiful. I found this stone on my first dive. I leave the stone atop his belongings and head into the darkness, alone.

The walk through the dark is excruciating, each step worse than the last. My pace is that of a snail. The stars begin to fade and a clear sky begins to break through the trees. I stop, taking a minute to breathe and check my bandage. The white cotton now stained red.

I take a deep breath and quickly tighten the loose material. "Geez, this hurts!" I bite out between gritted teeth.

When I get the nerve to start walking again, not ten feet in front of me stands my horse, Smoke. He munches on the grass; his tail absently swatting at pests. The sight of him makes me want to cry. I have never been so happy to see such a grumpy animal.

As I approach him, he steps away, lifting his head and shaking it wildly. "Are you mad at me?" I ask in disbelief. "If I remember correctly, you are the one who left me to die all because of the big scary dragon."

He lets out a loud snort of disagreement. I search Luca's bag, "Oh my dragons!" Enough money to feed a family for a year is hidden in the bottom. "He did sell me!" Another hot wave of anger settles in my stomach. "Whatever, he is gone now. It doesn't matter."

I close his bag and dig through mine. At the very bottom, I discover a small sugar cube; the perfect bribe. "Okay," I say and present the sugar cube. His ears perk up to attention. "Will you forgive me now?"

Gently, he takes the treat and pushes his long face into mine. "I missed you too."

I stare at my map, then back to the looming mountain in front of me. To the East, Rahkadyr sits like a violent storm waiting in the distance. Two options lay before me.

"The last thing my father told me to do was find Moir, and I don't have a sure plan for the King yet. On the other hand the great dragon may not even be in those mountains. I'm wasting precious time to find the King." I look down at Smoke. "You are no help." I rub between his ears and slide off, knowing my father's wishes come first. My leg healed days ago but I still find myself favoring the other one.

Both excited and terrified, I start up the mountain. Each step pulling me closer toward answers. Green bristle trees stand like spikey guards, the needles releasing a sweet aroma for visitors. Small creatures leave trails of slime and goo along the bark, and goats in the distance test their luck on boulders and tiny ledges. I leave my horse at a small patch of greenery and make my way up.

The sun makes its way over the horizon as I search for any signs of an Ancient lurking. Although, I am not sure what I should be looking for.

"Hello!" I holler. No one and nothing responds. I step forward, the edge only a few short feet ahead of me. I overcame my fear of heights a long time ago, but my legs slightly wobble and my mind refuses to let me creep any closer; instead, it plays my fall down the steep mountain side causing my chest to seize.

The breathtaking view expands for miles in every direction. Green trees fit closely together, like an army at full attention and mist lingers over the river as it snakes through the land.

"Fraya?"

My heart quickens as the voice dances through my mind. I've grown accustomed to the whispers, but here they are much stronger than hushed words and pieces on my inner thoughts.

"Moir?" I feel foolish speaking into the open air, waiting for an answer that may not come.

The earth tremors and as I step farther away from the edge, the ground beneath me falls away. I claw at the falling debris, trying and failing to find anything to hold onto. My voice escapes me as I disappear into the abyss.

I feel water calling me, ready to embrace me. Steadying my thumping heart, I call to it. I fall into the freezing water and it's like needles against my skin, the dark water engulfing me until I make my way to the surface.

I gasp as I pull myself from the spring. Five large marble pillars surround the spring, and large roots crawl down the ruin walls. The room is round with archways creating a narrow path around the room. Water drips from my clothes on the smooth floor.

I run my fingers over the rough walls. Three large dragons kneel in front of a gigantic dragon.

"The Ancients," I whisper.

My feet glide across the room, marveling at all that unfolds before me. All these forgotten stories and buried history. Faded patches of color decorate sections of the walls. I stop in front of a large etching of men and women standing in line with the dragons, weapons in hand. The next scene shows a large crack in the earth, swallowing men whole. I shudder against the image of men devoured by the pit. Hovering above is a creature that looks like a man, but has the wings of a dragon. I peer closer but am only left with more questions.

Deeper into the room, the walls unfold a story of love and pain, life and death.

"Some things should stay buried, Fraya. You shouldn't be here." The dragon whispers to my mind.

CHAPTER 25

Her words sting more than they should and now I know the gentle tug in the back of my mind has always been her, but . . . why?

"I am not leaving," my voice resonates off the walls.

There's no response, which doesn't surprise me. "At least I know I'm in the right place," I sigh.

I stop in front of a large hall that leads into darkness. My curiosity surfaces but so does my fear of small dark places. I need answers. No, I deserve them, and my gut tells me this is where they'll be.

Focusing my mind, I imagine pulling the fire into my hands . . . but nothing happens. After a few attempts, my forehead throbs from focusing so hard. *Why doesn't it come?* I can feel my heart race as my answers slip from my fingers.

My father's hearty voice flickers in my memory. *"Breathe, Fraya. Everything is hard until you learn it."*

Rolling my eyes the way I did when I was a child, I remember getting so angry when he would tell me that, but now it's all I can think about. I sit against the ground, "Concentrate."

I close my eyes and slow my breathing, trying to picture fire.

Instead, pictures of Klaus sleeping enter my head. The steady rhythm of his breathing, the scowl between his brows, and the feeling of his arms wrapped around my body. The safety I felt in those moments.

"Stop that!" I scold myself.

But when I try again, all I see are the letters with the blood red seal. I drop my head in my hands, the heavy smell of mildew creeping into my nose.

"Breathe, Fraya." Her voice is encouraging.

Her words are like a soothing ointment on blistered skin, a gentle nudge calming my anxious heart.

I picture myself being one with the earth, my heart starting to slow until all I hear is its gentle rhythm. I picture a single flame. The heat it offers and the hues of oranges and reds that flicker through it.

When I open my eyes, a single dancing flame sits in my palm. The heat provides comfort and security. I take a deep breath and head into the dark depths. The uneven ground is cracked under my feet, pieces of the walls are missing or crumbled on the ground. Beetles scurry along the stone floor and spider webs cling to the ceiling.

The story continues, the winged man always the center, until they just stop. The creature stands alone on one side while an army of dragons and humans are on the other. He stands alone against an army. A slight tremor rattles the ground beneath me and fear churns in my stomach until it passes.

Old torches line the walls until I reach a large room, far bigger than the one with the spring. Two large doors lean into each other, supported only by the vines that encase them.

"How did people open these?" I wonder.

Deep gashes cover one side of the foyer. "Claw marks," I whisper. The dragon that did this would be ten times the size of the one in the woods. I've never heard of a dragon reaching this size.

A narrow opening sits between the oversize doors. This is definitely not the time to have my wide hips. I manage to squeeze through the slit with minor scrapes and a bruised ego.

"Wow." I want to say more but words escape me. Remnants of the old city lay before me. I enlarge my flame and descend the broken stairs into the main city. Buildings lay broken and forgotten, crumbled foundations show a reminder of what was.

A few feet away sits an untouched marble statue. The dragon sits poised with a large tail curling around its body and wings tucked in. The face is slender and curves into a large crown of horns. Black gemstones fill the eyes.

In the middle of her forehead sits a mark. Immediately, my hand moves to my neck, fingers roaming over the different curves and edges. My other hand glides over the smooth cool stone, every intricate piece a perfect match. At the bottom of the pillar the word *Moir* is etched. My breath leaves my lungs. "This is who I am looking for."

More lonely pillars stand like skeletons throughout the city. Stairs leading to nowhere, pottery and tools left untouched, almost like the occupants left in a hurry. I imagine the people who walked these streets and lived in these homes. The old woman mentioned a war, is that what drove these people away?

I continue forward, finding more deep claw marks, these ones not as large as the previous. Evidence that humans were not the only ones who walked these streets. Thick vines claim the space, crawling down from the ceiling and entrapping old buildings.

A single book rests under a curtain of vines attempting to conceal the treasure. A cloud of dust puffs into the air as I lift the cover. Ancient words fill the pages and I wish I had paid more attention to my father's teachings.

I turn the page and see a dragon; images of water surround it. The Azule dragon. A mark sits atop his head as well but it is a circle with wave-like details around it.

The wings of the Noir dragon extend the next page; fire consumes her. I look at the flame in my free hand, careful to keep it away from the old pages.

My legs start to numb as I lean over the ancient text. A spider emerges from the pages, scurrying across the face of the old dragon.

"Ah!" I fall backward, my arms flailing to catch me before landing on my backside. I fall through nature's curtain, the room shrouded in darkness. Pieces of crumbled rock dig into my bruised skin.

The earth begins to groan, tiny rocks rain from the air, and dust fills my nose. The ceiling starts to give way and I brace for impact when suddenly I am dragged from the room by my legs. Alive . . . but not alone.

CHAPTER 26

I don't blink. I don't breathe. I don't move.

My body is a stone, except for my heart bouncing off the wall of my ribs, creating a deafening ring in my ears. Dust tickles the inside of my nose. "Don't you da . . ." A soul shattering sneeze erupts from me.

A hot gust of air pushes the hair from my face and I know I'm about to die. Squeezing my eyes shut, I wait for the dragon to swallow me whole.

But . . . it never comes. Instead, another blast of humid air sweeps across my face. I stare into the darkness, eyes wide trying to see what lies within it.

"Are you going to use your flame?" she asks.

My flame sparks, showing the silhouette of a massive dragon before going out. I try again, and this time the room lights up and before me is an Ancient.

The Ancient. Moir.

"Well done," her voice caresses my mind.

"I found you." Hot tears sting my eyes and the weight that's been sitting on my shoulders since my father's death, lifts slightly. I didn't realize I said the words aloud until she smiles.

Her toothy grin is terrifying, causing panic to twist in my stomach.

"You do not need to be afraid," she reassures.

I choke on a snort.

Her head quirks to the side, *"You don't believe me?"*

I look her in the eyes and realize the statue didn't do her justice. The night sky is held within her eyes, every tiny star twinkling against the consuming darkness. Her massive head is larger than my body, and her slender face bleeds into a crown of horns unlike anything I have ever seen before. She is terrifyingly majestic and bigger than I imagined. I am an ant at her feet.

The older the dragon the larger the horns, Luca had said.

"If I am honest, I don't know how to answer your question." I am quiet a moment before continuing, "You are the god of our people, but if that wasn't enough your size is quite intimidating."

She leans her giant head to the side. *"You are quite amusing."*

"How?" I ask confused.

"I am the oldest being in this world. I am known by many names, Fraya, but your mother called me Ciena, and so can you."

My heart kicks up at the mention of my mother. "You have been speaking with me for years and I never knew. Why?"

The Ancient is quiet for so long I begin to shift with unease. The crunch of rocks is my only distraction while I wait.

"Hmmm ... there are many ways to answer this question. But the simple answer is because your mother asked me to, but also because I am part of you and you are part of me."

"Alkazah," I say.

She smiles and nods.

"What happened to the others?" I ask.

"Others?" she asks.

I can feel a shift inside her. "Why am I the only Alkazah?"

"Your kind was hunted and killed after the great war centuries ago. People feared the power the Alkazah held and they eliminated it."

"But why?" I can feel she is holding something back, unwilling to give me the full truth.

"Why are you here, Fraya?"

The simple question causes my throat to swell. Grief wraps its ugly hand around my heart and doesn't let go. My body stiffens when the old dragon moves swiftly next to me. She lowers her large head and for a moment I stand, perplexed. But then her forehead is on mine, leaning into me. Our heads together; our grief shared.

We stay like this until I suck up my tears. I didn't ask for this, I don't want any of it.

"You are here for answers." She lets out a big sigh and I only nod, not trusting my own words.

"I am the beginning, I pieced together the world and all who inhabit it. The mark that lays against your skin binds us."

I trace the intricate designs on my body.

"Each of my children carry a piece of me. The Noir dragon carries fire, the Hausa carries healing and life, and the Azule ..." she pauses. *"She carried water."*

I don't lose the word *carried,* past tense. "Why didn't my father tell me?"

"I am sure he had his reasons."

"What if I don't want to be an Alkazah or the heir to a kingdom?"

"Your mother didn't want to be a princess or a queen. I think that is what made her so good at it. It was never about ruling, she just loved her people." She inspects me and says, *"You look so much like her."*

My father used to tell me I had her same wild hair and feisty spirit. I try to be happy I have some connection to the mother I never met, but it only brings more pain. A whole part of me is missing.

"And what does the Dark King want?" I ask.

"What he has always wanted . . . Me."

Anger boils within me and I struggle to keep it contained. Then it starts clicking together. "He wants your blood." I look up at her. "But why? If he can get power from any dragon's blood, why does he want yours?"

"The power flowing through an Ancient's blood is unlike any other."

"Who is the winged man?"

A deep growl vibrates from her chest. *"What do you know of him?"*

"Nothing, I have only seen the drawings etched into these walls." I point toward the ruins.

"He is Eternal. He is the creature our Ancient blood unleashes, and I will not let that happen again."

"Where were you when the Dark King killed my mother?"

"With you." She stares down at me with her star filled eyes.

"You left her to die?" My vision blurs, images of my mother dying all alone surface in my head. "She was fighting for you! Protecting you! And you were hiding?" My voice steadily rises with each word.

Her body tenses. *"It is not that simple."*

"You let her die! That feels pretty simple to me."

The anger I've buried inside radiates out of me. Her full size unfolds before me as she uncurls her body, her tail snaking across the floor, and her wings expanding. Her presence is consuming.

"Do not speak of things you do not understand!" she bellows in warning. I'm then lifted into the air, her tail snug around my waist.

I know I should be afraid but I have nothing left to lose. I thrust my palms toward the Ancient, a wall of fire following. Her throat begins to glow, revealing the same intricate designs that cover my body. Water spews from her mouth, drenching me and extinguishing my rage in the process.

"I loved your mother, Fraya."

"I wish I had been given the opportunity to love her too," I say.

CHAPTER 27

S uspended in the air like a wet rag doll, a giggle escapes my lips. Which quickly transforms into a fit of laughter at the insanity of this situation.

The Ancient pulls me closer to her, checking me over like I'm broken.

"This is ludicrous!" I wipe tears from the corners of my eyes. "None of this can be real."

A memory of my father calling me princess surfaces and I laugh harder with my grief. *Maybe I have lost it.*

"I assure you, it is."

I stare into her large black eyes. "Then I don't want it. I never did." I manipulate a ball of water, letting it roll between my fingers.

"You are much better with water than fire." The Ancient notices.

I gently nod. "I have had longer to practice with it."

She sets me down. *"Your father was a good man."*

"He lied."

"Everyone lies. What matters is why? Your father fought for his life for three days before he was found in the wreckage. The only survivor. When he realized your mother was gone, he walked away from this life and never looked back."

I ponder her words, still feeling betrayed and alone.

Her expression is kind. *"The right answer is never an easy one."*

"Killing the king won't be easy," I say.

"It will lead to your death, Fraya." Frustration creeps at the edges of her voice. *"You mustn't."*

I square my shoulders. "I will not cower in the dark while he continues to murder innocent people. Have you seen what is going on in your world? Children are starving in the streets, men ripped from their homes, women stripped of their dignity, and dragons are all but extinct!"

She flinches back, her head turning away from me.

She inches back slightly. *"I have heard."*

"And you do nothing?" I ask in disbelief. "You are supposed to love us."

She carefully sets me down. *"I learned long ago not to get involved in human affairs. Only more pain follows."*

"He took the only thing that matters to me. I won't stop until I have his head or I take my last breath."

"This is a dangerous path. You sound just like–"

Her words are covered by the earth and its need to be heard. I struggle to balance as debris falls around me and dust clouds make it difficult to see. A deafening shatter tells me the statue is no more.

"Fraya! Get on . . . now."

She lowers her head and I hesitate for only a moment before hoisting myself atop the Ancient. Chaos ensues around me as we weave through the old city, careful of falling debris.

My stomach turns as I cling to her. Every second I expect a large rock to crush us, but it never does. She glides through the air with little effort. A sliver of light cuts into the darkness.

"Hold on!" she yells.

"You can't be serious? That's a wall!" The words are just out of my mouth as we fly headfirst into the small opening.

The cave collapses as we emerge from the other side. The ruins now buried, never to be seen again.

The sun warms my skin and fresh air hits my lungs. I raise my palms to the sun soaking up the rays. It is a beautiful day . . . my father would say the best kind of day.

Birds call to each other and the breeze rocks the trees in a rhythmic melody.

I close my eyes. "I haven't changed my mind. I am going to kill the king."

"You have your mother's stubbornness."

I lower my outstretched hands. "I think it's one of my better qualities."

The dragon huffs and slightly nudges me with her snout. *"Your mother said something very similar many years ago."* She fails to conceal the sadness lingering behind her words. *"I promised I would keep you safe."*

"I've never been safe. I just never realized I was in danger."

The earth lets out another moan, but it remains still. "Why are you so angry?" I whisper and rest my hand against its surface. Concern sets on the Ancient's face but she says nothing. The old woman's warning rings in my ears, something dangerous lingers here.

"The rebels are working together to dethrone the king. They dwell between here and Rahkadyr." Her eyes bore into mine, holding many lifetimes of pain.

She leans down, again placing her head against mine. A greeting and a farewell. This time I lean in, placing my hands on each side of her face. "I will make her death mean something," I whisper.

"It will mean nothing if you die."

My heart tugs. "I better not die then." I give a halfhearted laugh but she doesn't find humor in my words. She seems lost in her thoughts, or possibly trapped.

"If you find the rebels, Ophius will help you." A single glassy tear slides from her eye. *"Get going, or I may change my mind."*

CHAPTER 28

As I reach the bottom of the mountain, I feel less confident. So many sacrifices were made to keep me hidden, but many more lives will be lost if I do nothing. Guilt washes over me followed by its close friend, Remorse.

"Lock it away, Fraya," I remind myself.

Finding Smoke where I left him, I start toward Rahkadyr.

I finally reach the trees that stretch to the gods. These were the first, planted by Hausa himself. I slide off Smoke and brush my hand against the bumpy bark as I walk around one of the giant trees; seventy-five steps. I have never seen anything like it. The sun warms my cheeks and the blue sky brightens my soul. It's so peaceful here.

A slight tremor runs over me and I slowly reach for the blade around my belt. I will no longer be running; I will no longer be prey.

"Please don't." I hear someone say. I turn, hand still firm against my weapon, to see a man. His hair is a shaggy mess atop his head and his round face makes him look younger than he is. He slightly tilts his head to the side, a boyish grin spreading across his face. "We have been waiting for you." He lowers his hands.

"I believe you have me mistaken for someone else." I grab onto the horn of the saddle.

"The old woman gave a pretty good description of you," he says.

I drop my hand at the mention of my old friend. "Is she here?" She insisted I go this way. The thought of seeing her again makes me smile.

He lowers his eyes. "No."

I pause for a brief moment, remembering Ciena's words about the rebels.

"What do you know of Ophius?" I ask.

His dark brows draw together. "What do *you* know of Ophius?" he asks.

I press my lips together, "Seems we may have more friends in common than we think."

A light sweet breeze weaves through the trees. "I have a letter for you, if you would like to read it."

I give a slight nod and he cautiously steps forward.

"Arik!" A deep voice comes from everywhere and nowhere.

I cut my eyes to the approaching figure. A tall, lean man appears with his blade drawn. "Arik," the stranger's voice raises in warning.

I grip the handle of my knife, my other at my waist. I can already feel the power running through me, ready to be released. Arik's chocolate brown eyes slightly enlarge as he glances between us both.

"Sven," his tone is cautious. "It's fine."

He still doesn't lower his weapon. He inches toward Arik, his eyes fixed on mine.

Arik puts his hands up between us, a small envelope extended toward me.

"I promise this isn't a trick, Fraya." His words are tender and his expression is soft. He shakes the envelope and I lower my weapon.

"What did the old woman say about her?" Sven nods his head toward me, his muscles still tense as he steps beside his friend.

"To be mindful of her dagger." He shrugs and a small laugh escapes my mouth.

Both men glance in my direction.

"It *is* her, Sven."

Sven clenches his jaw and his dark green eyes stare into my soul. I start to think it doesn't matter who I am supposed to be, he wouldn't care either way.

I slip the tip of my dagger under the sealed edge and remove the single piece of paper held inside.

If you don't trust them, trust me.
They will help you on whichever path you choose.
Until we meet again.

I look up at the two men in front of me. "I assume you are the rebels I have heard so much about."

Arik smiles broadly, but Sven says nothing. His jaw remains tight and his dark brows stay knit together.

"And you are the princess of the Western Region, daughter of Queen Ravina, Alkazah, and leader of our people." He bows and my stomach drops.

Arik speaks the words with such passion and everything in me wants to run. I can't be any of those things to these people.

"You don't need to do that." I clench my fist and swallow to try and stop the ringing in my ears. "Just call me Fraya."

He nods with a slight smile, "Of course."

Arik turns to Sven. "She asked about Ophius." Sven's eyes widen just slightly. If I hadn't been watching him, I would have missed it.

"No." He crosses his arms over his chest.

"No?" Arik and I ask in unison.

A silent exchange passes between the two but ultimately Arik says, "We should get going, camp is a bit of a walk."

A large drop of water hits my face, followed by a few more, until heavy drops drum against the ground in unison. I take in a deep breath and Earth's aroma fills my senses making me think of Klaus. I have always enjoyed the rain.

Sven leaves without a word, walking the way he came. I take the reins of my horse and follow. Arik stays close by. Twenty minutes into our walk, Arik looks up and says, "Don't mind him. He is just grumpy."

"He definitely isn't the most welcoming, is he?"

He looks at Sven and presses his lips together. "He will grow on you." He looks like he wants to say more but thinks better of it.

"I will take your word for it," I assure him.

Arik catches up with his friend and I watch as the tension in Sven's shoulders melts away like butter.

CHAPTER 29

T he Rebel camp is larger than I would have expected. *How do they hide this many people?* I could have never imagined what lies before me. At least a thousand men and women move about the camp, not including children. There are horses, supplies, tents, and structures built high up in the trees.

"This is impressive," I tell them.

Sven stops in his tracks causing me to run into his back. He faces me and says, "And you could ruin it all."

His words cut into me. They were meant to.

Many people stop and stare, others whisper among themselves, and a few bow in my direction. "Many of these people were loyal to your mother, or children of those who followed her," Arik says with pride. My cheeks redden and the overwhelming urge to flee rears its ugly head again.

"I just want to speak with Ophius. I will leave right after." I match his stare.

"Fraya!" A tiny voice catches my attention. I glance around trying to find the person when Lucy bursts between two people.

"Lucy!" Relief swallows me as I drop to my knees and wrap my arms around the child. "Thank the Ancients, you made it!" I pull her back to look her over and then squeeze her again. "I was so worried. Where is your mother?" I look through the crowd but don't see her.

Lucy's eyes fill with tears.

"What happened?" I ask her.

Her little arm runs across her face, streaking it with dirty tears. "She told me to run, so I ran." She sobs into my shirt. "I left her there; I left her alone!" she cries.

"Lucy, listen to me." I pull her away from me, my hands resting on her tiny shoulders. "You did the right thing."

A snot bubble pops onto her already tear-soaked face. "Will you find her?" she chokes out.

I look into her eyes and although I know the chances of me finding Maxine are slim, I will stop at nothing until I do.

"I will scour the earth until I find her." I fight back my own tears, knowing they will do nothing to help. An elderly couple stands behind her, their faces drawn and hands together. Lucy looks back at them and they give a halfhearted but warm smile.

The woman beckons for the girl to follow. She gives me one last squeeze. "I'm glad you got away." Her words are genuine but they stab me in my heart and I lose my breath.

I stand there like a statue, even after she is gone. Afraid that if I move, I will crumble to the ground and never get back up. I jump as a hand grips mine, and when I look Arik is standing beside me, his large eyes full of compassion and understanding. I clench my teeth, hating him for being so kind.

"This way." He motions to the right.

He moves a large tent cover and Sven stands looking over a table scattered with papers. He doesn't bother to look up.

"Why is she in here, Arik?" Sven's words, although stern toward me, are soft toward his friend.

"You know why. I am taking her to see Ophius." There is no room for discussion in Arik's words.

Sven lets out a deep breath, seeming out of options.

"Let me see it?" He finally looks up, his gaze hot with anger.

"What?" I ask.

"Don't play dumb. Your mark, let me see your mark," he demands impatiently.

"Excuse me?"

Sven stares at me with arms crossed, impatience dripping from him. "I want to make sure you are who everyone says you are."

"You want me to just rip my shirt off right here?" I throw my hands out in the open tent.

"Unless you would prefer to do it out there." He motions toward the exit.

"Why don't you like me?"

"I tend not to like people I don't trust." He leans against his desk, veins rippling out of his lean arms.

"You don't even know me," I scoff.

"Exactly," he snips.

"Sven." Arik tries to plead on my behalf but it is futile.

"Why are you here, anyway?" He throws an arm in the air. "You are supposed to be this *demi-god,*" he mocks. "But where have you been?" His voice continues to raise and my blood boils right along with it.

How dare he!

"You think I asked for this?" Before I can stop myself, a flood falls from my lips.

"You don't think I know I don't belong. Everywhere I go, good people die. I have nothing. No one! A title I don't want or deserve." My insides rip apart and faces flash before my eyes, the last one being Maxine. "If you think you can hate me more than I already hate myself, you are wrong!" The rawness of my confession leaves me breathless and broken.

I feel the heat rise in my body and I struggle to contain the raging inferno that threatens to spill out. I take a deep breath, and extinguish the tiny flames that lick my fingertips.

"Fraya." I put my hand up, stopping Arik from saying anything further.

"Can we go find this guy now?" I ask, exhausted.

"Guy?" Sven's lips curl into a smile and for a moment his sharp features are handsome.

CHAPTER 30

"Of course." I say and rub my hands down my face.

"She didn't tell you?" Ophius laughs and it is the most pleasant sound my ears have ever heard.

"That you are a dragon? No, she left that part out." The green dragon blends perfectly with the earth. Hidden in plain sight.

His piercing yellow eyes scan me curiously. *"So you are what all the fuss is about."* Each syllable strung together like a perfect melody, inviting me to sit and listen to its beauty.

Even Sven seems lighter. The earth hums around Ophius. When he breathes, the wind exhales.

"You are in pain," he notices.

I look down at my leg and move it around shaking my head. "Considering the number of times I have been stabbed lately, I think I'm doing pretty well."

I give a slight laugh, but neither Ophius nor my companions find my dark humor funny.

"I am not talking about your physical pain. The wounds you can't see are usually the ones that hurt the most," he says.

I swallow hard, that all too familiar sting hitting the back of my throat. I draw my brows together ready to ask a question when he asks, *"Why do you not use the Ancient's power."*

I must look as confused as I feel because he says, *"Come, sit."*

Ophius extends his claw and quickly slashes into my skin. I suck in a sharp breath as pain seers down my arm into my elbow. "What the hell?" I hiss.

"You will heal it."

"This will take a full day! And besides just because I can heal doesn't mean it doesn't hurt!" I hold my injured arm and step away from him.

"Come." He gestures for me to come close. *"I will show you how to heal instantly."*

I remember the soldier whose wounds stitched back together before my eyes.

"Why didn't Ciena show me?" I ask hesitantly.

Ophius nestles into the ground around him and extends his wings. The rain kicks up again and the blood washes down my arms and into the mud. Arik and Sven walk over to the dragon and rest under the canopy of his wings.

"She cannot heal you when she herself is not whole."

Reluctantly, I walk over to the dragon and sit in between his large legs. My backs resting up against his chest. Water splashes up against my legs and a river of red washes around me. "At this rate I may bleed to death," I mumble.

The dragon chuckles and it rumbles against my back. *"It is merely a scratch, child. Now, close your eyes and focus on the rain; the sound it makes as it meets the earth. The way the wind rustles through the trees. Align your heart with the beat of the earth."*

I breathe in, trying to find my peace, but the bug that struggles through the water drops grabs my attention.

"Fraya." Ophius drops his head on mine. *"Focus."*

I match my breathing with his. *"Good, now feel the energy of the earth and pull from it. Picture the energy flowing through your body and knitting your wound together."*

A familiar warmth washes over me, but instead of an angry blaze, a coolness spreads through my body, soothing the sting. When I open my eyes, I don't have to look at my arm to know there is nothing there besides smooth skin.

The pitter patter of rain has now ceased and my body feels better than it ever has. *"The outside may be better but your insides are still torn to shreds, little one."*

"That is not something we can fix in a day," I say through a forced laugh.

"We can start."

I shake my head, locking my bruised heart up tight. This pain keeps me going, I don't know what I would do without it.

Sven stretches his long slender body. "I think I have a plan and a way you can help."

"You want my help?" I say skeptically. I cross my arms over my chest. "Hours ago you were ready to throw me out."

"You are the rightful ruler of our people, he couldn't throw you out," Arik chimes in. Sven shoots a nasty glare over to Arik who only shrugs.

"I am no ruler, Arik." He has grown on me in the short time we have spent together. His optimism is infectious, and makes me wish I could be who he wants me to be.

"What is your idea, Sven?" I ask.

"The son has just returned from a task from the King," he informs us.

"What task?"

"No one knows for sure, but the King has not left the castle in months. No one has. There is a ball being thrown for his return. This is where you come in."

Sven outlines the plan, down to the very last detail.

"We will leave tomorrow, as soon as the sun disappears behind the earth, get some rest."

Sven stands in front of his desk once more. "You don't think I can do this?" I ask.

"I think you are the only one who can." He rubs his eyes and places his other hand on his hip. "That is the maddening part."

"So, it comes back down to trust then?" I look around the room, drawings of a castle and its inner workings fill the wall. "These are amazing."

"You don't have much time to learn the layout, so instead of gawking at them you should study them."

"You drew this as well?" I remove the tack, careful not to damage the picture.

Sven doesn't look up, "I drew everything up there."

"I have never seen anything like this. How did you capture his glow?"

His head snaps up and his eyes meet mine and then land on the drawing in my hands. He walks over to me, snatching the delicate paper from my hands. "You shouldn't touch things that aren't yours." He rips the castle drawings off the wall. "These are for you."

He drops himself onto a rickety chair behind the desk just as Arik enters with plates full of food. The spices make my mouth water and my stomach twists and groans.

"We can't plot to overthrow a King without food," he says with a bright smile.

Sven flips the paper over on his desk.

"Please tell me you aren't fighting again?" Arik drops his shoulder and sighs.

"No, actually we aren't," I say. "I was just marveling at Sven's ability with a pencil. I've never seen anything like it."

Sven throws daggers at me with his eyes and I can't help but smile. The devil does have a heart.

"He does have a special talent, doesn't he?" He looks up at his friend but Sven keeps his eyes on the desk, his jaw flexing.

"Whatever that is smells delicious." I rub my stomach, taking from the large mound of food and stuffing my mouth.

Arik and I sit on the fur rug and I scatter the castle drawing between us. I take a deep breath, "I guess we should get started."

"First, we need to do something about your hair," Arik says with a grin.

CHAPTER 31

Arik hugs my neck. "We will see you soon." I smile at him. How can he be so kind and optimistic? The more time I spend with him, the more I understand why Mr. Grumpy Gills likes him.

Sven nods. "Don't mess this up." Arik stares up at him in disbelief just before punching him in the arm. I fight back a smile as I crawl atop the dragon.

"Take care of yourselves," I say before we take off into the sky.

Flying with Ophius is smooth, and we blend into the backsplash of nature. His wings hardly startle the trees. The stars still line the sky when we land at our destination. I will have an hour's walk before I arrive, but I will rest tonight and head in first thing in the morning.

"The ball is in two nights."

I am not certain how he wants me to respond so I only say, "yes."

"You have one month," he tells me.

"I will be ready. I am beginning to think you are worried about me."

"Of course I am worried about you. He will know who you are the moment you walk into the door."

"That's the whole point," I insist. "And we went over the plan numerous times." I place my hand against his rough scales.

"This is dangerous and you can change your mind," he whispers to my mind. But we both know it isn't true.

"The moment he took my father, this was inevitable. Now I just have a reason to stay alive," I can tell my words bring him no comfort. "Besides, my new hair will hide me until I am ready," I say, exaggerating a hair toss.

"Don't underestimate him, Fraya," he warns.

"I will be okay," I reassure him. But, if I am honest with myself, I don't know if it's true.

He looks at me and gives a slight nod before saying, *"There is a book in the King's possession. I need you to find it."*

"A book?"

"It is a diary. The pages will be worn from centuries passing," Ophius says.

"Whose diary?" I ask.

Ophius pauses for a moment, careful with his next words. *"His name is Azius."* He explains no further and I do not push.

"Do they know?" I ask hesitantly.

"Know what, child?"

I look over the dragon whose beautiful mark is scared and mangled. "That you are Hausa, Ancient of the Earth?"

He doesn't seem surprised by my knowing. *"Humans see what they want to see. A god living among them seems too impossible."* He bows his large head and says, *"I should have known you would figure it out."*

"It took me a minute. You carry a different energy than Moir and your size does not compare but my father told me stories about you. Your lineage of dragons are peaceful but only you can feel a person's real pain. Only you can take it away."

"Your father taught you well."

A pang of pride fills my aching heart. "Yes, he did. I was so mad at him for leaving me in the dark, forcing me to figure this out on my own. I didn't realize he had been preparing me the whole time." The truth stings and is followed by the familiar ache.

"It is not your fault." His words whisper to the back of my mind, etching themselves on the locks of my heart. But, I keep the door closed, shutting it up tight.

"The diary, his weakness, and the blood bank." He reminds me of my goals.

"Don't eat my horse," I say, only half kidding.

"I can't make any promises," he says with a hint of laughter in his voice.

He leans forward, pressing his horned head against mine. *"There will be friends everywhere, Fraya."*

The trek into Rahkadyr is hot. The sun is unforgiving as the trees disperse and the terrain turns to rock and dust. I lift the hood of my cloak to keep my skin from scorching. There are men and women loading large crates into wagons. Rahkadyr lies on the other side of a thousand-foot bridge. The lone mountain floating in a sea of sand, engulfing the land in rolling dunes

Guards line the bridge, checking over the people arriving and departing. I take a deep breath. "Don't be awkward," I remind myself.

I walk past the first guard with ease as he searches through a fruit cart heading into the main city. Halfway across more guards weed through people's things. "Just keep walking," I tell myself.

"Hey!" I hear a guard yell from behind me.

"You." A hand grips my arms, halting me. "You can't pass through here without being searched." He lessens his hold on me but still holds me in place.

"I apologize." I lower my hood and look up at the man through my eye lashes. "This is my first time here and I was not aware."

"I have to search you," he says. His blond hair is cut short drawing attention to his strong chin.

"Of course." I remove my cloak. My leather bodice snug against my curves.

His large adam's apple bobs up and down as he pats my arms. His hands move down my waist, hesitating slightly before continuing. He stops at my thigh and looks up at me. "Would you mind lifting up your dress?"

"You haven't even bought me dinner yet." I place my hand against my chest. His cheeks flare red and I can't help but smile. He goes to open his mouth a few times but nothing comes out.

Someone clears his throat and the soldier straightens. "She is with me, Paul."

Paul's face returns to normal color as he goes to argue but is stopped in his tracks. He nods and moves on to the next person.

"Following me again, Litchska?" His voice is smooth and sends butterflies through my stomach.

"Again?" Are you sure you aren't the one following me?" I ask with a smile.

"I live here, remember." His eyes scan my body so quickly I think I imagine it.

"Ah, and is that why you are chummy with the soldier?"

"Paul? I grew up with him," he answers easily.

Wagons pass as we stride across the bridge nearing the city. The floating island is alive with people. Large buildings line the walkways, but the most impressive part is the castle nestled into the mountainside, overlooking the city.

"You dyed your hair," he states.

I glance over the side of the bridge, a three-hundred-foot drop makes my stomach flop.

"I tried something new," I say with a slight shrug.

The distance between us begins to grow. I pick at my fingers ignoring the strange tug in my heart.

"There is only heat and sand out here," I say.

"You would be surprised what survives in such conditions," he says.

I glance over hoping to catch his attention but his eyes remain forward. I pull at my clothes hoping to circulate some air against my skin. The heat is sweltering on the bridge, with nowhere to hide from its intensity.

"You okay?" he asks.

"Never better," I lie. The dry air stings the back of my throat and there is no moisture left in my mouth. I struggle between stripping my clothes or keeping them on to protect my skin.

"The evening is better." A smile creeps on the edge of his lips and my heart flutters.

My skin heats up and for the first time I am grateful for my sun kissed skin hiding the sudden flush running through my body. *This is not why you are here,* I scold. But I can't deny that a part deep inside me hoped to run into him.

A road cuts through the center of the mountain, overflowing with people. Different meats hang from hooks, the aroma of fried breads fills the air, and chickens cluck in cages. At each corner soldiers are posted, watching the crowd.

"Is it always this busy?" I ask, my eyes searching the crowd.

"Depends on the day." He pauses before we reach the mass of people. "You shouldn't have come here, Fraya."

His words sting more than I expect and my smile falters just slightly. How can he go from warm to cold so quickly? "It was nice to see you too, DG."

CHAPTER 32

A small dress shop sits at the end of the alley. It isn't as pretty as the ones on the main road, but it radiates charm and reminds me of home. The worn building leans slightly to the side and the door hangs off its hinges. It squeaks as I enter and I hear children giggle as a woman scolds them with a smile that radiates love.

The wood creaks under me and a warm glow casts in the corners.

"Hello?" I say.

Her attention turns toward me and the children scurry off in different directions. She smooths her skirt and smiles. "Yes, how can I help you?"

"I need a dress for the ball." I look around the small room and everything appears to be neatly tucked in its rightful place.

"I can help with that," she says charismatically and disappears into the back.

She returns with fabric of every shade and a few premade dresses. Laying the dresses out on the table and fluffing the skirts she asks, "You aren't from here, are you?"

"Is it that obvious?" I say with a laugh.

"Only slightly, dear." A hint of lavender and honey hits my nose and seems to linger.

I stick out like a panther among dogs, which is the reason I changed my hair. I run my fingers over the different fabrics; some soft, while others are coarse or silky. This close, I notice how frail the woman is. Her arms are thin and her collar bone protrudes from the skin.

I lift a dark green dress. "Can I try this one?"

She starts to take the dress from my hands. "I don't mind carrying it," I tell her and tug the dress back to me.

"Nonsense," she says, pulling the heavy dress from my hands and escorting me to a small room. She hangs the dress on a nail and closes the heavy curtain. "I will be outside if you need anything."

I stare at the green dress, with all its buttons and strings. *How do women wear these things?* I prefer my riding pants and boots.

After a few minutes, the woman asks, "Do you need help?"

I slide the dress over my head, struggling when the dress hits my hips. I shimmy the velvet dress down, mildly out of breath when I step from behind the curtain. The sleeves itch and the fabric is heavy.

"It is very beautiful, but it's not—"

"It's not you," she finishes.

"And it's so hot," I say.

"It isn't so bad in the evening," she assures me.

"That is what I have heard," I say.

Her eyes brighten up as she shoves me back into the changing room. "Get dressed, I have an idea."

When I step out, her long fingers are holding every shade of fabric to my skin and jotting down notes on a pad. Her brows wrinkle together as she works, a stunning dress unfolding before my eyes.

"What do you think?" She holds the sketch up for me to look at.

"It's amazing. How did you do that?"

"My mother taught me, and her mother taught her." She takes my measurements one last time. "I will have it ready by tomorrow evening."

"You can do that in a day?" I ask in disbelief.

"It may be tight but I will get it done," she reassures me.

"Thank you." I hand her a small piece of Luca's stash. "Would you happen to know of a place to stay?"

"If you don't mind kids, I have a spare room," she says and points upstairs.

"Not at all." I smile and soon hear a squeal and the pitter patter of tiny feet. She lets out a big motherly sigh and shows me upstairs.

A girl, no older than six, stirs a pot of stew. When she sees her mother, a large grin full of missing teeth greets her. "This is Fyre, Sarah, and Arthur . . . is around here somewhere."

Just then, a small boy burst through a door. "Here I am." He falls to the ground laughing as his mother places her hand on her heart.

"Arthur Spire!" His mother quietly yells. "How many times have I told you not to scare me like that?"

The boy continues to roll on the ground, his face and hands full of dirt from the days playing.

"Oh, Sue Bear." Her husband comes in and wraps his hands around her tiny waist. "Just scare him back." He quickly kisses her cheek and then snatches the boy off the floor. Arthur screams in delight as his father pretends to chomp his skinny belly for scaring his mother. His daughters squeal in unison as he scoops them up next.

"Sorry," Sue says with a smile. "I think they forgot their manners." Her fingers lift to her lips, concealing laughter.

"Never apologize for having a home filled with love."

"Mommy?" one of the girl's soft voice rings. "Do you know when sissy will be home?"

Sue moves her hands from her lips to her chest, holding it like a piece of her is missing. "She will visit soon enough." The child seems satisfied and runs back to play with her siblings, but the look in Sue's eyes tells me her daughter is not coming home.

She shows me to my room. It is barren except for a bed, a desk that sits in front of a window, and a few dusty books in the window sill.

"Thank you. This is perfect."

"Dinner will be ready when the sun goes down," she says and turns toward the door.

"Actually, I have a few errands to run tonight. I will grab something while I am out." She nods and heads down the hall while I prepare for tomorrow.

CHAPTER 33

As the sun disappears and the stars emerge, I slip into darkness and make my way around the floating city. The night *is* cooler and makes the hairs on my skin stand on end. After hours of searching, I gather the only way on and off the island is the bridge, unless I want to try rock climbing. I picture the drawings in my head as I near the castle.

People hustle in and out, preparing for tomorrow's celebration. Most of the roads end either at a building or disappear into the mountainside. *There is no way off this mountain except for that bridge.*

A dark figure moves through the buildings with ease. Curiosity gets the better of me as I duck behind barrels and buildings trying to keep up with the stranger.

Clouds conceal the moon, blocking its glowing light. Just when I give up my search, a noise comes from an alley close by. Silent as a mouse, I make my way over to the sound. Wooden boxes lay broken and a burlap sack lay in the dirt with fruit littering the ground.

"If you ever step foot down here again . . ." A man is lifted into the air by his throat. He slaps at the cloaked figure but he doesn't so much as budge. "You will find yourself begging for death," he spits. The moon reveals itself, basking the alley in its warm glow toward the men. The cloak slides down revealing black ink.

I press myself against the brick, trying to dissolve into the wall. *What is he doing here and why is he attacking that man?* A loud thunk comes from the alley and I run as quickly and silently as I can.

"You sleep a long time," a tiny voice whispers in my ear as fingers poke my face. "Ow! You don't have to hit me!" he says. I open my eyes and see Arthur rubbing his little arm.

"That is not polite," Sarah scolds. She looks down at me and says, "Are you hungry?"

"Ravenous, actually." I forgot to eat last night and my stomach is not happy with me this morning.

"Ravenous?" Sarah asks.

"It means I am super hungry." The aroma of hash and eggs drift through the house and my stomach growls. I place my hands on my stomach with wide eyes. "See? Told you I was ravenous." They squeal and run from the room. I chuckle and roll out of bed, my nose leading me to the table.

"I just have a few minor adjustments to make to your dress and it will be ready," Sue says as she places a plate in front of me.

"Perfect, I have one last minute thing I have to do then I will come back to the shop," I tell her.

"I will be ready for you." She beams with pride and says, "I hope you like it."

"I know I will," I say as I stand and stuff food into my mouth. "I will be back shortly." I take one more large bite of eggs and scurry down the stairs.

Pulling my hood over my head I head to the vendor tents. Luca's money sack sits between my chest. *At least this money will do some good.*

A familiar feeling washes over me and when I look up, I'm not surprised to see pensive eyes staring back at me.

"Why are you here, Klaus?" I ask and drop my eyes back down.

He continues watching me stuff the bag till it is overflowing. I keep my eyes on the vendors tables, trying to avoid noticing the way his muscles bulge through his shirt as he leans with arms crossed against a building. Today, his sleeves are rolled up to his elbows, revealing the thick lines that are etched into his skin. The same ones from last night.

I move about the merchants, every few minutes, I sneak a peek through the tents. His attention never leaves me. An image of my fingers running through his wild hair sneaks up on me and I swallow back the desire.

He seems to make some sort of decision and within moments he is next to me, plucking an orange from my bag. He begins to peel it, the juices sliding down his finger. "You are not safe here," he tells me.

"I am not safe anywhere." I hand him my bag and he takes it without missing a step, following me through the tents. Men and women stop and stare as we pass by, others avert their eyes. He says nothing until we reach the back alley of the dress shop. His fingers brush mine as he hands me the two sacks. I ignore the hot current as it shoots through my body and settles deep in my belly. "Don't come tonight."

"You know I can't do that." I squeeze the food sacks to my chest.

He steps forward, pushing me against the old building. "I can make you." His presence swallows me, and I watch as his eyes darken. A war being waged behind them.

"You can try," I bite back.

He growls and pushes himself away from me. I manage to catch my breath, but keep my distance.

"Our meeting wasn't a coincidence, was it?" I hate the way my voice drops and disappointment seeps through each word. I take a deep breath, centering myself. "It doesn't matter. If I must go through you to get to the King, I will."

CHAPTER 34

My body is still shaking when I leave the washroom to meet Sue. Why does this hurt so much more than Luca? How did I make this mistake twice?

"Your hair," Sue says.

"Yes, I didn't quite like the brown," I say and tuck my curls behind my ears.

"Are you okay, dear?" Her face is drawn with worry.

"Yes, I just have a lot on my mind." I give a big smile, smashing everything down deep. Tonight is do or die, literally. "Let's look at this dress," I say.

She sweeps the curtain to the side revealing the most exquisite piece of clothing I have ever seen. I brush my hand against the soft fabric. The gold sparkles in the warm glow of the candle light, like tiny diamonds on a fabric canvas.

"This is incredible, Sue. How did you do this?" I ask in awe.

"It's a gift." She chuckles at herself. "You deserve to wear something as beautiful as you."

My heart swells and I ask, "Can I try it on?"

"Yes." She shoo's me into the tiny room and I wiggle myself into the fitted gown.

Taking a deep breath I say, "Sue?" The delicate designs carved into my skin pop against the gold. There is no concealing them. My hair may hide the seal on my neck but the patterns that run down my spine and between my breasts will be visible to all.

"Yes, dear?"

I step from behind the curtain. "Can you button me?" I squeeze my hands together.

Her hand touches her mouth in awe. "You are a vision." She ushers for me to turn and then proceeds to cinch my waist. When I turn to face her, her eyes shine with tears.

"What's wrong?" I ask stepping toward her.

She nods her head, trying to compose herself. "You just remind me of my eldest daughter." She wipes her nose. "I am fine."

"Where is she?"

"She is with the King." My heart aches and I wince as I wonder exactly what *with the King* could mean. I notice small bandages on the tips of her fingers as she runs her hands over her eyes. "I made you something else."

She turns and pulls a stunning cape from under the remaining fabric. The gold matches perfectly, except instead of it sparkling like the starry sky, this is silky smooth. The perfect balance to the dress.

"It will help hide the mark of the Ancient one." Her kind eyes find mine and I am momentarily silenced.

I stare at her, my mouth slightly ajar. "How did you know?"

"I am a mother, dear. It is hard to truly hide anything from us." She stops for a moment before deciding to speak again. "I wasn't much older than you when Queen Ravina was killed."

My stomach turns but I say nothing.

"My family and I were a part of her Kingdom before it fell. My father and grandfather were slaughtered in the war."

"How can you be so close to him?"

"Keep your enemies close, dear," she says. But there is pain laced in her words.

"So, you know who I am then?" I drop my voice to a whisper, afraid someone will over hear.

She tilts my chin up. "I know there were rumors about a child born before the queen went to war."

"I'm sorry. I put your whole family in danger." I tuck the fabric in between my fingers, feeling the silk glide over itself.

A heavy sigh lifts her shoulders. "We are in no more danger than normal." She claps the cape over my chest. "It has been a pleasure serving you, your Highness."

My insides roll. *So many people are depending on me, if I mess this up it will be far more than just my life on the line.* The air feels tight and the atmosphere crushes me, making it hard to breathe.

"You can do this, Fraya." Ciena's words comfort my unsteady heart.

"I thought you were gone." I breathe a sigh of relief.

"We are connected until we each breathe our last breath, Fraya."

A smile pulls at the corners of my lips.

"Oh! One more thing," Sue says with a large grin.

CHAPTER 35

I tuck my hands into the pockets Sue stitched into my dress. The perfect surprise. She really did think of everything.

I flip a small knife through my fingers to keep my mind focused on the task in front of me. I stand at the bottom of the castle steps. My thighs sweat as I take each step, and the heat of the evening sun presses against my back as it tries to disappear for the day.

The night feels heavy, holding secrets just out of reach. A large door opens and a young couple stumbles out, their faces flushed as they giggle. From here, the castle is beautiful. A lot of care went into smoothing the sand stone and shaping it just so.

"You can do this," I tell myself.

The large foyer never seems to end, until I see two men standing in front of double doors. A large staircase ascends to a second level where it splits and two hallways lead to the heart of the castle.

"Would you like us to introduce you, Miss?" An older one bows slightly, keeping his eyes to the floor. The noise from the party inside makes my stomach stir.

"I would prefer you didn't," I say.

A gentle nod and the doors open, laughter floats through the room like a gentle breeze. I take a deep breath. "Here we go."

The aroma of wine sweetens the air. Sparkling chandeliers hang from the vaulted ceiling and candles give the large room an amber glow. I've never seen anything so grand.

A tall woman brings me a glass filled with red liquid and quickly saunters off, attending to the other guests. I lower my hood, my loose waves tickling my neck.

I focus on the swishing sound of my dress as it brushes against the marble floor. Men and women dance in a wide circle, celebrating amid a King who would just as quickly watch them starve tomorrow. How quickly things are forgotten and ignored.

"You look ravishing," a familiar voice says. The knots in my stomach tighten. "I have to admit, I didn't think you would come. At least, not walking through the front door." Luca laughs.

I face him and his eyes greedily drink me in, lingering on the long slit that exposes my thigh. "Who knew you had it in you."

His face is smooth and his dimples fully exposed. He looks like an entirely different person and I hate the way I take notice.

He runs his hands through his now short hair. "Seems I have left you speechless."

"Not speechless, just slightly disappointed," I say in disgust.

A deep laugh escapes his chest. "Only slightly?" The dimples in his cheeks shine back at me as a hungry smile pulls at his lips. "There she is. I have missed our banter."

He motions to the dance floor and I step back. "I would rather dance with a wild animal."

Something dangerous flickers in his eyes. "Let's not make a scene."

A near silent murmur fills the room. I clench my teeth and place my hand in his, digging my nails into his skin. "That a girl."

My jaw aches as he draws me close to his body and swings me through the crowd. "You don't look happy to see me, darling."

"I would be much happier attending your funeral, *darling*," I say with ire.

"But, I forgive you."

A loud laugh breaks through my chest. "You forgive me?"

His face curls in confusion. "You did try to drown me." He says as if it is a casual game we play.

I hate him.

"You have been practicing." He spins me in his arms with an easy smile on his face. The same smile that caused me to let my guard down. His jaw is smooth and square.

"I see even your clumsy feet were a lie," I swear with a sneer.

I scan the crowd, trying to hide my disappointment when I do not find gray eyes looking back at me. Luca gently tilts my head back in his direction. "It wasn't all a lie."

I jerk away from him. "You don't get to touch me like that."

I don't hear him approach, but I feel it . . . like an oil on my skin. A heavy arm falls on Luca's shoulder. "I am cutting in," a deep voice booms over Luca. The party stills and Luca tenses under the pressure the King places on him. His grip turns white and Luca drops his shoulder and steps back.

He wears a white suit with a blood red tie. "Welcome, I hope the ball is to your liking?" His eyes twinkle. He watches me like a wild animal watches his prey. His grayish-white hair slicked back and his salt and pepper beard lay against his face.

This is part of the plan, Fraya. I remind myself. The look in his eyes makes my skin crawl. He slides his hand around my waist, the form fitting bodice suddenly suffocating. I attempt to put space between us, but it is useless, his grip is like iron.

There is no life in his pale blue eyes, no kindness or evidence of humanity. A large gash decorates his face. "Did you have help finding your way here?" The way his voice lingers on the last word causes ice to run through my veins.

I say nothing, instead focusing on the cool steel against my thigh. *You can't kill him yet, Fraya.* I take a deep breath, cooling the anger that floods my veins.

We spin around the room.

"I heard about your father. A shame, really." He looks away, as if playing a scene out in his head. "I was hoping he would die at my hand."

A rage flares within me and then my dagger is pressed into his chest before he can blink; the tip sliding into his skin. His eyebrows arch. "Did you think I wouldn't know who you were the moment you walked through my door?"

He pulls me closer, his grip crushing my wrist. His lips are inches from my ear and I feel as the blade presses deeper into his chest. He doesn't flinch and his voice remains even as he whispers, "You didn't think it would be that easy, did you?"

He squeezes my wrist, my bones cracking under his grip. I grit my teeth and my hand releases the blade. "Can't blame me for trying," I sneer.

"On the contrary, given who your mother is, I would have been disappointed if you hadn't."

I try to hide the sting of his words. He gently slides the tiny dagger from his chest, the edge stained with blood. "So, you do bleed."

His pale blue eye winks. "Don't tell anyone." A cold finger runs over the marks on my flesh and my skin crawls.

"What do we do now?" The ball continues around us, as a small war happens in front of them without notice.

"Those marks sure are beautiful." He turns the sharp edge of the blade across my flesh and I let out a soft cry. "Don't scream, I wouldn't want to have to murder all these people because you didn't know when to shut those pretty lips."

His eyes never leave mine as he drags the blade down, like he plans to rip my heart out of my chest. I trap the scream inside, clench my jaw, and blink back tears. I will not give him the satisfaction of seeing me cry. His eyes twinkle in excitement.

"Interesting," he says. "Your mother never cried either."

"I will enjoy killing you," I bite out.

Just when I think I can't take anymore, he withdraws the knife. The front of my dress is seeped with blood. He put his finger across my open flesh. His eyes brighten as my ruby red life source slides down his finger. He is more beast than human.

He closes my cape around me, hiding his artwork. "Enjoy the evening. It may be the last one you have, Princess." He turns back to Luca. "I would say I am proud, son, but I am more embarrassed you let her get the upper hand."

"Son?" My mouth falls open and my heart shatters.

"Pick up your mouth, girl." He drags his finger across his tongue. "It isn't becoming of you." His pupils dilate and he sighs in pleasure, licking his lips. He extends his arms wide and walks through the crowd.

Luca's eyes are to the ground. "You are a coward!" I spit through gritted teeth.

CHAPTER 36

The room feels small and sweat trickles down my spine. My breathing is uneven and labored, and my heart flutters in my chest.

Oh no! Not now. I fight the impending doom as it settles in my stomach and pushes its way out of my body. A mass of people begins to fill in the space the King left.

I try to move past but Luca stops me. "You are not allowed anywhere but the ballroom." He doesn't look at me.

"I need air, Luca." His chest rises heavily but he steps out of the way and I scramble to the door. The foyer is filled with guards, blocking my way outside.

I start toward the stairs, making my way up as the edges of my vision start to blur. Deep down the hall, I smell water. A cool breeze floats through my hair and the hall opens. Below me, a crystal-clear spring reflects the moon and stars.

Stairs descend to my left, and by the time I reach the ground my body shakes from pain. All-consuming pain, physical and emotional.

Plants grow up every pillar and flowers bloom beside the still water. I expand my lungs, letting the water calm me. How does anything grow in this wasteland?

"You are not supposed to be in here," a deep voice rumbles from the corner. A voice that draws you in and leaves you begging. I don't see him; he stays hidden in the corners of the atrium.

I drop to the water, removing the cape. The room feels tight and I am trapped. I try to push down the fear that nips at the back of my mind. Ruby-red blood droplets fall into the water, the impact creating tiny ripples over the water's surface.

I am surrounded by the smell of him, like a freshly lit fire after a heavy rain. I scoop the water into my hands and let it run down my chest, the pool of water now a slight pink.

A low growl comes from within the darkness, as I continue to let the cool water run over my chest.

"There she is." The jingle of weapons clang louder as he descends the stairs. A beady-eyed guard tracks my movements. "You are not supposed to be down here, girl."

I stand and try to back away, but my dress catches a rock and rips the bottom of my skirt. He grabs my broken wrist and I hiss in pain.

Klaus steps from the shadows like a dark angel emerging from the ashes of his enemies. My insides twist when I see him, his eyes dragging over my body and fury burns in them. Power rolls off him in waves and I struggle to not cower beneath it. His dark hair is pulled up tight on his head and his suit is all black.

My skin flushes and I drop my eyes, *what is wrong with you?*

"Your Highness? I wasn't aware you were here." The guard stumbles over his words.

Highness?

The word hits me like a brick. Klaus' eyes slide to me momentarily, but I can't read them. The air prickles and an unease settles between us.

Quick as a snake, Klaus extends his blade. A thin line of red appears across the guard's throat who has yet to realize his fate. The faint line grows larger with each passing second until he plummets to his knees. He gapes at his neck and I stare in disbelief as he crumbles to the ground.

He hollers to the remaining guard who scrambles down the stairs, his eyes lingering on the dead man at my feet. He lowers his top half in front of his future King. I feel sick.

"Take her to my room," Klaus orders.

"Absolutely not." I hold my throbbing wrist against my bloody chest.

"Klaus!" Luca's voice echoes against the walls.

Who are you?

Klaus leans in close to the guard. I see his jaw moving and the slight hand tremor the guard develops.

"Do we understand each other?" he says to the guard.

"Yes sir, absolutely sir." Sweat beads up in the corners of the poor man's temples.

Now, Klaus turns to me but I avoid his gaze. "Go with him."

Again, I hear Luca holler but it is close this time, his words more slurred than earlier. "And if I don't?"

He doesn't have time to answer before a drunk Luca leans over the edge of the second story. "You found her!" he says.

"Now, Fraya." His gray eyes pierce through me and his jaw is wound tight.

As much as I hate it, I have no other options. Klaus nods toward the guard averting his eyes, instead staring at his lifeless com-rad.

"Where are you going?" Luca points his finger at me.

The guard steps into view. "I have orders to take her, sir." He dips his eyes but does not bow as he did to Klaus.

Luca leans back over the half wall. "And does that blood . . ." He points to the fallen guard. "Lay on our guest's hands?"

I have never seen him like this. He takes a step toward me and the guard inches in front of me, stiff as a board.

"Luca!" Klaus' voice bounces off the walls of the atrium, deep and commanding.

"Brother!" he calls. And although I know it to be true, a part of me can't help but hope this is a bad dream. I go to step around the guard and he practically jumps out of his skin to avoid me.

A deep growl comes from the atrium and I freeze and my escort trembles. "This way, ma'am," he says. He points down the hall, visibly taking a step away from me.

I stare at the large double doors in front of me. Pacing and waiting for Klaus to explain himself. Preparing speech after speech about his betrayal. I think of every possible retort when a light tap sounds on the oak.

My heart jumps out of my chest when a young girl steps inside, eyes cast to the floor, and finger locked around the basket in her hands; my heart softens. She can't be more than twelve.

"I have come to help you out of your dress," she says.

"I may be stuck in this dress for all eternity, if I am honest," I say. "I am pretty sure I stopped breathing a couple hours ago."

A small smile creeps up on her lips, but her eyes remain downcast. *Poor girl.*

"What is in the basket?" I ask.

"Oh yes!" she exclaims. "I have your evening gown, bathing supplies, and I was instructed to bring pain medicine." She looks up and horror fills her youthful face.

I look down, seeing what she sees. I quickly turn, giving her my back. No child should ever see something so horrible.

"Just the dress will do," I say.

"Are you okay?" her voice is just a squeak.

"Just a little cut. Nothing to worry yourself over," I reassure her.

I hear her feet shuffle forward. "It was the King, huh?" She is right beside me now and I look down at her, her eyes burning with hatred.

"What is your name?" I ask.

"Astrid," she says. More confident.

She seems so familiar. Her lashes are long, fluttering against her rosy cheeks. Light freckles sprinkled all over her face and her fingers are calloused from years of hard work.

"How old are you?" I ask.

"Old enough." She straightens her back and lifts her head.

"You know how to unhook this thing?" I realize I couldn't get this dress off by myself even if I wanted to.

She nods and I take a deep breath. "Why do women wear these things?" I say. "It's like voluntary torture."

Another laugh, but this one is more genuine and her small fingers make quick work of the suffocating corset.

"How did you do that so fast?" I ask.

"I grew up in a dress shop." She shrugs.

My mouth falls open and she stares at me waiting for me to explain. "Is your mother Sue?"

Her green eyes shine with unshed tears, "You know my mother?"

"That will be all, Astrid." I never heard him enter.

CHAPTER 37

"**W**hy haven't you taken the pills?" Klaus asks.

I glance over to the basket with the painkillers but say nothing.

He walks around the room, undoing pieces of his clothing. His jacket falls away, and suddenly my throat turns dry. *He is trying to distract you.* I close my eyes and repeat those words over in my head. He unbuttons his dress shirt, each button slipping through his fingers.

"I know you are in pain," he says.

I am used to pain, I want to say, but I don't. Instead, I hold my dress to my body and count my breaths. My heart thumping against my rib cage enrages my cut-up sternum.

When I open my eyes again Klaus is kneeled in front of me, watching me. A flutter escapes in my chest. *He killed a man right in front of you!*

Only after he hurt you. My mind argues back.

I listen to the splash of the rag being wrung out over the warm bowl of water. His tan skin glows against the black cotton shirt he now wears. The tattoos on his arms look like shadows absorbed into his skin.

I flinch as he places my nightgown and medicine next to me, hurt flashing in his eyes so quickly I am sure I imagine it. His touch is gentle, sending sparks up my arm. His thumb brushes over the fingerprint bruises and warmth spreads across my chest.

Silence hangs like a thick fog rolling in from the ocean. Although I had so many things I wanted to say to him, now that he is here nothing comes out.

"Fraya–"

I interrupt him. "Why did you save me that day? To get me here?" I motion to the room.

"Litchska," he attempts again. His voice deep and gentle.

He lied to you. The thought stirs in the back of my mind. *This is all a lie.*

I take the rag. "I can handle it from here, Klaus."

His eyes harden and the mask he so carefully constructed slides over his face, expression cold. He stands. "No one will touch you again." I drop my gaze. *Why does part of me ache at the hurt in his eyes? He is the enemy.*

A soft click tells me I am left alone.

I scour the room, looking for anything that could be useful but it soon proves pointless. A warm bath removes the blood from my skin but not the memory. I look at the mirror, pieces of the bottom shattered, reminding me of the web of a spider. Dozens of my reflections stare back at me, none of them I recognize.

I close my eyes trying to focus on pulling the pain from my body but every time the pain eases, guilt floods through me. *I deserve this pain.*

Tempted by the cool breeze that skirts across the room; I let my feet lead me to the balcony. The cool evening air is a refreshing break from the scorching mid-day sun. The ground feels miles away. Laughter floats up to me, bellies full of food and wine. If only life was so simple.

I lean my head back and gaze at the stars when I see something glide across the sky, blocking the stars from view. I crane my neck as the dark blob blends in with the night. The only thing that would be that high up is a dragon.

"What is it?" a small voice asks.

I nearly jump out of my body. "Bless the dragons, you scared me to death!" I wince against the flash of pain that rips through my torso.

"I am sorry." Astrid's eyes drop to the ground.

I look down and Astrid is twiddling her fingers, eyes cast to the floor. "I won't do it again."

"No. No, no, no," I stutter. "I am okay, everything is fine. Just a little jumpy is all." I feel awful. Poor girl is scared enough. "Astrid, I promise it's okay."

"You aren't mad?" Her voice is hushed.

I shake my head. "Not at all, I was just a little startled."

"You should really get some rest, miss."

I look down at the girl, whose gaze is to the stars. "I will try," I tell her.

The sun glares through the open balcony doors. I curse as covers stick to my skin for choosing to keep them open. The little sleep I did have was filled with torment. Nightmares I am too familiar with; my father dying by a sword I shoved through his chest and Maxine being dragged into darkness.

If my nightmares didn't keep me awake, the creaks of the castle did. Every time I closed my eyes, I expected to get hauled into the deepest part of the dungeons, but it never came. Astrid sits at the table, scribbling in a journal with a tray full of eggs and bacon beside her. My stomach makes a loud groan.

Astrid looks up from her writing, "Miss, you are awake!" When I sit up, my chest wound opens and blood leaks, splotching my gown bright red. Tomorrow it will be healed; no scar, no pain, just a memory. My wrist is just a mere sprain.

You should have healed them last night. I try to push the thoughts from my mind but they plague me.

"Can you tell me how my family is?" She is on the verge of tears, her voice waivers heavily. I nod and begin to tell her how it all transpired and she wipes away the silent tears.

"Why are you here?" I ask.

"When the King said he needed a maid for a guest, I came. He promised extra food for my family." Her voice is low, defeated.

"How long have you been here?"

"Five full moon cycles," she confirms.

The room starts buzzing. *That can't be right.*

CHAPTER 38

For the next two days, I'm locked in this room like the kidnapped princesses. I can't help but chuckle at the irony. None of those women intentionally walked into the devil's den, as I have.

I check the door periodically, but it remains locked. I suppress a frustrated scream at being trapped within these four walls. Alone.

My only visitor is an older gentleman, who says nothing when he brings my meals. I lay on the bed with my fingers laced behind my head and my feet crossed at the ankles. Looking up at the ceiling, I spot spiders have made homes in the corners and a thin layer of dust is just visible.

Five months the King has prepared for me, but it has been no more than three since my father was murdered.

The weight of the blanket increases around my sides. "Wake up sleeping beauty." My eyes shoot open to find Luca leaning over me with an obnoxious grin on his face. "We are going to be late." I jerk my head forward sending it flying into his nose. "What the hell, Fraya!" His hands wrap around his face and blood creeps through his fingers.

"No! What the hell, Luca! You creep! Who leans over someone like that while they are sleeping?" Astrid stands off to the side looking scared and horrified. She runs in the washroom coming back with a gray towel.

"Here, sir." She hands it to him without keeping eye contact. He snatches the towel, wincing when it touches his face.

"Have her down in ten minutes, maid." The door slams so loudly the room echoes.

"You shouldn't have done that," Astrid whispers.

"He will be alright. His ego is hurt more than anything." I throw the covers off.

"What am I getting ready for?"

"I am not allowed to ask questions ma'am." She picks at her fingers. "We should get you dressed."

Astrid pulls out a lightweight blue dress and I manage to run a brush through my hair before I am being ushered down a long hall. Muffled voices echo down the long corridor.

"Ah, the guest of honor." The King sits comfortably in front of me, my father's dagger sliding between his fingers. His face is leather, weathered by the sun.

My clenched jaw aches, I was reckless.

"Sit . . . Eat." He motions toward the buffet of food sprawled across the long table. If he is in pain from my assault at the ball, he doesn't show it.

My stomach groans but my feet don't move. Tension vibrates through the room.

Anger flashes in his eyes but a sly smile follows. That single gesture fills my body with fear.

"Your pain is only momentary." He motions to the freshly grown skin on my chest. No evidence of the torture he inflicted.

"What is your point?" I glare at the King and the air feels thicker.

"The point is, there is no denying who you are.," he says and my blood boils. It was a game for him, a test.

"However." His eyes flick up to me, his icy blue eyes holding me in place. "The pain I inflict on *others* . . ." He leans his head to the side, a malicious smile creeping over his face. "May motivate you to obey."

I look between the brothers. Luca, whose face is already starting to bruise, touches his broken nose and Klaus sits still as a stone, no emotion.

The Dark King lifts from his chair and lets out a cackle that soon turns into a coughing fit. All eyes are on him, and then his face rages with anger. "Bring her in!" He bellows, his eyes slightly bulging from his face.

My face pales and my hands sweat.

The table is lined with food but no one dares touch it, waiting for the King to finish his theatrics. Three men I don't recognize sit at the far side of the table, dressed in their military best.

Astrid enters the dining hall, her head bowed. Her body trembles. She is tiny compared to the brute who ushers her in.

"I will sit," I say. I fumble to one of the empty chairs, dragging it across the stone floor.

"Too late for that." The King is almost giddy with delight.

"Maid, you are assigned to," he points the dagger toward me, "this thing, correct?"

"Yes, King." Her eyes are still on the floor and my heart slams in my chest, so loud I am sure everyone can hear it. I look from the King to Astrid, she is wringing her hands together. I glance around the room and no one is saying anything.

"Guard." The word is lazy, as if a young girl's life is not worth the breath it takes to give the order.

The guard grips her by the back of the neck and her body stiffens, tears filling her dark green eyes. "Hands!" he demands. I look in horror as she displays her hands in front of her.

"King!" I yell, but he doesn't acknowledge it.

He ignores me and brings his eyes back to Astrid. "Do you think this young girl heals as quickly as you?" Of course she doesn't, but I know this isn't a real question. Astrid starts to pick at her fingers again, a nervous habit. She knows something bad is about to happen. "I think we should find out."

Astrid's eyes open wide. "What do you think?" the King asks. Tears brim her eyes but just as they are about to fall her face falls.

"Whatever you see fit, Dark King." Her voice is shaky, but her eyes glaze over.

The guard grabs a whip from his belt and grips it tightly. The sound of the leather tightening under his hands makes me nauseous.

"No." I step back in front of her. "Whatever the consequences, I will bear them."

The king now looks at me, his eyes piercing my soul. I swore to myself I wouldn't be afraid when I got here, but I am. I hate that I am. "You will sit, or I will make sure this beating kills her!" His eyes lock me in place and I don't know the right answer. I cannot watch her get whipped but can't see her killed.

I feel hands pushing on my back, I look behind me and Astrid stands with shoulder back. Her eyes tell me to sit down and I hate myself more with each step I take toward the decorated table.

I will kill him. And I will make sure I enjoy it.

He nods to the guard, pleased with himself, stabbing my precious dagger in the side of a pig.

"Eat!" he demands, as the first crack splits the air.

CHAPTER 39

"Have you found them yet?" The King picks apart a roll waiting for his reply.

"We have not, Your Majesty." He lowers his gaze, hoping to avoid the King's wrath. "The rebels are still evading us, but we managed to capture one."

My ears slightly perk up but I keep my eyes down, my fork sliding through my eggs.

"You will make him talk." It is not a question; it is a demand. "They have been a thorn in my side for far too long."

My heart rate increases, I can only imagine what's in store for the poor fellow who got captured.

"You are not eating," the King says.

Only now, do I glance up. "Seems I have lost my appetite." I bite back the words as soon as I say them. Instant regret fills me and I picture Astrid's bloody hands. I look up but the King doesn't seem bothered by my flippant words.

"What do you think of the rebels?" His brows raise and I have no doubt this is a trick. He is playing a game and I am going to have to learn the rules.

"I don't know much, just a group of people who oppose your rein."

"Reign of terror." Ciena's thoughts slip through my mind and I fight to stay composed. The King eyes me suspiciously.

"I didn't get out much, as you can imagine." I flip my fork up and a sausage rolls off my plate.

"Ah yes, your overprotective father." He crosses his fingers and leans his elbows on the table. "I was disappointed when I didn't find him amongst the dead all those years ago."

I clench my hands together and bite my tongue. A copper taste filling the back of my mouth.

"Temper, child." Ciena whispers to my mind.

I clench my teeth. Now she chooses to speak with me. Not when I was getting my chest carved for his enjoyment.

A deep cough rattles his chest. I raise my brows and lean back against the chair, its large back extending above my head.

"You are claiming ignorance then?" he asks with raised brows.

"Since I know nothing, I must."

"You have some nerve!" The commander bellows, slamming his fist against the table. His eyes bulge slightly and his neck swells like a bullfrog. There is nothing scary about a bullfrog.

I turn my attention back to the King.

"Sit," he says calmly. The vein in the commander's forehead throbs but he does as he's told. The King needs something from me, otherwise I would be dead. I am in uncharted waters with a predator circling, and I need to figure out how to stay afloat.

"Luca." The King stands, the screeching of his chair assaulting my ears. "Take the girl." Klaus visibly tenses.

"Where, sir?" Luca stammers.

The King's eyes bore into him, like the sun on a scorching day.

"Yes, sir." Is all he says.

Luca strides casually beside me. "Are you taking me to the dungeon now?" I can't hide the snark in my voice.

"Do you want to go to the dungeon?" He raises his thick brow at me. "Maybe we could go together?" The edge of his voice slips into flirtation. Falling back into the same patterns that caused me to let my guard down in the first place.

He motions to turn and we pass the Atrium. The square space is still just as breathtaking as it was the first night. So full of life given that it is in a desert wasteland. Earthy splotches of green come to life around the spring.

Men and women scurry about and guards linger around, but no one looks at me. I take in every turn, entrance, and doorway; memorizing it and comparing it to the drawings Sven gave me.

The aroma of fresh bread fills the hallway. My stomach knots together, I should have eaten when I had the chance.

"Left," Luca says.

The clank of pots and pans rattle behind double doors. Luca pushes through the doors, disappearing into the kitchen. Moments later, the doors swing open and he steps out with a handful of assorted breads and muffins in his arms.

"You didn't eat much, figured you may be hungry." Luca mumbles with bread in between his lips.

I try to suppress a smile at the sight of a flaky, stuffed pastry hanging out of his mouth. He raises his brow right before I pluck the sweet treat from his mouth.

The pastry melts on my tongue. "That is my favorite one," he pouts.

"Which is why I took it." I smile with delight. "It is delicious."

Luca picks at a muffin, huffing in displeasure.

"Where is Astrid?" I ask.

Luca's shoulder tenses and he takes another bite to keep from answering my question. I stop and he runs into me, eyes wide and mouth full.

"I tried to kill the King and instead of repercussions I got food and a warm bed?"

"You tried to kill him?" I am not sure if I hear shock or awe in his voice, possibly frustration. "Fraya." He runs a hand through his hair. "Why do you insist on making this more difficult?"

We pass a large wood and metal door with no knob. "Is that the dungeon?"

"Why are you obsessed with dungeons? Do you want to stay in one?" He storms off and without thinking, I reach for him. His attention strays to my lingering fingers. Only inches separating our bodies. His eyes soften and for a second I see the man I spent weeks traveling with, the one who wrapped my blistered feet and spent many nights under the stars with.

His finger glides over my forearm and when I look up at him all I see is the man who lied and betrayed me. I step back but trip over my feet, the bread falling to the ground. His arms grip my elbows, stopping me from hitting the floor. "As graceful as ever." A light chuckle escapes his chest. He tucks a stray curl behind my ear and I shrink back. A flash of disappointment quickly passes through his face, but a lopsided boyish grin spreads over his lips, quickly covering it.

"Why did you lie?" I hate that I ask, but I have to know.

"Your room is the third door down the hall." He points toward the empty hall.

"What if I get lost?" I muse.

His eyes bore into mine and I see the man behind the boyish grin. The real Luca. "I wouldn't."

CHAPTER 40

I hesitate in front of the large oak doors for only a second before pressing through. Astrid sits on a small table. Instead of writing in her journal, her tears fill the pages with unspoken words.

Worry and guilt sits like a stone in my gut.

"Astrid?" I whisper, my throat catching just slightly. "I am so sorry." I don't know whether to rush to her side or give her space.

"She is a child. She's hurt and alone, Fraya." Ciena's calming words tell me.

"But, I caused this." My insides hurt.

"Child, you are not responsible for the actions of evil men."

I take a deep breath and sit beside Astrid. "Are you really who they say you are?" She turns and looks at me, her face blotchy and puffy from crying. How long has she been here like this?

"Depends. Who are they and who do they say I am?"

She sits up straight and wipes her face with her wrapped hands. I can't help but wince at the sight of them. Her wounds may heal but the scars will remain. A constant reminder of the Evil King's brutality. "The old maids tell stories of a time before, when dragons and humans co-existed. They said you are chosen . . ."

A light tap rattles at the door. I put a finger to my lips, stopping Astrid from continuing.

Klaus stands at the door; his eyes look tired. He hands me a small basket stuffed with fresh rags and ointments.

"Are these for Astrid?" I ask.

He nods. "I came to check on you."

"How do you think I should be after watching your father torture an innocent child!" I hiss. I step into the hall leaving Astrid to rest.

His eyes are bloodshot and hair a mess. "I am not a good guy, Litchska. There are things I have done that I can't take back."

My heart races in my chest. *Why is he telling me this?* I look at his bruised and bloodied knuckles.

I step farther out into the hall. "Klaus? What happened?" I try to take his hands in mine, but he steps away, eyes hardening.

Only now, does he really look at me.

"Caring for people is a weakness, Fraya. He doesn't have to kill you when he can just as easily break you." He straightens his back.

I shake my head, biting down the part of me that agrees with him. Getting close to me has resulted in too many innocent lives getting hurt, or worse. "Why are you telling me this?"

"Because, I told you not to come."

"I want to help," Astrid insists.

"Absolutely not. No chance." I shake my head at her request. "It's too dangerous." I squeeze the warm rag, letting the water run over her angry swollen skin.

"Why?" she demands.

I look down at her trembling hands. The skin is still newly open and slightly bleeding. "I am looking at the reason, Astrid. No." I gently rub ointment on her hands and wrap them before taking the rose-colored water to the washroom.

Keeping her wounds clean is the least I can do.

When I turn around, Astrid is behind me with her eyes to the floor. "What's wrong?" I ask.

"Prince Luca requests your presence in the other room," she says.

My insides burn with anger. "Please, stay here."

Luca sits on the bed, smiling when he sees me. *I hate him.*

"Why are you here?" I ask.

"That is not the way to treat a guest." He rises and strides over to me. Clearly enjoying his taunt.

"You are no more a guest than I am." I reign in my tongue, remembering Astrid's bloody hands.

He shrugs slightly. "I wanted to check on you."

"I will tell you the same as I told your brother, I am not the one who was beaten for no reason." His calm composure slightly cracks as the mention of his brother. *Interesting.*

"He would have beaten you until you begged for death and I made sure he didn't."

I draw my brows together and pull back. "What do you mean?"

"I just told him hurting *you* is pointless." He shrugs and paces around me.

It wasn't Klaus. I hate the relief I feel at the realization, but it quickly turns into seething rage. "She is a child!" my voice raises. "How could you?"

"I didn't know he would hurt *her,*" he says, like it makes it better. Like what he did was okay. "I thought you would be grateful." He steps forward and his proximity makes my stomach churn.

"Get out," I hiss.

"Excuse me?"

"Let me slow it down for you. Get . . . OUT!" I yell through gritted teeth.

"Why are you so angry?" he yells.

I consider hitting him in his already broken nose, but I can't risk Astrid being hurt for my recklessness. I need to breathe.

I run my hand down my face, forcing myself to calm down. "Why are you really here, Luca?"

A smile spreads across his face. "I am taking you out."

"No," I say.

"I wasn't asking."

CHAPTER 41

We walk in silence, the shuffle of our feet the only sound. We turn down numerous hallways, circling the same area a few times before returning to the main hall.

"Are you trying to confuse me?" I say from behind Luca.

"Only if it's working." He turns and smirks.

The stairs spill out before me and a small door sits to the left, unremarkably plain. Meant to be unnoticed, but that is the very reason I notice it.

Klaus exits the door to my left, momentarily stopping at the sight of us. His eyes quickly scan me from head to toe causing my insides to flip. He lowers his gaze and shuts the door, his hand tightly clenched over the handle.

"After you." Luca motions his hand down the flight of stairs.

I stare at him. "I prefer not to turn my back to a traitor, one knife in the back is plenty."

His hand slaps against his thigh in defeat. I glance up at Klaus who walks away, but not before spotting a smile creeping over his lips.

"Ouch, darling. That one stung a little."

We descend the stairs and he pushes the large castle doors. The suffocating heat hits me in my chest, taking my breath away. The air is dry and the breeze is non-existent. The hoots of owls catch my attention. Two stunning white owls sit inside a stone building. The yellow in their eyes both haunting and beautiful.

The bright yellow eyes are the same ones that stared down at me from the perch in the tree the night I met Luca. The wound reopens and the sting feels as fresh as the day I found out. From day one, I was targeted. The question is . . . how did they find me; how did he know?

The closer we get into the middle of the city, the more people roam the streets. The aroma of spices and livestock fill my senses. Many stop and give a slight bow to Luca, who beams at the attention.

I manage to stay in the shaded parts of the road, avoiding the unforgiving sun like the plague.

Dozens of people loiter in the dark alleys, others beg for food, while many rest against the buildings giving shade. Many of the townspeople look malnourished and my heart aches. How can a King sit by while his people starve? Where is all the food and supplies going that he steals from the neighboring towns and villages?

My insides twist. "Where are we going?"

"I thought you would want to get out of that stuffy room." I look into his sea blue eyes and he really believes he can ignore everything. I can't, but I also need answers and if I must play nice, I will.

"Thank you. I am having a good time." I force myself to soften the words.

Luca lets out a laugh from deep in his belly. "Don't start lying to me now."

"You don't like when people lie to you?" I tilt my head to the side. "But, you do it so well." I cross my arms over my chest, leaning my weight to one side.

"What's your problem?" he snips.

"My problem? Really?" I throw my hands up, looking at him as if he has three heads. "Do you not see these hungry people? Do you not think it's evil that your father pumps his army full of dragon's blood? And what are his plans for me? Is this my last day out before the King decides I am no longer useful?"

It is his turn to look at me as if I have three heads. He stands there processing everything I exclaimed.

"He isn't going to kill you, he needs you. He needs the Ancient," he says.

My heart slams in my chest. "And why does he need us?"

"Because he's . . ." Luca stops mid-sentence. He presses his lips together and his eyes widen.

"What, Luca? Am I a prize to be won? Sold to the highest bidder?" I try to get a rise from him but he doesn't budge. I am so close.

"Because killing you would be too easy." His eyes harden as he hides behind his sharp tongue.

"I feel bad for you," I say without remorse. "You are a pawn in your father's game, just like I am. Which means you are lying to yourself as much as everyone else."

His eyes burn with rage. I hit a nerve and it has shifted something inside him. He steps forward, backing me against one of the buildings. My stomach dips. People rush by, eyes to the ground.

He towers over me now, his eyes boring into mine. "You tried to kill me. I could have your head for that, but instead I forgave you. And this is how you repay me?" He pins me to the wall, his hands on either side of my head. The scent sun-tanned skin washes over me.

I bite my lip but refuse to drop my gaze.

"I thought I could trust you!" I bite out between gritted teeth. "I thought we were . . ." I stop. My heart squeezes. "If you want to kill me, you can try."

"You thought we were what?" his voice softens and his blue eyes shine down on me.

"It doesn't matter what I *thought*, Luca. Because now I know what you are. From day one, it has been a lie!" I take a deep breath, trying to still my racing heart.

"And do you think my brother is any different? I see the way he looks at you." He flexes his jaw.

"Are you jealous?" I ask in disbelief.

Luca smashes his fists into the wall and I flinch. "Dammit, Fraya!"

My heart hammers and I swear he can hear it. His hand drops to my face, cupping my cheek in his calloused hand. The familiar flutter settles in my stomach as his hand brushes my cheek.

The image of Klaus leaning over me, his body inches from mine makes my skin flush and Luca's eyes light up in pleasure. "Fraya," he purrs.

"Luca." I push my forearm against his chest.

He swallows, his hand slowly makes his way to my hip and for a moment I wish we were back in the woods, before I knew what he was, what he is.

"No," I tell him.

His body turns rigid but he doesn't move, his body still draped over me. "We can go back to before, pretend at least."

I clench my jaw, staring up at him with seething anger. He doesn't realize as my hand slips into his belt, retrieving his dagger. I slide my free hand up his chest watching desire flood his greedy eyes.

Before he can register what I did, his blade is to his gut and his eyes go wide with surprise. "This is your problem, Luca. You can pretend like evil is not breeding before you but I cannot and will not."

His face falls into a wicked grin, the same one he makes when he is about to say something off the rails. "You know I like it when you play rough, darling."

I dig the blade just deep enough to cause pain. "Touch me again and it won't be a watery grave I bury you in, it will be a fiery one."

I turn back to the castle, catching a flash of gray eyes watching me through the darkness, sending a tingle down my spine.

CHAPTER 42

I storm back to the castle. The bridge sits to my left and the urge to run and fall back into the habits I have grown up with makes my legs throb. But ultimately, I let my feet guide me back to my prison.

When I reach the stairs, Luca lays lazily on the steps. "How?"

A sly grin spreads over his thick lips, "you are not the only one with tricks."

"Why are you here? I didn't run away."

"I still can't figure out why you haven't killed us all. I would like to think it is because you are irrevocably in love with me." He puts his hands to his heart. "But, given the knife to my heart moments ago, I don't think that is it," Luca says.

"I can confirm you are correct," I sigh. "I am definitely not in love with you." A flash of hurt crosses his face but quickly dissipates. I stand beneath the scorching sun as it cooks my delicate skin.

He holds his hand in front of me and when I continue to stare at him . . . he shakes it. "My knife."

I look down at the blade still clutched in my hand. Klaus passes, his muscles flexing with each step. My eyes follow him until he reaches the large castle doors.

He *was* at the market.

I hate the way my insides betray me at the revelation. Luca steps in front of my line of vision, blocking my view of his brother. His face is red, his fists clenched tight, and his teeth bared. He grabs the hand that holds his blade and rips it from my grip.

"I don't mind fighting for your affection, Fraya." His tone is a mixture of anger and resentment.

I push past Luca, the heavy doors swinging open as I approach. The man who brings my dinners stands in the large doorway, his fragile frame struggling to prop the door. "The King requests your presence, miss." He dips low, keeping his eyes to the ground.

"Tell him I will bring her shortly, Sigmond. We're not done here," Luca says.

"You may not be, but I definitely am," I hiss.

"The King has been waiting and demands I bring her immediately," Sigmond says. His graying hair has started to thin but his green eyes still have life in them, watchful and alert.

Luca gives a tight nod, deciding not to tempt his father's anger. Sigmond ushers for me to follow him. The King's study is on the second floor behind the plain ordinary door that drew my attention earlier.

My ears ring as I look at the wood door. *What does he want.* Sigmond's cold hand reaches for mine, and when I look over at him, he gives me a reassuring smile. "Breathe . . . and mind your temper," he says quietly.

I choke on a laugh. He drops my hand just as the door swings open and Klaus looms over me. The Dark King stands behind Klaus. When they stand together, I realize how similar they look.

Klaus is broad and tall and wears his shoulder length curls pulled up; his father's hair is less curly and lands just below his ears. The beard on Klaus' chiseled jaw is smooth and black as ink while the King's is peppered from age.

I think of Luca and his short blond hair and smooth face, but his frame matches his fathers. I wonder where Klaus gets his height and stature?

"Leave us," the Dark King barks.

Sigmond leaves without a second glance. Klaus' feet don't budge.

"You too, boy," the King orders.

Klaus presses his lips into a tight line and his boots stay glued to the ground. "You have someplace to be." The King glares at his son. Klaus' jaw tightens and he closes his eyes, stepping into the hall.

The King saunters over and sits on an oversize black leather chair and above him, mounted on the wall, is the head of a dragon. My breath hitches and the King smiles in delight. Taking pleasure in my discomfort.

"Come in." He displays his hand to the room, beckoning me to come and sit. The dragon was an Azule. Its blue scales without their glow. I step closer and see a missing horn. My heart drops. *Trusting people will get you killed.* She warned me. He killed her.

My fists clench at my sides. The king stalks toward me. "I see you are admiring my trophy. Her blood will feed my army for weeks." A glass of ember liquid sits on his desk, and the spicy aroma of alcohol seeps from his breath. "Seems you had a run in with this beast? So, you understand how dangerous they are?" His lips curl into a wretched smile.

"You are vile," I bite out between gritted teeth.

He chuckles, low and deep. "Ah." He steps behind his large wooden desk. "I am much worse. Sit."

I could kill him right now, end this. I think about watching the life drain from his eyes as I did my father. There is nothing in my head besides murder as I fly over the desk, my hands around his throat before he can blink. The book shelf behind him rattles in protest.

My heart races in my chest as I squeeze tighter. I look into his beady eyes waiting for fear to arise but it never does. Instead, as the veins protrude from his forehead he only smiles. "You look just like her. You have her temper, too," he chokes out.

My grip loosens and his fist slams into my chest, knocking the air from my lungs. A knife sits at my throat. "You also have the same weakness." He backs away from me, dropping the blade from my skin. "You won't kill me, because you can't. I know things about your mother no one else does."

Quick as a snake, he slices my hand and grabs my wrist. My blood pooling into the spiced wine. When he is satisfied, he slings my hand back, falling into the oversize chair, air rushing from the cushion as he does. He mixes the drink, his hand slightly trembling.

"Sit," he demands.

He dips his finger in the concoction and slips it in his mouth. My insides protest. He shoots the drink quickly, his pupils dilating as he lays his head back and sighs. My face twists in horror.

"You get used to it," he says. I watch as the trembling in his hands settle.

Ciena? I let the thought flow through my mind. I am still not sure how our connection works but if she can reach out to me, maybe I can reach out to her.

"How do you keep the blood from curdling in this heat?" I ask curiously.

"Courtesy of minds far superior than mine," he says. My eyes slightly widen. "You look surprised. I recognize I need people around me who can do things I can't. The trick is, making sure they stay in line." He picks up the knife, twisting it on his finger tip. "Wouldn't you know, it only took sacrificing one of their families for my friars to stay in line."

I say nothing, hatred spinning a spool in my stomach.

Kill him, Fraya. The thought plays in the back of my mind. *It can all be over if you just kill him.*

"For ninety years, I have walked this earth. Dragon's blood can do a lot of things, including expand a lifespan but unfortunately, it does not make one live forever. I was so close to finding Moir, so close to achieving eternal life but your mother snatched it from me." He slams his fist on the table.

Ninety?

Anger passes over him, but something else lingers there . . . loss?

"I was wondering when you would call on our link." Ciena's words flow through my body and I feel as if I can breathe again.

A devilish grin spreads across his lips. "Your mother shared the same expression when she communicated with the beast."

I take a deep breath. "I'm afraid I do not know what you are talking about."

"No need to hide it." He shrugs and pulls out a drawer in his desk.

He slams an animal skin book on the table. Twine wrapped around to keep it secure.

I nearly jump with excitement but instead I stay seated, trying to keep my eyes from flicking to the journal.

"Did you know there was a man who killed an Ancient and became a god?" He casually flips through the old pages.

He waits for me to respond. "No?" He nods. "That is not surprising. It is the Ancients biggest mistake and greatest loss. Azius murdered the god of the sea in a fit of rage, consuming her life force and her power."

"Why are you telling me this?" I shift in my seat, he is lying.

He ignores me and continues, "They locked him underground, punishing him for all eternity. This journal is his life story but most importantly, how he did it. I need your help and if you help me, I will let you live."

"I will never help you," I spit.

"But you will, because I have the one thing you won't say no to." He grins, proud of himself.

"And what is that?"

He shoves the journal back into the desk, "I have your mother."

CHAPTER 43

I try to keep my chest from heaving. He said he *has* my mother. Not that she is alive. For all I know, her bones are scattered somewhere as a permanent trophy. Just like the dragon head that hangs on his wall.

"Nice try, but I have no attachment to a woman I have never met." I shrug my shoulders.

"He says he has my mother." I hate the plea that seeps from my mind to Ciena.

A desperation sweeps over me, followed by pain, and a fleeting sense of hope. I clutch my chest as my heart nearly explodes from my chest. These emotions are not my own. Panic rises like bile in my throat.

"Stop!" I plead.

Instantly, my heart slows but my body is in a cold sweat, my head is spinning, and my breathing is still labored.

"Fascinating," the King says in awe. He almost seems happy and it feels wrong.

He stands and I follow, unwilling to get caught underneath him. "You will help me."

"I won't." My legs wobble beneath me. He grips my jaw, squeezing just enough to cause pain.

"You really have no choice." The Dark King's eyes bore into mine.

"There is always a choice." I spit in his face. All humor slips away before sending his free hand into my jaw. My head spins as I spit blood onto the floor.

Kill him. Kill him. Kill him. The thought burns into my mind like a prod used to mark cattle.

"I know you want to kill me. Rip my heart from my chest. It is what I would do." He shoves my face and says, "but you won't. You can't." He turns his back to me, making his way back to his desk. "Think about my generous offer." He motions for me to leave with his hand.

I place my hand on the door handle, fighting the words I so desperately want to ask. The vulnerability that they hold. "Is she alive?"

"What fun would it be if I told you that," he smirks.

"I will kill you," I say as I push the door open, my arms quivering under its weight.

"We will see."

I stumble as I close the door behind me. A guard waiting with his arms crossed reaches out, but quickly stops as I brace myself against the wall. "I am here to escort you back to your room," he says. He is the same man from the ball. I wonder if the man Klaus cut down before his eyes was his friend.

"Of course you are," I sneer.

The room is dark and cool and I allow it to consume me. Tucking myself under the covers. *What did you do to me?* My body continues to jump and twitch against my will.

"Hello?" I scream but it comes out brittle and broken, just like me. "Lock it away, Fraya," I whisper into the covers.

Just before the darkness takes me Ciena whispers, *"I'm sorry, child."*

A knock rattles my door. I stay locked in my bed, unwilling to pry myself from its comfort. Another knock, this time slightly more urgent, but I remain.

"Fraya. Please." The slight plea tugs at my heart and I let my legs lead me to the door.

"Leave us." He doesn't look at the guard who he orders away, nor does the guard protest.

Klaus has both hands against the frame, his hair falling into his face. My heart skips. "I needed to see you." He drops his hands and I look up at him.

His hand finds my bruised face and I lean into it. I ache for comfort, his comfort. Klaus steps into the room shutting the door behind him. The scent of him envelopes me. Like I am in front of a warm fire on a cold evening.

"Did you know?" I hate how pitiful my voice sounds. I hate that the King has this much control over me.

"Know what?" he asks.

"That my mother may be alive?" I can't get my hopes up, I can't let him get into my head.

He says nothing, each minute ticking by feels like an eternity. "I could never keep something like that from you."

I let out a breath. *The king is lying. She is dead.*

"Litchska." He steps closer and a flutter caresses my spine. The sound of my special name on his lips ignites a flame in my chest. *I should step away.* The thought is fleeting and I push it way down deep; letting myself enjoy his closeness, relishing in his touch. I hear him swallow as he wraps a finger around a wild curl. I stay trapped in his eyes, locked in the storm that rages within them.

He traces a finger along my collar bone and up my jaw, sending a wave of desire crashing into me. My breath hitches as he tilts my chin up gently. I place my hand against his chest and he tenses, his heart thumping wildly.

Before I can say anything the door creeps open and Astrid walks through the door, stopping when she sees us. "Am I interrupting something?" she says.

Klaus quickly steps away from me. "Not at all, I was just leaving."

CHAPTER 44

As soon as Klaus is out the door, Astrid squeals. "Nope," I say and tuck myself back into bed, my body still alive from Klaus' touch.

Hours later, I am combing my thick hair back into a ponytail and Astrid comes in with a smile on her face. I search for Ciena, but she is nowhere to be found. Somehow, I feel more lonely than ever, barren. I never realized the effect her presence had, until it was gone. Many questions rattle around in my mind, but images of Klaus and the feel of his skin on mine keep intruding on my thoughts.

"*Ciena?*" Again, I try our connection but she is silent. Anger swirls in my stomach. How can she leave me like that?

Astrid bounces through the room with a large smile on her face. "What has you so happy?" I ask, a little harsher than I intend.

"Two things. One, the cook has made fresh sweet rolls and we are going to get some and two, I think I figured out a way to help."

"Astrid," I warn.

But she ignores me. "Let's go. Once they go cold, they are not nearly as good."

My mouth starts to water as we enter the hallway. The guard trails behind leisurely. He is a mammoth of a man; his hands could easily squash a watermelon if needed. *Where does he find these people?*

The fragrance from the kitchen wafts through the hall and my stomach gurgles in anticipation. My mouth waters as Astrid pushes through the door. Sigmond sits on a stool in front of a round woman with an apron that was once white.

"Miss Fraya?" Sigmond says.

"It's Fraya, Sigmond," I tell him.

Astrid hops over to the cook and smiles a contagious smile. "We came for sweet rolls!" she exclaims. Her excitement is infectious. The cook grins, her hips bumping into the counter when she turns to pull out a tray of mouth-watering, cinnamon, sugary, sweetness. Sprinkles of white pop out amongst her jet-black hair.

"So, you are Fraya! You are a pretty thing," she says.

"Yes ma'am," I reply. "Thank you."

"Oh no, no, no. Call me Tainya." She lays the large tray on the open counter. "Or Momma T, whichever you prefer, baby."

Her accent is thick and not one I have come across before. "Come, eat." She ushers us closer.

"I don't think she should be . . ." Sigmond starts.

"Shhh, nonsense. The girl is hungry." She swats him with a towel and he throws his hands up in surrender. The soldier hovers in the corner, his eyes watchful but relaxed.

"Thanks," I say before I stuff an entire roll into my mouth. "Mmm. How are these so good?"

I grab three more. "Here," I say, plopping the delicious forbidden sweet roll into the hands of the guard.

A door swings open in the back as I lick the sweet sauce from my fingers, and a sweaty Klaus walks into the kitchen with the same burlap sack I saw him with the first night I was here.

My heart jumps into my throat. Even with a cover over his face, he is unmistakable. He quickly turns his face from me and I feel foolish.

"It's delivered then?" Momma T asks.

He nods. Astrid and Sigmond stand and bow in his presence. I catch his eyes on me for a moment and my insides squirm. "You should be in your room," he says. Cold and callous. I hate the way my heart sinks at his rejection.

"No sir," Momma T snaps. "You may take her back to her room."

I nearly choke on my food and the room becomes tense.

"It's fine. The guard can take us back," I assure her. "Ow!" I hiss at Astrid. My skin burns where she pinched and I glare at her.

"I need both Astrid and the guard to help with food delivery." She doesn't look at me as she speaks, instead she stares at Klaus with her hands resting against her wide hips. I am in awe at the gall of the woman before me.

The guard finishes his dessert and heads into the storage without a word, grabbing a large bag of potatoes. A scheming look passes over Momma T's face and Astrid fails to hide a grin. I look at Sigmond who only shakes his head in defeat.

A heavy sigh rises my chest. I grab a few more rolls. "Well, let's go," I say, pushing through the kitchen door. Klaus soon follows, a cold glass of milk in his hand.

Momma T's doing no doubt.

The silence is painful. Each time I go to speak, words fail me. My inner torment screams at me to get answers while the other part of me is angry and embarrassed.

How can he be so cold only hours after touching me so gently.

I lift the dessert to my lips and catch Klaus staring. I calm my heart and ask, "Want one?" I hold it out in offering.

"You are a distraction I cannot have right now." His words are clipped and hurtful, and I board up the doors of my heart.

I don't know what I expected him to say but it wasn't that. "All you had to say is no," I murmur.

He pauses before deciding to take the cake, his fingers brushing mine. I stiffen and the cakes plummet to the floor.

The heaviness of this moment is suffocating. Something unfurls within me as I stare into his stormy eyes, but I can't let it take hold.

"I owe you a dessert," he says quickly.

"You owe me nothing." I walk to my room and shut it behind me and slide to the floor. The plan hasn't changed, even if my heart beats like a caged bird in my chest when he is near. It is easier this way.

CHAPTER 45

When I am certain I am alone, I gently open the door. I half expect the guard to be at his post but he is still with the cook. *It's now or never.* I race through the open hallway, keeping in mind to stay away from the kitchen. The castle is enormous and finding out where to start is almost overwhelming.

Without knowing how much time I have left, I start with the closest rooms. After seven chambers, tombs full of dust and spiders come up empty, I move to the next floor and it is more of the same. Reeking of dust and age. I start to feel discouraged after another row of doors proves fruitless.

Voices creep down the hall and the blood rushes to my ears. I take the first door to my left, the soft click sounding like an alarm in my head. I stay there for a moment, paralyzed with fear, trying to force my breathing to even out.

A few minutes pass and I take in the room. Like the others, this room is covered in grit. Floor to ceiling curtains hang around the room, creating a heavy darkness. But after my eyes adjust, I realize a lone green chair sits in the corner with a table off to its side. An oil lamp sits half full in the center but it is too dark to see anything else.

A surge of adrenaline passes through me. *This is important!* My insides scream; but how? The door jolts and I freeze, fear tearing a hole through my chest.

"Move your legs," I plead to myself. *"Move, or we're dead."*

Just as the door opens, I slide behind a heavy curtain. Heavy footsteps get closer and my heart fights to escape my chest. Something tickles my arm and I trap a scream as it grows in my throat. The footsteps cease and the lamp flicks on. I risk a glance, and spot salt and pepper hair leaning against the back of the chair. The Dark King sits just a few feet away from me. His head disappears for a moment and then a deep sigh escapes his lungs.

The minutes ticking by feel like hours. My muscles jerk, a warning I will not be able to stay in this position forever.

"It didn't have to be this way," The King says. The unexpected tenderness is jarring. But the affection soon leaves his voice, a sneer replacing it. His words are harsh and angry but sorrow fuels them. Pain is laced between each syllable, holding it all together. I hear him crush whatever he is holding and quickly smooth it out.

Who is he talking to?

He slides down into the chair and I hear the clink of his glass as he sits it on the table. My calves start to burn and my toes have gone numb from holding my weight. The temptation to place my feet flat is all I can think about. My legs continue to throb, my muscles screaming for release.

A deep unsettling growl comes from his chest as he gets to his feet.

Sweat trickles down my temple as I helplessly cling to the wall. Seconds tick by until finally the light flickers out.I sigh in relief as his steps near the door. But . . . it never opens. Uneasiness fills my gut; *he knows I am here.*

Slowly the door opens and closes, but the panic flowing through my veins only increases. Like I am trapped in a cage with a wild animal. I squeeze my eyes shut and I do not breathe, afraid he will hear even the slightest breath. A shiver runs down my spine and I know he is standing right in front of me. My heart beats so hard it hurts and a knot forms in my throat as alarms go off in my head. But I remain still and reach deep within myself pulling from the power that runs through my veins.

I will not go down without a fight.

His heavy footsteps fade, the door slams, and my legs give out. I rub my throbbing legs. "Ow, ow, ow," I whisper as I pound the ache from my calves. I furiously scour the chair, hoping whatever he grabbed from here; he also left. I slide my hands under the chair, ignoring the webs my fingers catch on and feel a letter-sized paper in a small opening.

I frantically light the lamp, half expecting him to emerge from the darkness, but I am alone. I carefully open the wrinkled letter and a small picture floats to the ground. I hesitate only a moment before turning it over. My mouth suddenly feels dry and time seems to slow as I stare at the faded crumbled image.

Her smile is like that of a spring rain after a harsh winter. Her golden hair falls in waves around her shoulders. However, what stops my breath . . . are her eyes. They shine like freshly cut emeralds.

"You have your mother's eyes, sweet girl." I remember my father saying. She couldn't be more than a couple years younger than me in this picture.

Hot tears sting my eyes and the picture blurs. I blink a few times, fighting to clear my vision, and slowly open the letter.

I read and re-read the letter from my mother, running my fingers over each stroke of the quill. The words, now faded with age, are beautifully written. But, something about it feels wrong. An invasion of privacy.

My Dearest Zekiah,

The nights have been lonely since you left.

I miss our late-night strolls in the garden.

Yours forever.

-Princess Ravina.

Then, like a punch in the gut . . . I know. The King has a weakness. *My mother.*

CHAPTER 46

I hurriedly tuck the letter back into its hiding spot and blow out the lamp, shaking from the new information. I rush from the room, the heavy door slamming with a thud. Sigmond turns the corner as I do, his eyes widening. "Miss Fraya, I think it wise to return to your room. *With haste.*"

He turns back the way he came and I dash up to my room. Keeping my feet as silent as possible. When I see my hall, I let myself breathe a little easier. "Almost there," I say. But two voices stop me.

So close. I can see my door, safety only a few feet away.

Astrid's voice floats through the air alongside the occasional grunt from the guard. If I am caught, she will be punished. I scratch my brows and rub my face in frustration. Carefully peeking around the corner, Astrid seems to be watching for me because her eyes immediately find mine.

She stops and grabs the guards arm. "Oh no," she says. The guard raises his eyebrow. "I forgot the dress!" She gently steers the man around and gives me a slight nod. I run without breathing.

"I must check on the girl," he says and tugs away from her.

Faster, faster, faster. My insides cry.

I slip through the door only a few seconds before the guard knocks. "She may be sleeping," I hear Astrid say.

"It's after noon," he says dryly.

A louder knock echoes and I do the only thing I can think before the door pushes open. My cotton dress is partially over my head when the guard and Astrid step in. Heat rises on my skin. Both Astrid and the guard stand surprised as I struggle to hide my exposed body.

The guard throws his hands over his eyes and turns. "I didn't see anything."

After I slide the dress over my head, I can see Astrid fighting with herself to rein in her amusement. I roll my eyes and step toward the door.

"Please don't tell his highness." The guard's back is still to me but his shoulders are tight and he tugs at the bottom of his uniform.

"I am dressed, you may turn around," I say.

He vigorously shakes his head. "I will never look upon you again, I swear it."

"Word spread pretty quickly that Klaus sliced the throat of the last guard to lay a hand on you," Astrid says.

I should feel ashamed at the titillation that flickers through me, swirling in the deepest parts of me, but I don't. *"No one will touch you again."* I remember the fear I felt in that moment, the anger that seeped off him.

"I will say nothing," I assure him. His shoulders relax slightly, but he keeps his back turned and says nothing more. I will not have this man's blood on my hands as well.

As soon as I shut the door, Astrid breaks out in a fit of giggles. "Of all the things you could have done, you decided being half naked was the best choice." Her giggles continue until she is wiping tears from her eyes. "Good thinking though, no guard will set foot in here without permission again."

"Thanks for the help," I tell her.

"It was nothing." She shrugs. "Such a small thing to do for you, your Highness."

I stop and stare at her in disbelief. "How do you know that?"

"I told you, I want to help," she says simply.

She looks so much older than when I first arrived here. Her shoulders no longer slouch and her eyes hold a determination along with a hint of sadness. She has been through too much in her short life.

"Did you know that I turn twelve in a few days," she says with glee.

Images of my twelve-year-old self fighting against the water surface, the fear I felt that day but also the power I found. "Twelve, huh?" I say peeking over at her.

"Yup."

"Are you changing the subject?" I accuse.

"Nope," she says sweetly.

The door swings open and both Astrid and I jump out of our skin. "Interrupting something?" Luca says.

As the door closes, the guard still has his back turned toward the door, his head cast to the floor.

"I see you still don't know how to knock." I shoot daggers with my eyes.

"I take it you are not happy to see me, then?" He strides closer and Astrid sinks away from him.

"I am never happy to see you," I bite back.

He is inches from me now. His rough hand slides under my chin lifting my face up to look into his eyes. "You know I like it when you are mean to me." A wicked grin spreads across his lips and his eyes drop to my mouth, so quickly I think I imagine it. A small tug pulls at my stomach.

I narrow my eyes and press my lips together. "What do you want?"

He suddenly drops my face. "We're going on a little trip."

"Why?" I ask skeptically. "Are we going to the dungeon?"

He gives an exasperated sigh. "Why do you have to ruin this? I am not taking you to the dungeons."

"So, you admit there is a dungeon." I can't help but smile a little at his frustration. He is so easy to mess with.

"Get dressed," he demands.

"What does one wear to a dungeon?"

"Fraya," his tone rises in warning.

Leaving now gives me less time to find the blood storage and look for my mother. A strange hope surges through me but I quickly taper it down. *That's what the king wants, to get your hopes up. You can't fall into that trap.* I remind myself.

I feel Ciena in the corners of my mind but when I reach for her, she pulls away. A painful isolation snakes around my insides, pulling me into the darkest corners of my mind. *"More people will die because of you. You are a failure."* The assaults bombard my mind, trapping me. *"She is not alive."*

Air is trapped in my lungs, but Ciena's pull gets stronger. *"The girl will die because of you, too!"*

"Ciena!" I cry.

"You promised you would protect my daughter." The words are like a blow to the stomach. Something is very wrong. These are not my torments, they are Moir's.

CHAPTER 47

A tug on my arm brings me back. "Are you okay?" Astrid says. Her eyebrows drawn together in worry. "I have been talking to you for a few minutes. Where did you go?"

The suffocating grief of the Ancient still rattles my bones, making me shudder. "Luca is waiting for you."

"Okay." I dress quickly, Ciena's misery still hitting me in waves.

As I open the door, I see Luca leaning against the wall, the juice of a fresh orange dripping down his fingers. The guard quickly turns his back to me. "What did you do to him?" he asks, brow raised.

"He isn't an ass, unlike some people," I snip, staring accusingly.

Luca places his hand over his heart and winces like I stabbed in. *If only I had stabbed him.*

Outside, a group of soldiers wait with their horses and wagons ready for travel. "Where are we going?"

"Supplies," is all he says as he loads himself on top of his horse. I recognize a few men from around the castle. The most recognizable though is the large man I shared sweet cakes with. I thought he was large before but dressed in full armor he is a mammoth of a man and equally as terrifying.

Luca drops his hand to me.

"I am not riding with you." I cross my arms over my chest.

"Unless you plan on riding with one of these fine gentlemen." He motions to the surrounding officers, many of which turn their heads or begin to move their horses, including the large one. If Luca notices, he says nothing.

I walk over the empty carts. This will be an uncomfortable ride but riding up against Luca for an unspecified amount of time is not an option.

"You can't be serious?" he says.

Folding my arms over my chest I say, "Dead serious, actually."

After hours over bumpy terrain, my body screams at me for being so stubborn. At this point, I am sure the soldier is making a point to hit every hole, rock, and divot in the road. My skin, blazing and red, tells me that pain awaits me in the morning and it will be unpleasant.

"Had enough yet?" Luca asks as his horse prances alongside the cart.

"I am fine where I am," I say just as the cart dips, sending me crashing into the side of the rough wood. I hear a snicker from Luca and I glare at him through squinted eyes.

Luca trots on, his body smugly swaying with the movement of his horse. I look down and a scratchy blanket lays over the side of the cart. When I look back up to see who valued my comfort, there is no way to tell who my sneaky friend is.

I try to relax as the cart jostles me, my thoughts drifting to my father. On days like today, my father and I would watch the clouds drift through the sky. He would tell me to make sure to always find at least one beautiful thing around me, as it could change my whole perspective on my surroundings.

I close my eyes, listening to the sound of hooves beating on the ground, men talking, and birds chirping. Letting my thoughts drift to Ciena.

"Ciena?" I am hesitant at first, fearing the pain that wreaked havoc on my body not too long ago. I search for her in the very corners of my mind, imagining a wall around my heart to help shield myself from her pain.

"Ciena, it is not your fault." A silent stirring rustles through me.

"Child, it is all my fault." The depth of her sadness is etched into every word.

"You couldn't have stopped my mother, any more than you could have stopped me." The weight she carries is suffocating.

"It is not just your mother. All of it, from the very beginning. I thought . . ." I feel her slipping from my mind.

"I think she is alive." I blurt out the words, hoping that it will ease some of her pain. I don't know what happened to the god my father told me stories about, but this is not her. Pieces of her shield crack and her pain and anger start to seep through, taking my breath away.

"You do not want her to live, child. Death would have been a mercy."

"How could you say that?" I demand.

"Sleeping, are we?" Luca's voice stirs me as I fight to maintain my connection with the Ancient. But I feel her pulling away, shutting me out, protecting me or possibly herself.

I grunt and sit up. The sun has begun its descent, allowing the moon to show its face. *I just closed my eyes.*

"Seems like you made a friend." Luca nods to the blanket and I roll my eyes.

"Glad someone here has manners." I rub my sore joints.

He snorts, and I roll over to look at him.

"What?" I ask.

"You have zero manners." His horse keeps pace with the wagon. The horse pulling it pays no mind to him.

I shrug. "Like I said, I am glad someone has manners."

A dimple emerges on Luca's face and I avert my eyes. *Damn dimples.*

"We are making camp." He slides off his horse and offers me help. I am too stiff to say no. I place my hand in his, ignoring the heat that runs up my spine. *I hate him,* I remind myself.

The group of men quickly set up camp and within the hour I am sitting in front of a fire with my belly full. There are fifty of us gathered around multiple fires. I try to focus on anything other than the thirteen faces staring at me.

"Did you really try to drown the prince?" A kid no more than seventeen blurts. The camp goes quiet, all except the crackles of the fire. Everyone waits to breathe until I answer.

I take a deep breath. "I saved his life and he returned the favor by betraying me. When I found out, I tried to kill him." His brown eyes widen. "But . . . as you can see, I failed."

All eyes fall to Luca, who only nods his head in agreement.

"Are you really the long-lost princess?" he asks. The words come out soft and uncertain. Luca shoots him a look that silences him immediately.

"Why are you here?" I ask. Luca eyes me suspiciously but stays quiet.

"I was given an order to come on this supply mission, Prin . . . ma'am," he quickly corrects.

"Why did you choose to become a soldier?" I ask.

"To help feed my family," he says, like it is the most obvious thing in the world.

"How long have you been a soldier?" I pry.

"Six months, ma'am," he says, but a sadness hangs in his words. What has he been forced to do in these last six months? I watch the men pass the meat around, tearing off bread and dipping it in soup. None of these men seem like the cruel ones I have encountered. "Your hair glows in the moonlight," he says sheepishly.

A deep, hearty laugh bursts from the large soldier.

He smacks the kid on the shoulder. "Are you smitten, son?" The large man bellows but Luca looks less than pleased.

"Shut up, Rayne." He nudges the man's large hand off his shoulder and all the men laugh together. All, except Luca. I feel him looking at me, his eyes scanning every inch of me. I resist the urge to fidget and instead meet his gaze. The flames of the fire reflect in his eyes. For a moment, we are in the past. Before his betrayal, before he was a prince, when he was just a traveler and I was lost. But, that was before.

I break eye contact and go back to the conversation with the soldiers. The older men are speaking of their wives. A few have kids, and one refuses to settle down. He says settling for one woman is an injustice to the women he hasn't encountered yet." Then you haven't found someone who stops your heart and makes it thunder wildly all at the same time," says Rayne.

"Awe," I say.

Another man chimes in, "The only thing I need is for my . . ."

"Nope!" I say cutting him off. "With that, I am going to call it a night." I slap my thighs and stand.

The stars light my path back to the cart. I lay on my back, my arms under my head. I stare at the millions of stars, each one proof of the Ancients' power.

"You would think you would be finished with this little cart after traveling in it all day," his voice is deep, inviting. He leans against the wheel, the wood creaking against his weight.

"I won't sleep with the bugs again unless I have to," I say. "What do you want, Luca?"

"I don't have a lot of regrets, Fraya. But . . ." He turns toward me.

I cut him off before he can finish his sentence. "You seem to be the only one."

"Fraya, please . . . listen." He turns toward me. How dare he do this to me. How dare he make me remember the good, only for it to get clouded by the awful truth.

I jump up and the cart rocks, sending me barreling forward. Luca catches me effortlessly, and for a split second I notice myself wanting to stay in his arms.

"Nothing you say or do can take back what you did . . . Who you are," I say, straightening myself. "Is this why you brought me out here? So you could manipulate me?"

"Your hair really does glow in the moonlight." He lifts his hand and brushes it from my face. I carefully move back, cautious of the wobbly cart.

"How many nights did we spend together and you just now noticed." He drops his hand. "You offer nothing but pretty words and false promises," I hiss.

I gather the blanket and head back toward camp.

CHAPTER 48

Only myself, Rayne, the kid, and a few other soldiers are left to pack up camp the next morning.

"There was an urgent matter he had to attend to, miss. That is all I know," the kid says when I ask where Luca went off to.

I roll the blanket up and walk over to Rayne. "Thanks for this," I say as I hand it back. "It did make a world of difference."

He stares down at the scratchy cloth in my hand, his braided beard falling against his chest. "How did you know?"

I point to his horse's rump. "You're the only one without a roll."

"His highness would kill me if I left you without a sleep sack," he says, no malice in his words. I look into his ember-colored eyes and realize he isn't referring to Luca.

The supply station is the size of a small city. The unmistakable sounds of a blacksmith echoes through the air, and the hammering of metal rattles my brain. Soldiers march around giving orders to half-starved slaves. Both men and women wear clean shaven heads, sunken eyes, and bruises.

Anger swells in me as I move around the camp. Crates of vegetables and fruits from all over the region are stacked three feet high. Beautiful colored tapestries and fabrics lay out in the sun. A beautiful coral jewel is sewn into one of the tapestries and I pluck it off, tucking it in my pocket. "This will be perfect!" I say with a smile.

A strange white smoke creeps along the ground like a heavy fog. It circles my ankles and I squat, letting the man-made fog whisper through my fingers. "I see you have found the fish," Luca says.

"Fish?" I ask confused.

He opens the crate and sitting on a bed of smoke are dozens of fish. Each one still looks like the day it was caught.

"How?" I ask.

"The King made it happen," he says.

I notice, not for the first time he calls his father King. *"Minds far superior than mine,"* I remember the King saying. This is how he keeps his blood cold! I nearly jump from excitement.

An apple hits my foot and when I look to find its source, a woman is down on hands and knees trying to collect all the runaway fruits. A soldier grabs her by the neck. "Useless woman," he says between clenched teeth. I don't hear the rest of his words but the fear in the woman's eyes tells me all I need to know. He kicks her to the ground and her face slides against the rough ground.

"Get up!" the soldier yells.

I look over at Luca, expecting him to do something. But he only says, "It's best not to get involved."

My anger boils over as he kicks the woman in the stomach, a stifled grunt breaking my heart. "Stop!" I yell.

I feel Luca place his hand on my arm as a warning but I ignore it. I yank free from him and rush to the woman. I ignore the whispers and the stares and rush to her side. But he pays me no attention as he raises his hand, ready to strike the woman.

A heavy slap crashes against my face and I spit blood to the ground. "Feel better?" I ask, wiping my mouth. He blinks rapidly, glancing between me and the woman on the ground.

"My turn." He has no time to react before my fist smashes into his nose. He stumbles back, shock written on his face. He holds his face; spitting a tooth on the ground. He reddens as blood rushes to his cheeks from anger and embarrassment, he steps toward me and Luca clears his throat.

We have an audience now. Soldiers and slaves alike have stopped working to watch the spectacle. Rayne stands close by, his hands clenched into fists. I turn and let the woman lay into me, her body almost weightless.

"Fraya?" My blood runs cold and her raspy voice whispers my name.

"Maxine?" I whisper, tears threatening to spill over my eyes. I look at her bruised skin and fury rattles through me.

"Lucy." She presses her lips in a line, unable to say anything further.

Dread sweeps over me as Luca pins me with his gaze. "Maxine, you don't know me. Do you understand?" I hurriedly whisper.

I have no time for a response before Luca is standing over me.

"Who is this?" he asks, but there is something hidden behind such a simple question. It is never simple.

"I was just asking her name?" Her once full face stares up at Luca with no fear.

"Maxine," is all she says.

"The guard will be removed from his duties, you should have no further incidents," Luca says. It is my turn to wear a bewildered expression. I give Maxine to a nearby woman, who gladly takes her.

"I need a word." I take Luca's hand and guide him away from the crowd that has gathered.

"What? I removed the soldier, what more do you want?"

"You see this, right?" I throw my hands out to the sea of malnourished, bruised, and beaten bodies. "This is the same argument we had at the castle."

"They are slaves of war." He doesn't back down. "These people are enemies of the King."

"What war!" I scream. "There is no war, they aren't one sided. No one is fighting you."

He grabs my arm and pulls me close. "Enough!"

I inch closer, my face almost touching his. "She is coming back with us."

He laughs in my face. "No, she is not."

"I am not leaving her here to suffer when we leave, Luca. I won't."

"You have no choice," he says between gritted teeth.

I clench my fists at my sides. "Then I will burn this place to the ground. The only thing left will be ashes." My nostrils flare as I try to control my breathing.

"You wouldn't," he challenges.

"Watch me." I dare to step closer to him, already feeling the flames lick my fingertips.

We each stare without blinking, waiting for the other one to relent. He lets out a low snarl. "You may be seeing the inside of that dungeon really soon if you are not careful." He storms off and I let out a long, slow breath.

I scan the dispersing crowd for Maxine, hoping I am saving her life and not ending it.

"I took her to our camp. She is safe, for now." I turn to find Rayne beside me. I never even heard him approach.

"Thanks. But . . . how did you know?"

"Just a hunch," he says with a hint of amusement.

"Thanks, Rayne."

I start toward Maxine when Rayne says, "We aren't all monsters. At least, we don't want to be."

CHAPTER 49

Maxine sits with her legs crossed against the cart stuffed with food. Other carts are full of weapons and fine linens. I realize my mode of transportation up here may not be an option on the way back, but I can't dwell on that now.

I drop down beside her, my arms resting on my knees.

"She's fine," is all I say to avoid listening ears. Those two words are her undoing, her arms now slick with tears.

"Thank you," she chokes out between sobs.

My butt and back begin to ache and I begin to fidget when Rayne approaches, his footsteps oddly loud; almost like he is trying to let me know he is approaching.

"We are loaded and ready to go," he says, his eyes darting between the two of us.

"Let's go." I help my friend stand, her hand still clutching her bruised abdomen.

I wish I would have killed him. The thought doesn't surprise me but the one that follows does.

Who's the monster, now?

"I don't think the prince has decided about her yet," Rayne says.

I look over and see Luca pacing. I picture steam bursting out his ears. "Leave him to me." Rayne hesitates before approaching the scared women. The instant panic that rises within her is evident as she shakes against me.

"It's okay. Rayne will not hurt you," I say hoping to calm her fears.

Raynes' expression is almost unreadable, but I see the lines of worry in his forehead.

Luca stares at me in disapproval as I approach. "This isn't a good idea, and you know it."

I look back at Rayne who only gives me an *I told you so* shrug.

I ease my tone and place my hand against his forearm. He glances down but says nothing. "And you know I can't leave her here to die."

"Dammit, Fraya." He runs his fingers through his thick hair.

"Please, Luca." My voice is just below a whisper, a plea for him to listen.

Something dark flashes through his eyes, "I am not responsible for what will fall upon her when we get to the King."

I try not to flinch at his harsh words, but he is right. I may have only prolonged her death. "Thank you." I place my hand against his chest and feel it thunder wildly. For a split second I feel a twinge of guilt using him this way.

I am forced to ride with Luca, my back pressed up against him. His arms are against my thighs, the leather reigns relaxed in his palms. Rayne has not left the cart Maxine is squished into.

Hours into our trip, I realize this is not the way we came. A body of water calls to me from somewhere close. Only a small path cut through the foliage. The tiny hairs on the back of my neck raise.

"Luca, something is not right." A flock of birds erupt from the trees, their wings beating heavily, spooked by something.

"Everything is fine. This is just one of the paths we use for the trip home. We are not lost." He sounds more irritated by my concern than alarmed by it.

I turn as much as possible to him, my shoulder hitting his chest. "Stop the horse, right now," I demand.

"Your manipulation won't work a second time. We are not stopping," he bites out.

The earth holds its breath, not even the wind stirs. "Luca," I warn, but it's too late. Arrows rain from the heavens as Luca pulls me off the horse, shielding me with his body. Luca starts barking orders as another assault of arrows are released. These arrows are wild with flame.

I make my way to Maxine, her body shaking with fear. Rayne stares at me for a long time before sliding me a dagger. "Keep her safe," he says, then runs off.

The weight of the blade feels off and it doesn't fit snug in my hand like mine does, but it will work. "I just want to see my daughter," she cries.

"You will," I say. "But I need you to get under the cart."

A large group of people advance, the tree line beginning to bleed people. I see Sven burst through the bushes and my heart both leaps and plummets at the same time. These men are not the raiders, they are rebels.

They will get themselves killed.

Another group of them come from behind, removing items from the last of the carts. Then it clicks, the fight is a distraction, they just want the supplies. I use the chaos to edge Maxine toward the back of the caravan.

The last two carts are already cleaned out by the time we get there. Food and weapons like they were never there.

"We are going right toward them!" Maxine hisses.

"This is where Lucy is staying. Go with them." I look back, making sure to keep my head down, begging to stay unseen.

Hope springs in her eyes as a group of rebels come into view. They see us and draw their weapons. Recognition flashes through a woman's eyes, her sword drops and she bows. My face flushes with embarrassment and Maxine stares at me, questions on her lips.

I shake my head. "There is no time." I quickly embrace my friend. "Keep her safe." I tell the woman before hurrying back to the fighting, looking for Sven. *He better not get himself killed.*

When I finally find them, he and another man are tucked behind a group of trees. When I see who he is fighting, I sprint, jumping over bodies and other objects trying to get to them.

"Stop!" I yell, but they do not hear me. Each of them locked on the threat in front of them. Luca plunges his sword into a rebel whose last breath is a cry and my heart squeezes as he makes his way to another man, cutting him down easily.

Rayne and Sven match blows, each clash brings them closer to killing each other. A deep anger drives Sven. Neither man notices as I approach. A broken arrow protrudes from Rayne's shoulder and Sven bleeds from multiple wounds.

I dig into Ciena's ancient power and pull the water from deep within the earth, the air, and the nearby creek. "Enough!" I yell. Water slams into each man's chest, sending them stumbling backward. "I will not let you kill each other."

Their weapons fall to the ground, and they stand with their mouths open and eyes wide.

"Take your people and go. There are too many people dying," I say to Sven.

Rayne watches our exchange, wearing an unreadable expression.

"They have Arik," Sven says between clenched teeth. The fury he fought with is replaced with grief. A deep ache I am all too familiar with.

The rebel the commander caught was Arik. My heart sinks and I finally understand Ciena's warning about killing my mother being a mercy. If Arik is alive, he will never be the same.

"Your people are being slaughtered," I tell him. Sven's jaw clenches then he lets out a loud whistle that catches the wind and the rebels disappear as quickly as they came. These woods are theirs; we won't find them unless they want us to.

I take a deep breath and rub my eyes. When I look up at Rayne, he won't meet my gaze.

"She's gone?" he asks.

I nod.

"Is she safe?" His eyes still have not met mine. His shoulders are rigid and his expression remains blank. I nod again.

"There are men who would risk the King's wrath by taking your head. Right now, your identity is a rumor. Keep it that way," Rayne says and stalks off toward the convoy.

CHAPTER 50

Although the death total is few, it is still too many. I stare down at the kid; his eyes are open to the sky but there is no life in them. He was so young. I bend down and say, "Until we meet again." Then, I close his eyes.

"Did you do this?" Luca's anger boils over and his men clear a path to me.

"Of course not!" I fight back. "I told you to stop and you didn't listen."

He is on me faster than a snake, my jaw in his hand. "If I find out otherwise . . ."

"It seems you are more like your father than I thought," I say between gritted teeth.

"Sir, she saved my life." Luca looks over at Rayne, then back at me. Putting more pressure on my face.

"I will make sure your pain is drawn out. Do you understand?" His nostrils flare as he waits for a response.

I push down my pride and hateful remarks. This is not the time to poke the bear. "Understood."

"And the woman?" he asks.

"She is gone," I say. He presses his lips together.

"Of course she is," he scoffs.

We lost twelve men and Luca wears it on his face. We load the men in one of the now empty carts, so their families can give them a proper burial.

"What about these people?" I point to the dozens of fallen rebels.

He doesn't look at me as he says, "They are animal food."

We push through the night, finally reaching the castle just as the sun hits the highest point in the sky. The villagers stop and stare, whispers breaking out among them. The King flies toward us, meeting us halfway over the bridge.

Fear snakes its way through my stomach as the King's impending wrath approaches. The King finds me amongst the men, his ice-cold stare sending shivers down my spine.

He needs you alive, I try to remind myself. But, *alive* doesn't mean free from pain.

"You!" the King sneers and dismantles his horse.

"It wasn't her," Luca says.

The back of the King's hand meets Luca's face with a deafening crack. He doesn't do anything but move his head to the side. Blood pulls at the corner of his lip, next to an imprint of the King's ring. "Are you so blinded by her?" he yells.

He looks up and finds Rayne standing behind me. "Interrogate our prisoner."

Rayne takes off without a word and my gut twists. The King's sword clings at his side as he mounts his horse.

"What's wrong?" I never heard Luca approach; my mind fixated on Arik. He is alive but I am not sure for how much longer.

"Nothing," I lie. I look up and see his eye already beginning to swell.

"You always play with your necklace when you are worried or thinking about something." He nods to the hand that is slowly spinning my mother's necklace.

I didn't even realize I was messing with it, though I'm slightly annoyed that he recognized that detail.

I stare at the pile of bodies on the cart. "He was a nice kid."

"He knew the risks," his voice is hard and flat.

"That seems a bit harsh." I pull back and look at him, somehow surprised by his callousness.

He stares after his departed father. "It is reality." He glances down, his gaze passing straight through me.

"And what about his family?" I ask.

His eyes fall to the ground. "The King expects you in his chambers immediately." He stalks off without another word.

The Dark King circles me like a predator. I stand there under scrutiny, waiting for whatever he is going to do. The eyes of the blue dragon haunt me, staring at me from every direction. "Do you think I am a fool?"

"No." The King has not become the most feared man in the region by being a fool. He is cruel, calculating, willing to kill whoever gets in his way. But a fool, no.

"Where are the rebels?" he demands.

"I don't know." The words are hardly out of my mouth before the King has me pinned to the wall with my hair knotted in his hands. Leather and spice singe my nose as he pulls my hair tight, his fist resting against my scalp. He pulls until my neck is fully extended and when I swallow, a gurgle is released.

He runs his ring over my skin, nicking it in the process. "I think you are lying," he snarls. He releases me. "You could put an end to the young man's suffering. Tell me where they are and I will have his death be swift."

He speaks as if he is doing me a favor, a simple transaction and not a life hanging by a thread.

"I still don't know where they are," I tell him.

The same hand that bit into Luca meets my face. The pain is immediate and my head swims.

"This doesn't have to be difficult." He drags me to the desk, slamming my hand down on the solid oak desk. "I will only ask one more time."

"My answer will be the same," I sneer.

The King looks me in the eyes and says, "Your father hid you well. But, it was only a matter of time before he slipped up and it is only a matter of time before the rebels get sloppy as well."

I clench my teeth together. *Ignore him*, I tell myself.

"Do you know how I got this scar?" he asks. A blade pointed at the gruesome gash down his face. When I don't answer he continues, "I underestimated my enemy."

The wavy bladed dagger sinks into my skin, pinning me to the table. I bite my lip, swallowing the cry that bubbles to my lips. More of my blood spills and I wonder if it will eventually run out. "The dragon fooled me into thinking he was dead. I didn't know the beasts were capable of such a thing."

I fight to keep my composure, as sweat beads at my temples.

"I learned to never underestimate my prey."

The Dark King sits in his chair and plops his feet on the desk, jostling my hand. I hiss as pain shoots through my hand and up my arm. I look at the monster that sits before me.

"Pain is my only comfort, so give it your best shot."

His lips turn into a vicious smile as he leans over and plucks the blade from my hand. My breath slightly catches in relief. "Do you ever wonder about the old woman from Pendshire?"

I feel my eyes enlarge. How does he know about her? My stomach rolls.

"I don't want to ruin it for you but if you want to know the gory details, you should ask my youngest son." His eyes glisten with pleasure. "She is not the only death he left in his wake."

My heart pounds. The King delights as he watches the horror that fills me, swallowing me whole. *He didn't.* But, I know deep down the King is speaking the truth. Lying would be less painful.

CHAPTER 51

I can't get out of the door fast enough. My feet slide as I round the corner, a blood trail following me. Everything speeds up and slows down at the same time. My world continues to spin as I search for Luca. I try to call for him but my throat burns and no sound escapes my lips. I throw open every door in my path, but all I see is empty rooms and stunned maids.

Hot tears stream down my cheeks. Flames start to lick my fingers and fear grips me. *I can't control it.* "I don't want to control it," I breathe. I nudge open a door and let the flames swallow me.

"Fraya?" A deep voice says from behind me.

I bury my face in my knees, ignoring the figure at the door.

"Litchska," his voice is gentle.

"Did you know?" My voice comes out muffled against my knees.

"Look at me," he says and I hear him edge closer.

"Did you know!" I yell. The heat becomes more intense as I meet his gaze, anger pooling off me, looking to devour all in its path.

"Know what?"

"About the old woman? About my father?" I am standing now, shoulders back, ready to strike. But he only looks at me with confusion.

"I know your father died and I don't know any old woman." He continues to move toward me, ignoring the flames that dance at his feet.

"This is what he wants. He wants to break you," Klaus says.

He is now standing in the flames, amongst my grief and pain. "I can't control it," I sob. "He killed them and it's all my fault. What is the point of these powers if I cannot even protect the people I love?"

"Breathe." He takes a deep breath in and slowly lets it out. His eyes are locked on mine the entire time, like he is approaching a wounded animal. He is now in the midst of my torment, the flames inviting him as if they were his own.

His arms wrap around me and pull me to his chest. I fall into him, my head resting against him, the thump of his heart soothing me. Slowly, my power dwindles until all that's left is the tingle of my skin.

Klaus rests his head atop mine and a strange sound rings in my ears. It takes me a minute to understand that it came from me. My rage comes out in sobs, but still his arms don't leave me. Instead, they tighten, securing me.

When my body has nothing else to give, we sit there. Wrapped in each other until my breathing slows and the smell of him consumes me, like the first rain after a dry spell.

He runs a single hand against my cheek, wiping away my tears. Where his fingers trace, electricity ignites my already warm skin. The scent of burnt cloth lingers around us.

"How are you not burned?" I place my hand against his bare skin and he flinches under my touch. I pull back but his arms tighten around me once more, refusing to let me go just yet. He relaxes slightly and when I look up, his eyes are fixed on me. A deep pain flashes in his eyes.

"I don't know," he admits.

"You confuse me," I whisper.

"You bewilder me," he says as he runs his thumb under my jaw.

The door creeps open. "Fraya?" The voice is hesitant.

I still, and Klaus slowly turns, keeping my exposed body behind him.

"You," I bite between clenched teeth.

He opens the door and the little light from the hallway seeps into the room. Luca stops when he sees his brother, pain flashing across his face. I try to move around Klaus but his hands keep me in place.

"Brother, I would leave." There is an undeniable warning in his tone, but it only angers Luca.

"So you can keep her to yourself. Usually, you are not a one-woman man, *brother*." Luca's words slice through the air and they hit right where they are supposed to, like a punch in the gut. I don't want to be a notch on a belt.

I fight off his hands, my body suddenly cold where his grip was. "I am not some commodity to be passed around." When I finally see Luca, his hair is a mess and the rims of his eyes are red.

I fight with my clothes to keep my intimate parts mostly hidden but I see the way Luca absorbs every inch of me. Klaus steps forward and I shoot him a glaring look which makes him remain where he is.

"Please, listen," he begs.

"So, it is true." I know the King told him I knew. He wanted us both to suffer. "It was you in the woods?"

"I didn't want to." His hands are in front of him, pleading with me.

I inch closer. "And my father?" I swallow the lump forming in my throat.

He slides a mask over his face, emotionless and withdrawn. "Fraya."

"Answer the question." I feel the flame again. The power coursing through my veins.

"I didn't kill your father. You killed the man who took his life," he reminds me.

The memory of my father taking his last breath sends a sharp pain to my heart. "Did you give the order?" I wait for his answer, holding my breath. Hoping, even now, that it isn't the truth.

"I didn't have a choice." His eyes fall to the floor.

"There is always a choice," I snarl. My pain rips open like an old wound and bleeds out by way of flame.

I thrust out my hands, greedy for his death. He shields his face but not fast enough. It singes his face and the cry of pain that he releases only fuels my need for revenge.

My insides hurt. *How many more will die because of me?*

At least one more, I tell myself as I beg for his death.

"I will never forgive you for this." Deep down, I know I deserve this pain. This is my fault.

"Fraya, please," Luca pleads.

Luca meets my gaze, the side of his face singed.

I charge at him. "You're a monster!" A strong arm wraps around my waist. I thrash against Klaus. He tightens his grip, struggling to keep me away from his brother.

"Breathe, Litchska." He looks at his brother, the desperation in Luca's eyes only infuriates me further. He is not the victim here. "You should go, Luca."

As soon as he leaves the room, I swivel around to Klaus. "Why?" I pound against his chest. "You let him go!"

He takes my hands gently. "You would have hated yourself later," he says, his voice calm.

He lifts me into his arms. "I hate him," I cry. Something about the way his grip tightens around me makes me slink into him. Into the safety I feel when he is near.

CHAPTER 52

Klaus doesn't take me to my room. Instead, he lays me down in his bed, and brushes my hair from my tear-stained face. *How many more tears will I spill?* He turns and I grab his hand, pulling myself from the bed. "Please, stay." I hate the way my voice sounds. The desperation lingering behind those two simple words.

I stay trapped in his eyes, locked in the storm raging within them.

He traces a finger along my collar bone and up my jaw, sending a wave of desire crashing into me. My breathing hitches as he tilts my chin up gently. I place my hand against his chest and he tenses, his heart thumping wildly.

One hand slides down my curves, my tattered clothes exposing pieces of my smooth skin. A deep growl vibrates in his chest and he pulls me against him. My hands search the ridges of his body and end up tangled in his hair as his hand tightens around my hip.

"That is a bad idea," he growls, his lips inches from mine.

"This is the only thing that makes sense to me right now." I lean into him, pressing my body to his. My skin flushes as his grip on my hip tightens.

"You're in pain." I can see the war raging inside him.

"I want to forget. If only for a moment," I whisper.

"I love the way your body responds to my touch, Litchska." His voice comes out deep and heady as he leads me back.

Just as I think his lips are finally going to meet mine, he pulls back and my heart sinks. Embarrassment drowning me.

His eyes flicker with lust, but he clenches his jaw and says, "Not like this. You don't really want this. Not right now."

"I want this," I say. Touching him again, my hands exploring his exposed skin. "I want to feel you, to feel anything but pain."

"Fraya," he warns. I see his body trembling under my touch and my insides squirm at his desire. "When and if we do this, I don't want anything other than me to be on your mind." He touches me again, a wave of pleasure rolling down my spine as he runs his finger between my breast making me gasp.

"I want you to be lost in me, not your grief." He cups my face in his large hands, and I melt in them. His thumb slides over my cheek and a slight smile turns the corners of his mouth.

Gods, he is suffocatingly handsome.

"Get in the tub," he says.

I slide into the hot water, relaxing my achy muscles. Klaus slips out of the door, leaving me alone. I dunk my head, the sting from the boiling water a welcome pain. The water turns pink from the hole in my hand, but I can't bring myself to heal it just yet.

Luca killed my father. He may not have been the one to stab the sword through his heart but he gave the order, and that is no different. All that time we spent together, I feel like an idiot.

The water glides over my skin and puddles around my feet as I slip Klaus' shirt over my head and inhale his rich scent. I step out into the room, the stars peeking through the balcony doors. Klaus sits with a leg over his knee, watching me. He is always watching me.

"I don't think you have ever looked better, Litchska." The way Klaus looks at me makes me feel naked.

My skin flushes. "Are those Momma T's sweet rolls?" I eye the three desserts and the large glass of cold milk on the side table.

"When my mother was upset, she always wanted sweets." He shrugs.

"You have never told me about her," I say. He remains silent.

"What was her name?" I probe a bit more.

"Ismene." The way he says her name tugs my heart. "There is not much to tell." He pulls me to his bed. I hiss when he grazes my punctured hand. "Who did that?" His eyes darken.

"Your father." I look down and move my fingers. Each tiny movement sends a new throbbing spark through my hand.

His features relax and Klaus' presence fills the room until it's thick, dark, and suffocating. His anger is almost tangible. "It's fine. See?" I focus my attention on the pain and pull on my power, watching as my skin knits itself back together.

He watches my every movement. "Will you stay with me?"

His lips twitch up in amusement, the darkness in him slipping. "I thought we decided . . ."

"Just sleep," I quickly finish before he embarrasses me further.

He is up and removing his shirt in an instant. I swallow hard as I look over his skin. It looks like shattered glass that someone attempted to put together again. I look up, asking for permission before I touch him. He nods and I run my fingers over each scar, each broken piece of him. Some are jagged and angry, while the rest are just visible.

"Who . . . who did this to you?" Tears sting the corners of my eyes. I look down at his arms, the dark wisps moving up his forearms.

"You are not the only one my father tortures." He wraps me in his arms. "It's time to sleep."

I want to protest, but I have no words and my eyelids are heavy.

"Klaus?" I ask.

"Hm," his chest hums in response.

"Thank you." I whisper.

The steady rise and fall of his chest soothes me and just before sleep takes me, Klaus whispers, "*Preima Ti'stin*" against my hair.

I wake alone. Crawling out of bed, I see the stars still shining against the sky's black backdrop. When I open the door, no guards greet me. The stone floor is cool against my feet as I move through the darkened halls. I continue until nothing feels familiar, my gut tugging me deeper into the castle.

"If I was being interrogated, where would I be?" I say aloud. *Or if I was the long-lost queen?*

I quickly realize I may not be able to do this on my own. Already, I can feel the castle heating up as the sun births a new day.

"Ms. Fraya, you will find nothing down this way." Sigmond stands behind me, his arms clasped behind him.

How does he always find me?

"You better hurry back to your room, the castle is starting to stir," he says.

He walks me back to my room, ushering me through the door. Astrid sits on my bed, eyes red and puffy. When she sees me, she flies off the bed wrapping her arms around my neck. "I thought he killed you."

Sigmond bows and closes the door.

"I am fine. Everything is fine." I pull her back. "Are you okay?"

She nods her head, snot dripping from her nose. I didn't even think about what it would look like if I didn't return.

She slowly backs up and looks me over, her brows furrowing. "Who's shirt is that?"

"It's a long story." I sigh.

She straightens up, squaring her shoulders. "The maids have been gossiping. One of them overheard the King whispering about the blood moon. Whatever he plans to do, it will be then."

The blood moon is just over two months away, why the blood moon?

"I thought I told you not to get involved?" I give her a disappointed glare but she ignores me.

"I didn't listen," she shrugs.

My eyes roll. "Why?"

"Would you have?" she asks, crossing her arms.

I scoff. *She's got me there.* "It's dangerous."

"Just living is dangerous," she says. "My mother lived in Rindon. A small village in the Western region before the war. When the King came, he slaughtered thousands. They barely got out." I have gone through Rindon a few times. The city is still a broken shell, fighting to rebuild itself.

"Why are you here?" I ask, obvious disbelief on my face.

"Because, Your Highness, this is where we are needed."

Who is this person in front of me? I glance around with fear of being overheard. "Are you . . ." I drop my voice hardly above a whisper, "a rebel?"

"Keep your enemies close, it's the only way to stay ahead of them." Her mother had told me something similar.

"You're a child!" I hiss. Even as I say it, I realize how perfect the plan is. No one would suspect a child of such things.

"There are no children under the tyranny of the King. For twenty years, we have struggled under oppression, and now we finally have a chance. My life for hundreds of thousands seems like a small cost."

Conviction seeps into her words and guilt creeps over me like the early morning fog. A heaviness weighs on my shoulders.

"You're not alone in this fight," she says.

But I am. There is none like me. I am the only one who carries this burden. I can't tell her the faith she puts in me is misplaced. I was born to run, not rule. My own father didn't trust me enough to tell me who I was. No one should put trust in someone who doesn't trust herself.

Instead, I look at her with a soft smile and say, "Let's burn this place to the ground." I let the flames trickle between my fingers and watch as she stares in awe.

I can destroy. That is what I was born to do.

CHAPTER 53

Astrid works on the location of the blood and I try to find Arik and my mother. She said only a few guards know where the prisoners are held, and I know one that does. Sigmond nudges through the door, a tray in his hands. "I was told you may be hungry," he says. He sets the food down and bows before starting to leave.

"Sigmond?" He turns, his hands behind his back. "How long have you been here?" I ask.

He pauses and looks up to the ceiling. "Twenty years." He looks tired as he says it. A sadness settles over him as he keeps his eyes toward the ceiling, trapped in a long-ago memory.

I tread carefully, Sigmond has never been anything but kind to me. Something about him feels so familiar, like it is staring me straight in the face but I'm missing it.

"Did you know my mother?" I ask.

"There are not too many who didn't," he says. He makes his way to the door, his hand lingers over the knob, and I think he is about to say something but he doesn't.

"Do you think you could get this to someone?" I ask before he leaves.

He looks at the name on the letter and smiles. "She will be sending something back."

He nods and disappears through the door. I wrap my fingers around my amulet then run my hand up my neck, massaging my tense muscles. Alone with my thoughts, nightmares, and fears.

Rayne stands guard outside my door. I inch the door open and he peers down at me from the side.

"No," he says before I have a chance to speak.

"So, you're not still mad then?" I ask with a grin.

His eyes narrow and he turns his face back toward the wall. "I need to stretch my legs," I say.

"You have a whole room," he says bluntly.

I bite the inside of my cheek, a few minutes pass. *I only have a few more days.* I push through the door and start down the hall. It only takes him a second before he is quickly following beside me.

"Have you lost your mind?" he scolds. "Stop right now."

I continue to ignore him until his meaty hand wraps around my arm, just firm enough to get me to stop in my tracks. "You are going to get me killed," he hisses. He drops his hand. "Then you're going to get yourself killed."

"Either turn me in or escort me." I plant myself firmly in front of him. "But, unless you plan on dragging me back to the room and locking the door, I am not going back."

Something dark flashes over his face and for a second, I think he is about to throw me over his shoulder kicking and screaming.

"One lap," he says.

"Three," I counter.

"Two." He sets his jaw. "Or I will drag you back right now, damn the consequences."

The *consequences* being Klaus.

I nod and he exhales sharply. Neither of us walk leisurely, I have a goal. I smell the fresh air and feel the spring in my bones, finding myself longing for the ocean and mourning the moments I took for granted.

One large square later, we pass several guards, seven servants, and too many rooms to count. "What is this place?" I ask.

Rayne grunts at the colorful linens that hang from the ceiling, each one more elaborate than the last. I run my fingers over the material, some rough and others are feather soft. "The castle was never finished. These hide the ugly rock walls."

"These are beautiful," I gush in adoration.

"They are," he says before we move to the next corridor.

Each time we near a soldier, I see Rayne's finger twitch toward his weapon. When we pass the King's office, there are no guards. *He probably thinks no one is dumb enough to enter his space.*

I hear Rayne swallow. "We are going back."

"We still have one lap," I protest. I need more time.

He clenches his teeth, his eyes boring through mine. I know that look, fear. His hand grips the hilt of his sword. "Now!" He snatches me up, his grip biting into my skin. My heart slams in my throat. Two men step around the corner, one with long blond hair and another with his hair cut short, his ears sticking far from his head.

"I said . . ." Rayne's face is close to mine, his breath unbearably hot. I flare my nostrils.

"I heard she was a wild one," one of the men say. "Did you see the prince's face?"

My face burns, and I struggle against his grip but it is useless. I scratch at his skin but it is like leather from the harsh sun.

"Be careful, the last person who touched her got his head removed." Big ears chuckles. "Poor bastard."

"You got her?" the man with long hair asks. His voice is sweet like honey, but he sends a wave of unease through me.

Rayne shakes me, my head flopping around like a rag doll. He looks at the two men, hatred filling his eyes. I stop struggling, *that hatred is not for me.*

"I think she gets it now, gentlemen. But, thank you for the assistance," Rayne forces out.

I let him drag me back to the room, on my tiptoes the whole way. When he shoves me into the room, I leave the door cracked and slide down the wall, resting my head against the wall.

"Rayne?" I don't know what to say, he warned me. I massage my aching temples.

"What are you doing down there, miss Fraya?"

I roll my head to the side, Sigmond's golden brown eyes stare down at me. "Contemplating my life choices."

A low chuckle vibrates his chest and I can't help but grin. I have never seen him so much as crack a smile.

"Don't we all?" He pats my head like I am a child. "I just came by to let you know your message was delivered and we should have her reply tomorrow."

"Thanks," I say.

When he leaves, I stare through the small crack in the door. "I know it was to protect me." Rayne stiffens but says nothing. "Thank you."

CHAPTER 54

Astrid sits on the edge of the bed waiting for me. "You know, it's creepy to watch people sleep," I say in my scratchy morning voice.

"I found it," she says.

"What?" I rub my eyes and sit up. My eyes catch the white envelope on the nightstand and I smile. *Thanks, Sigmond.*

"The dragon's blood," she says. She has my full attention now. "There is a hidden door that leads under the mountain."

"Of course. He wouldn't risk someone stumbling upon it." I throw the covers off. "Where is the door?"

"The incomplete part of the castle. Those curtains are not just for decoration," she squeals.

"I was right there!" I smack my head. "What is back there?"

She shakes her head. "No idea. No one's ever been inside. A previous maid was cleaning and found it. She left a few days later, but not before she asked a few of the other maids about it."

I watch as her face morphs into understanding. She didn't leave, she was murdered. "No more, Astrid. You have done enough."

I put up my finger. "Promise me." I stare into her soul like my father used to do to me when he was serious.

"Fine," she murmurs.

"Good. Now I have a surprise!" I say as I grab the small parchment. "Happy birthday, Astrid. You are the only part that has made staying here bearable."

She pulls the necklace out first, moving the jewel between her fingers gently. "I saw the stone and knew you were meant to have it."

She smiles from ear to ear. "It's so pretty." She hands me the necklace and I clasp it around her neck.

"Hurry, now the letter." I can't help but wiggle in excitement. This was the trickiest part of her present. I consider getting up and letting her read in peace but when her teary eyes find mine, her arms sling over my shoulders.

"How did you do this?" she asks before going back and re-reading her family's letter.

I laugh. "I can't give away all my secrets."

"Mom says thank you." She turns the letter around and says, "Look, even Arthur gave his own squiggle."

"I am glad you like it. It is the least I could do."

Getting past my new guard was easy. "They always underestimate me," Astrid said before she dragged the older guard away from his post, ranting about sweet rolls and monthly cycles. The guard was so red I thought he would burst. I laugh as I slip between the heavy fabrics.

I stare at the wall cursing. *Where is the blasted door?* My heart races, someone could walk by at any moment. I run my hands along the rough rock, pressing firmly until one of the stones gives under my fingertips. My mouth drops open as a piece of the earth relaxes, allowing me to push through.

"*Minds far superior than mine.*" I remember the King's words and marvel at the contraption before me. I step inside and the door closes behind me, enclosing me in complete darkness. I let the fire flow to my fingertips and in a moment a path lays before me.

I keep my flame small, in case someone is near, but move as swiftly as possible through the bug infested tunnel. The cool air is a nice relief to the inferno outside. Beetles and other insects scurry along the path, fighting to escape the flame. The earthy aroma is not overpowering, but soon a metallic smell hits my nose.

Whispers in the distance make me stop, my heart pounds in my ears. I have nowhere to go, so I continue forward, pushing my feet faster. Hoping to find a divot in the wall I can squeeze into.

A white smoke lingers around my ankles and I feel a flush of excitement courses through me. A small cave to my right gives off a warm glow. I drop my flame and inch closer.

Farther up, warm sunlight breaks apart the darkness.

"You are sure?"

"Of course," a familiar voice says.

"Your brother had almost gotten himself killed twice. You better not fail me. We are so close," the King says.

"Of course, father. She keeps asking about her mother." Klaus' voice is hard and void of emotion.

"Good. Let her stay distracted. We only have two months until the blood moon," The King tells him.

"And then you kill her?" Klaus asks.

My throat catches and I throw my hands over my mouth.

"Don't tell me you are getting attached?" The king laughs. "I made that mistake once."

Feet shuffle around the room, shadows dancing along the walls. "This isn't going to be a problem, is it?" The King asks.

"I am not Luca, and I am not you." Something lingers behind those last words but as soon as it is there it vanishes.

I feel numb. The clang of tiny bottles rattles and when I peer around the corner, their backs are turned. I dart across the small opening and run toward the light. A man sized hole drops into nothingness. I just miss falling to my demise.

"I hear you, human. You are playing with death," a voice whispers to my mind.

I hesitate for only a moment before I continue. I know what lies beyond this opening, but I don't believe it. Laying curled in on itself is a dragon, the same one from my first night here.

"By now, death and I have become close friends," I say.

CHAPTER 55

H e lifts his large head and tilts it to the side. *"It is a pleasure to finally meet you."*

"Finally?" I ask skeptically.

"I have been told many things." He raises and I realize there is no chain holding him in place. He is free to leave if he chooses. *"Just because I am not chained, does not mean I am free, child."* His voice is stern, angry. *"Much like yourself."*

My mouth falls open. "How did you know what I was thinking?"

"Your face wears your questions openly," he says.

"Why do you stay?" I ask.

"Mmm," the dragon says. *"Complicated questions get complicated answers."*

I walk closer, keeping my eyes on the monstrous black dragon. His scales are the color of the night and the spikes coming from his face look sharp as a blade. His eyes are the color of lava as it cools.

"I stayed because a human I loved asked me to. I stay, because a human I love needs me to." He seems somber and far away.

"How long have you been here?"

"A long time," he says.

I look back the way I came, listening. Half expecting the King to burst around the corner, but it is silent.

"I can smell our creator's blood running through your veins," he says, but not menacingly.

"I am not sure how I feel about that," I admit.

The dragon laughs. *"It just means that all dragons know you, feel you. We are a part of you."*

A howl of pain comes through the dark, echoing off the walls and escaping out the mouth of the cave. I put my hands over my ears, the blood curdling scream tearing through me. The voice sounds familiar and my insides twist. *Arik?*

"You should leave this place," he says, but there is age in the way he says it. A heaviness.

"Where are they keeping him? How do I get down there?" My voice is creeping on the edge of panic.

He stares at me as if I lost my head. *"I am not sending you to your death. You are the last of your kind, your people need you."*

"I wish people would stop saying that. I have a choice." I raise my voice slightly but quickly rein it back in, careful of listening ears. Sadness fills his large orange eyes, his features pained.

Footsteps echo down the hall and another cry comes from the earth but this time it is lacking life, more death moan than pain. In a few steps, I am next to the dragon. "You say my people need me, but *he* needs me. He is my people; I can save him."

"You cannot, he is already almost gone. I know you hear it." He lowers his large head back to the earth.

"Tell me!" I demand.

He straightens his neck. *"I led your mother to her death, I will not do the same to her child. Leave."*

I stumble backward, praying my ears have heard wrong. "She is alive," I say, but listening to them come from my mouth, I realize how it must sound. "He loved her."

Pain settles in the dragons eyes. *"When evil men find their weakness, they destroy it so it can never be used against them."*

I hate myself for believing for one second, he would spare her life. "I will find him on my own."

Two soldiers stand with arms full of dragon's blood. They never see me coming. I shut off the part of me that feels. "This is the only way," I tell myself. Their screams join with Arik's as I burn through the room, destroying every vial of blood in the process. When I enter, I am in a throne room of blood and fire. My stomach rolls.

One man groans, and I end his life swiftly. A mercy, I tell myself as I remove his blade and stab him through the heart. I try to dismiss the fear in his eyes moments before his death. I rush as quickly as possible through the dark cave.

It only takes me a few seconds to find the secret lever. The passage edges open and I am running. The sun starts to dip below the horizon. I slide around the corner and Rayne stands mouth agape. "I don't have time," I tell him.

I burst through the door causing Astrid to jump out of her skin. "I need you to meet me at the kitchen door." Her brows draw together. "I do not have time to explain, please just gather your things and meet there. I will come for you."

A knock sounds at the door and Klaus walks in. I stand in front of Astrid. "What are you doing here?" I ask. He looks slightly confused as he approaches. "You don't have to pretend anymore."

"What are you talking about?" He asks confused.

"I heard you. You are just like your father, worse even. At least he is honest about how vile he is. You walk around pretending." The words sting and I feel Astrid tense behind me. "Leave."

He looks as if he is going to say something but decides against it. When the door shuts behind me, I let myself breathe again.

"Fraya?" Astrid's voice is heavy.

"Meet me at the door," I tell her.

She reaches into her pocket and pulls out a skeleton key. "Sigmond brought it by and said you would know what to do with it."

I take the key. *Crazy old man. This will get him killed.* "If I am not there when the bell chimes, leave without me. Cross the bridge and head west, I will find you." She nods her head vigorously and scurries out the door.

That leaves me with Rayne. As if he heard my thoughts, his large hand pushes open the door. "Rayne," I warn. "Please don't make me kill you."

He sighs. "There is only one way in and out of those cells." I pause, not understanding at first.

"Where is it?" I demand.

"Under the atrium," he says. "But it is a suicide mission."

"Then I better not get caught."

CHAPTER 56

The door is just where Rayne said it would be and he was right, there is only one way in. The spiral staircase leads to a door. I can't believe I didn't see it before. I hear footsteps above me, soldiers on rounds. I hardly missed them in the halls. Staying quiet, I wait for them to pass before creeping open the door.

The spiral stairs descend steeply. The deeper I descend, the more wary I become. Just when I think it couldn't possibly go anymore, the staircase ends and torches flicker violently on the walls. It's damp and musty down here and the lingering smell of death has penetrated these walls. I hear the groans of tired and broken men.

I reach the first cell and only remnants of a body remain. I turn away, but the next cell proves no different. One disappointment after another. I come across a few cells where men are tied to the walls but when I get closer, they are not Arik. I round the corner and my ears catch subtle moans. The smell of rust is so thick I can taste it.

Arik hangs suspended from the ceiling, his shoulders in an awful twisted position. His chin rests against his chest and the blood dripping from his face is deafening as it hits the ground, the steady drip maddening. My stomach clenches as I near his still body.

"You better not be dead," I hiss at him.

I see a subtle rise and fall of his chest and breathe a sigh of relief. "Arik?" I whisper. I don't hear anyone else down here, but that doesn't mean there aren't any. He slowly spins away from me. Gently, I turn him and look at the rope that rips into his wrists. "How am I going to get you out of here?"

His eyes flutter and a gurgling sound comes from his throat. "It's ok. Don't say anything." He lifts his head slightly, his swollen eyes unable to focus on anything.

"Leave. Please leave." He drops his head back against his chest. "How am I going to get you out of here!" *Think, Fraya.* I walk around him a few times, trying not to jostle him more than necessary. Arik flinches as the rope pulls his skin but otherwise stays silent.

I move the barrel sitting against the wall until it is next to Arik, pulling the dead soldier's blade I steady myself before slicing the thick rope. Panic causes me to hack faster, which makes the skin on his wrists separate further.

The sound of metal scratching against rock startles me. "Come out and play," someone hollers.

I look around frantically for a place to hide but find nothing. I'm completely exposed. "I know you are there. I saw you come down."

"Hold on Arik, I have to deal with this." I say as I crawl off the barstool.

A man comes around the corner with a gruesome smile on his face. "I have been hoping I could get you alone. I knew it was only a matter of time before you slipped past your guard dogs."

I remember him, his long blond hair is half up half down and his sharp cheekbones highlight his jade-colored eyes. His sword drags against the ground lazily. "You are not supposed to exist. You are a monster, you upset the balance of nature."

"Seems like you think very highly of me," I sneer.

Anger flares in his eyes as he swings his sword. I duck, and the metal smashes against the rock sending sparks flying in the air. I back deeper into the dungeon and his eyes brighten with excitement as he tries to trap me like a caged animal.

A pair of shackles rest over an iron gate. I sheath my dagger and grab the chain wrapping it around my fists. My blade will do nothing against his sword. I swing the cuffs waiting for him to strike again.

"I admire your attempt to save your life, but you only prolong the inevitable," he says. His words aren't harsh, but he believes each one.

He fires another attack and I send the chains toward his sword. They wrap around it, stopping his sword from breaking through my skin. I twist the chains, ripping his blade from his hands. He quickly pulls another knife, crouching before he takes a few more jabs.

"Nice trick," he snarls.

I let my flame bleed down the chains. He takes a step back, the blaze dancing in his eyes. I strike and the chain meets his face. Again and again the metal meets his skin, each time he tries to deflect but the flame bites at his flesh.

"You vile abomination," he hisses, fear breaking through his hatred.

I whip around, bringing the chain down on his head. His eyes drift to the back of his skull and he crashes to the ground. His blond hair now matted with blood.

"Stop!" A soldier's eyes are wide with terror, looking from me to the body at my feet.

I look up to see an arrow pointed at my heart. I drop the shackles slowly, one hand raised in the air.

"In the name of the Dark King, I-" A blade rushes through his chest and Rayne's giant body fills the space behind him. As he slides his blade free, his unsuspecting victim collapses at his feet.

"Why are you here?" I ask as I scramble back on top of the barrel. Arik falls over Rayne's shoulder.

"Klaus would kill me if I let you die down here," he mumbles.

"Why, so he could kill me himself?" I utter.

Rayne gives me a sideways glance. "Kill him."

"What?"

He motions to the blond-haired man unconscious on the ground. "If you don't make sure he is dead now, it will bite you back later." His voice is flat as he says it. A soldier trained to kill. "Hurry up," he demands.

I don't have time to dwell on it as I slide the blade into his temple, ignoring the wave of nausea that rolls through me.

CHAPTER 57

Rayne carries Arik up the staircase with ease. "Do you have a plan?" he asks.

I glance back at him. "Not a good one." The second floor is eerily quiet, fraying my nerves. "Astrid is meeting me in the kitchen. A supply wagon is waiting."

"You are right, that is an awful plan," he says, shaking his head.

I pause and look at him. "Thank you, Rayne. Just load him in the cart and leave, no one needs to know you were a part of this."

"Are you not coming?" he asks.

"I have one more stop." He starts to interject but I turn and run as fast as my feet will carry me. I stand in front of the King's office, listening for only a second before I slide the key Sigmond retrieved through the lock.

The click is so loud, I wait for someone to notice but no one does. I slip through the door and head to the desk. The book is exactly where the King left it. I'm tempted to read its pages but I tuck it in my pants instead.

Bu-bum bu-bum bu-bum.

I freeze, place my hand over my heart, and listen. *Bu-bum, bu-bum, bu-bum.*

As I near the door, the sound softens. I search the desk again; the beating grows louder. I think of the hidden door and slide my hands under the desk until I graze a latch. The soft click releases a compartment under the desk.

A precious dragon egg sits nestled against a pillow. I frantically search the office until I find a satchel and slide the egg into the pouch. The egg is no bigger than my hand. A small shell for such a large creature.

"You're running out of time!" A warning in the back of my mind screams at me. I round the corner and see a blood trail that leads toward the kitchen. Panic surges through me.

"Find her!" The King's roar is unmistakable. My blood turns to ice when a shriek pierces through the hall. *Astrid.* I turn down the hall and meet the King's deadly gaze.

"Ah, there you are. You have been busy, but I knew you would come running when I made her scream." He twists her arm in an unnatural position and she yells again. Her eyes brim with tears but they don't fall. "I see you have made yourself at home in my study." He points to the satchel around my shoulder.

"Let the child go," I say. His eyes are black holes. *Dragon's blood.*

Blood drips from Astrid's fingertips.

"Now, why would I do that? She is my leverage." He shakes her for emphasis.

I stalk forward. "I will kill you." My jaw aches from clenching it so hard.

"Not before I kill her."

"You play a game you can't win, *Zekiah*." I let his name drip off my tongue with venom. He is silent for a moment, his face blank.

"Check the tower," he says to one of his guards. A large vein pulses in his forehead.

The tower, what tower?

"But, sir." He has no time to finish his thought before a knife sinks into his gut. He gives the order again and two men disappear.

"You left quite a mess in my storage room. I didn't think you had it in you. Murdering men in cold blood. I am impressed."

"Astrid, look at me." Her jaw flexes as she bites down fighting the urge to cry. "Zekiah." I watch his left eye twitch at the mention of his name. "Did you ever love her? My mother?"

"I loved watching her suffer," he bites out.

Ciena's power fills me, I listen as the rage within me pulls on the inferno within.

"Incredible," he says. "Now hand over the bag."

"If I give you the bag, you kill her." I move closer and his hand travels to her neck, squeezing until she is wheezing.

"If you don't, I will kill her." He grips her tighter, lifting her body off the ground. Her feet dangle loosely in the air, her nails scratching at his hands.

"Okay!" I yell. "Put her down."

His brow raises and he lowers her. "You are weak," he spits.

"Astrid, it's going to be okay." I console her.

She presses her lips together, the tears now falling from her eyes. They sparkle like jewels. *Save her!* My entire being screams.

"One life for thousands," she says softly as a fat tear trickles down her cheek.

"No!" I lunge forward but am not fast enough. A tiny dagger falls into her hands as she elbows the King in his stomach. He grunts and she slams the knife into this thigh. I reach out and grasp her fingertips as the King hollers and snatches her up with one swift, merciless motion then he snaps her neck. The crunch of her neck will haunt me until I pass from this world. Her body slumps and I catch her just before she hits the ground, her necklace breaking off in my hands.

The guard grabs my arms and I twist around, grabbing the King's sword and severing his head. The King stares down at the head as it rolls in front of us. A battle cry comes from within me as I bring the sword down on his shoulder and then shove it into his gut.

He hisses in pain but the wound is already stitching itself back together. He falls to his knees, holding his stomach together.

I crumble to the ground holding Astrid's body in my arms. "Astrid," I whisper and brush her hair from her face. If I didn't know any better, I would think she was sleeping. Tears stain my cheeks and I grip the coral necklace I had just given her this morning.

Images of my father's lifeless body surface and my heart is now a hollowed-out tomb, full of sorrow and grief. I lay her lifeless body down and see the King attempting to crawl away. My body shakes violently and I slowly walk over to him. "She was a child!" I bite between gritted teeth. Sweat ripples from his forehead and fear causes him to shake. I let the flames creep across the floor until it licks at his feet.

Faces of the people who have died at the hands of the King rush through my mind. My heart races and the flames creep over his legs. I hardly register his screams and cries as my thirsty flames devour his body.

"Fraya!" Luca's voice rocks me from an enraged state and his sword almost meets my shoulder. "What have you done?" Again, he wildly thrusts his blade in my direction, but it's sloppy. He looks more like his father now, each man adorns a scar. I realize the only way his face would have healed this quickly.

"You are a spineless roach," I spit.

His nostril flares at me as he drops to the ground next to his father.

A group of thirty plus men rush down the hall, weapons drawn. His chest heaves up and down. "Leave." He turns his back to me and drops to his father's side. As I turn the corner I see him pulling a small blood filled vial from his pocket.

CHAPTER 58

I fall out of the kitchen doors as an ear shattering alarm rings through the town. Men will begin pouring into the streets.

"It's about bloody time!" Rayne hisses. "We are never going to make it off this wretched island."

He takes in my blood splattered clothes and I immediately say, "It's not mine."

Doom settles in the pit of my stomach. "Astrid?" he asks.

I drop my eyes to the ground and clutch her necklace in my hands. He picks up the cart, he knows there is nothing he could say to make me feel better. "Both of you get out of here. I will cause a distraction."

Rayne shuts me down. "Absolutely not."

I lift Arik, wrapping the satchel around his broken body. "Do it!" I demand. "Please." I call the water from the earth. The springs below groan as they bend to my will. She feels like an old friend. She is comforting but deadly.

Rayne's jaw clenches as he looks between me and the cargo in the cart. "Take him to the trees that reach the heavens." He lets out a large sigh and leaves with Arik.

Rayne nears the bridge, his slow pace wrecking my nerves. Fear wraps its greedy tentacles around me. If I die here, it will not be without a fight. The center is chaos as soldiers bleed in from all sides. Innocent people trampled in the process.

Rayne is stopped on the bridge, and anxiety creeps in my mind, whispering its chilling tale. The weight of uncertainty and death swirl through me, *everyone will die.*

I call to my fire; the element responds immediately. In the night sky my light is a beacon for all to see. Citizens stop. *Witch, chosen one, monster,* and more whisper through the night but the one that brings me the most comfort, *Alkazah.* Rayne squeezes through the soldiers as they rush toward the alarm. He turns, our eyes locking for a moment. He bows deeply and I choke on tears.

"Fire!" Luca's anger is unmistakable as he gives the command.

Screams fill the air as people rush to safety. An arrow lands in the back of a woman who shields her kids. *No, no more innocent deaths.*

"*Ciena, I need you.*" I call on her power.

As easy as a breath, her presence floods me. My flame grows hotter and the water flows easier. I reach toward the man whose arrow hit the woman, his eyes wide with fear as the water envelopes him. I sling him off the island. His cries disappear into the evening air.

My flame is a creature, seeking and finding its prey. More screams, less arrows. The King's men cautiously approach, weapons drawn. Luca emerges from the group. "You cannot win," he says.

The King's blood is still wet against my skin. "I have already won," I say with a grin. "Even if I take my last breath today, I got what I came for."

An arrow lands in my shoulder, I never heard it coming. I stumble back, the edge of the cliff creeping closer. I break the end of the arrow off, flinching as the pain creeps down my chest. The next arrow is slowed by my water shield but it still nicks my thigh. Three more follow, one landing with a sickening thunk into the soft tissue of my belly."

Fury rolls off Luca, anytime he nears the flame he flinches. He has already been burned twice. He is scared.

Another man is thrown off the cliff and the fire snakes closer to the men. *How many have I killed?* The word monster consumes me. When a man walks through my wall of fire, my breathing hitches. I let my flame burn hotter, the blue hues beautiful against the night sky. Luca watches in envy as his brother escapes the flames without so much as a singed hair.

I can't look away from him.

"Fraya," he says, his expression blank.

I hate the way my stomach flutters when he is near, the way my insides twist when he says my name. I push the thoughts away, focusing instead on my deep hatred.

"Jump." That comforting lull tugs at the back of my mind. His shoulders slightly relax but just as quickly he is tense again. I shake my head, pushing the thought from my mind. *"Jump."* Again the thought kisses my mind.

Klaus is so close; I can reach out and touch him. But I can't move, I am stuck. My heart hammers in my chest, why can't I move? My fingers twitch as I fight for control over my body.

"I'm sorry," his words are a mere whisper only meant for my ears.

"I hate you." Tears sting my eyes. How could someone who held me so gently, who kept my pieces from falling apart, be so cruel.

"I will carry your hate," he says.

I break his hold on me, my fist flying into his jaw. "I will *never* forgive you for this!" I hiss. His betrayal presses down on me like an anchor. I hold his gaze, refusing to let the fear growing in my belly be seen.

His face is inches from me, his heart beat banging against mine. "I can live without your forgiveness, Litchska." His soft lips whisper against mine. For a second, I think I see pain or sadness but just as quickly as it was there, it is gone. Panic slides down my spine and he places his hand against my chest, then he is stone as he pushes me over the cliff.

CHAPTER 59

I don't scream, I can't. It's locked within my throat. *Now the pain will stop.* I close my eyes, my father rubbing his scratchy beard against my face to wake me up in the mornings my last thoughts.

Right before the hot sand claims my body, I'm plucked from the sky. The arrow digs deeper into my flesh. We are part of the night. "Rayne. Arik," I say before I slip into darkness.

"If she doesn't wake up, I will kill you." The voice is familiar but I can't place it.

A deep growl comes from beside me. "She risked her life to get *your* friend out. If she doesn't live, you will suffer the consequences of her death, not me."

Rayne? I want to say, but everything hurts.

"Enough," says another voice, a woman's voice. "You two bickering is not helping. Here, put this in her mouth." A scratchy piece of fabric is stuffed between my teeth. "Hold her down." Hands wrap around my upper body and someone lays across my legs. Warm liquid pours over my torso.

A searing pain jolts through my body and I struggle against it, grateful for the cloth stopping me from biting through my tongue. I try to get away from the burning that rips through my chest, but it is useless. The pain is everywhere. A monstrous cry fights its way out.

"Keep her still," the woman's voice is stern.

More hands press against me. "This is going to hurt," she says. "I am so sorry."

What could be worse than what I am experiencing now? My eyes flutter open and I try to beg them to stop. Big brown eyes, stare down at me. "Maxine?"

She looks around. "One, two."

I want to scream at her to wait, but it doesn't come out.

"Three."

Stars explode in my vision. I fight the darkness trying to pull me under. *Stay awake, Fraya.*

A warm sensation tingles throughout my body. I struggle to keep hold of it, coaxing the power to the pain, but too quickly I am gone again.

Visions of Klaus' face, my body immobile when I'm locked in his gaze, and the feeling of falling fill my nightmares. Just before I meet the earth, I shoot up. My breath comes out labored, my head dizzy.

"Easy." A gentle hand touches my shoulder.

I throw the blanket off me and feel my stomach, expecting to still have a hole in my side. "You healed most of it and Ophius finished after you passed out," her voice is gentle. "We thought we lost you for a second. There was so much blood," Maxine says.

"It seems I am not that easy to kill." She doesn't find my joke amusing. "And Arik?" I ask.

She motions to the bed at the other end of the tent. I see him breathing, his wounds freshly wrapped. "How long have I been out?"

"Three days," she says.

"Three days!" I start to stand and she firmly presses me back into bed. I shoot daggers at her with my eyes but she only shakes her head.

"That does not work on me." She points back to the bed.

I look her over. Her cheeks are full and her hair is starting to thicken. "Did they find the satchel?"

She points to the end of the bed where the satchel lays, still closed. I pull it toward me, crossing my legs and opening the top to find its hidden treasures. The egg feels surprisingly warm in my hands, its rough exterior adorned with vein-like ripples.

Maxine's eyes light up. "It's beautiful," she says.

The soft *bu-bum* throbs in my chest. I feel her, as if she was mine. The purple egg pulses with power unlike anything I have ever felt before.

"You're awake!" Sven walks through the door, his eyes falling to Arik. There is a worry that lives there but when he glances back at me, there is no more anger or resentment. "The big guy was going to have my head if you didn't wake up soon."

Rayne enters the tent, relief softening his features. "Thank the Ancients," he says. His eyes dart to Maxine whose dark skin flushes. I tilt my head and look between the two.

"You're alive!" I choke out. How did this brute of a man become such a close friend in such a small amount of time?

"Nice to see you too, Your Highness." I roll my eyes but he only shrugs.

"Where is Ophius?" I ask, standing. I roll my shoulders, surprised when I feel no pain. I grab the bag and tuck the egg back safely. Klaus' face flashes before my eyes for a moment but I shake it away, I don't have time to think about that right now. A war is coming and I need to know how to stop it.

Sven points outside. "Out there," he says.

Pushing through the heavy tent flap I find the great dragon relaxing in the middle of camp. Occasionally, he snorts smoke at the children running around him and they burst into a fit of giggles. Lucy is amongst them and when she sees me, she waves fervently.

"Alkazah." He slightly bows his head toward me.

"I have the book, and I found something else."

"Come," he says, rising from the children who groan in disapproval.

We walk through the forest, and a peace envelops me. The earthy scent of the damp soil and decaying leaves blend with the sweet aroma of blossoming flowers. The birds harmonize with each other in the treetops, as sunlight breaks through the thick canopy overhead.

"This is your doing, huh?" I ask, motioning to the peace settling over us.

"Your mind deserves rest."

"But, this is a lie. You are manipulating how I feel." A spark of anger fills me, but it's quickly soothed away. Like a healing salve over a burning wound.

"This is not a lie. I am just merely making you feel what you are running away from."

I want to tell him I don't deserve peace, that the blood I have spilled will haunt me until I die, but instead we walk in silence.

"Her heartbeat matches yours," Ophius says, glancing at my bag.

I cradle the egg in both hands. Ophius tilts his head to the side, studying the exquisite shell. *"She will be the first of her kind, as well."*

"I am not the first Alkazah."

"But you are the first of Moir's bloodline. Moir is the beginning, all life flows through her and now you." I stare down at the egg, feeling slightly less alone.

"What is in the book?" I ask, tucking the egg into the bag.

He is quiet as he sits to the ground, his long tail wrapping around his body. His features are somber. *"This is the diary of Azius. The first Eternal."*

Chapter 60

Ciena's words come back to me. *He is Eternal. He is the evil our blood unleashes and I will not let that happen again.*

"The creature in the ruins."

"He was the first bleeder. He murdered thousands of our kind, draining them and gaining power. But it was never enough, his hatred for our kind only burned brighter."

My gut twists. The old dragon is not giving me the full story, I can feel it.

"Why are you telling me this?" Guilt washes over his face and makes me take a step back.

"Fraya!" a broken voice yells, but I pay it no mind.

"You should go to your friend." The gust from his wings causes my hair to fly wildly around my face.

Arik wobbles toward me, a crutch under his arm. His slightly swollen mouth smiles at me.

"You look like hell," I say as I laugh.

"I knew I liked you. Sven was worried, but I always knew." He hobbles closer and wraps his arm around me.

"How are you feeling?" I squeeze gently, careful of his bruised body.

"Thanks to Ophius, better than I look," he says with a laugh.

"Thanks for coming for me." Arik stares down at me with his chocolate brown eyes and my throat tightens. I said those exact words to my father mere hours before his death.

"I am just sorry I didn't get to you sooner," I say.

Sven leans over his table with his shoulders tensed, but when Arik and I enter, they relax a little. I lay the book on the table, trying not to think about its secrets and focus on our plan to stop the King.

Arik delicately picks up the journal, flipping through its old pages, scanning each symbol gracefully. "I destroyed the blood supply."

Sven nods and his eyes soften. This man is far from the same one I met all those weeks ago, or maybe this is who he was all along and I never saw it. "He will bring everything he has to us. We must be ready."

"Sacrifice and rebirth," Arik says.

Sven and I both gawk at him. "What?" we say in unison.

"This passage says, *Naiemty Ravierm;* sacrifice and rebirth." When neither Sven or I say anything, he continues. "My mother and father lived in Arcaneum before it fell. The queen made the ancient language available to everyone, my mother was one of its teachers." Sven looks at Arik, his own torment reflected in his eyes, an understanding. "My father, Samuel, was Queen Ravina's second, he was with her giving people like my mother an opportunity to escape."

"I am so sorry." I sigh and drop my eyes.

"We have all lost something," he says. "But, I don't want it to be in vain."

I nod and look down at the book. "Does it mention anything else?"

He scans the pages. "You aren't going to like it." He points to an image in the book where a man stands over a slain dragon.

"What does it say?"

"He murdered Azule." Arik's eyes grow wet. The Ancient Azule, the god of the sea whose scales blended with the ocean. *The Dark King was telling the truth.*

The pain I felt with Ophius makes sense, and I understand now why Ciena wouldn't save my mother. When he turns the page, my heart stops. The creature from the ruins stares back at me, his wings expanding the page and the ink black marks that run through his veins.

CHAPTER 61

For twelve days we plan, gathering men and supplies. Rayne leads a group into the King's supply stations. The first few raids met resistance, but soon most of the soldiers were called back to the King and we encountered blood baths. The prisoners slaughtered.

Arik hardly leaves my side, which has been oddly comforting. He begins to fill out and his clothes no longer hang from his bony form. Sven forces him to train, but outside of that he is with me. If he's anything like his father, I can see why he was my mother's second. While he is with me he studies the book, making sure we are aware of what we will be walking into.

The egg sits in the middle of my desk, wrapped in blankets. I can still feel her heartbeat in my chest but I do not know what it means, or when she will be here.

Ophius has been sparse around camp. I am not sure where he goes but he is absent.

More often than I would like, I find my thoughts drifting to Klaus and the look in his eyes as he pushed me over the edge. The icy stare, void of any emotion, still makes me shudder.

Arik sends out messages to all the rebel camps, and slowly our camp grows to ten thousand, but a sickening feeling tells me it won't be enough.

"What troubles your mind?" Arik asks. Thunder booms outside and rain pelts against the tent.

"We aren't ready. I can't ask all these men to march to their deaths." I take a deep breath, the weight slightly lifted at my confession.

Arik is silent. I wonder if my mother ever second guessed herself before going into battle, or if my father ever wanted to run. I can't picture him wanting to run from anything.

I think about Astrid and her family. How am I going to tell them I could do nothing but watch as their daughter was taken too soon. *If they are even alive,* my thoughts shout at me.

He places his hands on my arm, and although I have learned to keep a strong grip on my emotions in front of my people, Arik sees straight through it. I hate him and love him for it. "It's a good thing you don't have to do it by yourself."

"Your Highness!" A beautiful blond haired, blue eyed killing machine walks in. She arrived with the first group of rebels. She bows.

"Yes, Kamari." Rain streaks down her face. She wears her hair in multiple braids knotted down her back.

An ear-splitting crack vibrates through my chest. *Something is wrong.* A deep growl rises over the blanket of rain and a roaring flame lights up the night sky. Two dragons circle each other, locked in a deadly fight.

Onyx?

A group of a dozen men emerge from the trees. *How did they find us?* Rain pelts me from all sides. My men stand ready and I pool the water around the soldiers, stopping them in their tracks. A flash of lightning reveals their scared faces.

"Enough!" Ophius commands the dragon. Onyx falls from the sky, bowing his head in reverence. The Ancient hovers above him, ready to kill.

"Fraya!" I hear. My heart thuds heavily. I would know that voice anywhere.

I edge closer to the enemy and Sven grabs my arm. "This could be a trap."

I nod. "Have the men ready." He doesn't like it, but he quickly gathers our soldiers. I hold the men in place, my water an unforgiving force. As I near, the soldiers kneel and I try not to show my confusion. Sigmond stands when he sees me, his old man smile making me falter.

"Sigmond?"

"Miss Fraya." I drop the barrier and look at the dark figure of my friend.

My men flank me on all sides. "Stand down," I say.

I hear Sven growl but he lowers his weapon, only slightly. Rayne stands behind me, as big as an ox. My hair clings to my skin and rain drips from my lashes.

"Can I approach?" he asks.

"No one else moves, or I order my men to kill you all," I shout over the rain. Sven raises his bow again and Kamari readies her sword.

Sigmond seems older, more tired. Sven's grip on his bow stumbles as he looks at the old man. "Dad?" The crack in Sven's voice tears my insides apart.

Sigmond turns his attention from me to Sven, and now I know why Sigmond always felt so familiar. They have the same eyes. He falls into his father's arms and Sigmond sobs into his son's shoulder. He pulls back and looks at his boy, an exchange passes between them and Sigmond nods, new tears springing forth.

"Ophius." I look up at the old dragon who hovers above the threats. "Release Onyx, he saved my life."

The black dragon rises, shaking his large head. "Strip them," I yell. I see the silver in Klaus' eyes as the moonlight gleams off them. I am free falling again and I bite down to center myself. "Except Sigmond, leave him be."

I look to Sigmond. "Momma T?" I ask.

Sigmond shakes his head. "He slaughtered everyone. I just escaped with my life." He grabs my hand and pats it. "I am sorry about Astrid."

Tears swell up in my eyes. "What about her family?"

"I don't know," he admits.

The soldiers do not protest as their weapons and armor are stripped from their bodies. The men shiver under the harsh rain. A skirmish erupts from the middle of the men, and I don't need to guess to know who causes the issue.

"Enough, Klaus!" I yell. I walk past the men and they divide until I am standing face to face with him. "Why are you here?" I growl.

Being this close to him, smelling the richness of his skin, hurts in ways I didn't think possible. "We are here to fight beside you." I look around at the dozens of men who stand beside Klaus. I recognize the man from the bridge, Paul, I believe.

"You pushed me off a cliff." I fight the urge to yell at him. I cannot lose my temper.

"You wouldn't jump," he says.

"Tie them up," I say and turn away from him, marching back to my tent.

I rub the stone I gave to Astrid for her birthday, her death still a raw, gaping wound. I swallow my grief and throw my shoulders back.

"Who is the handsome one?" Arik says as he strides in from the rain.

"I don't know what you're talking about," I mumble.

"Your body language says otherwise." He pokes at me. "And the way he looked at you says you . . ." He looks me up and down with a grin, his eyes enlarging.

"Would you like me to comment on the stolen glances between you and-"

"Okay." He throws his hands up in surrender. "But . . . the tension is intense."

"What do you want?" I groan as I pace around the small tent. I do not have time to be distracted, and Klaus is a distraction.

"He wants to speak with you." He lifts his brows.

"Absolutely not," I say.

"He said you would say that." Arik shrugs, trying to keep the smile from his lips.

I clench my teeth. "Anything else?" I snap.

"Do you want to keep them tied up in the rain?" he asks.

I drop my head in my hands. "When is Rayne due back?"

"Tomorrow, before the sun rises," he says.

"Good. Put them in the dinner tent until the morning, with our best men guarding them."

"And the one with smoldering eyes?" Arik says and wiggles his brows at me.

"He can wait too," I tell him.

"He asked me to give this to you." He pulls out my father's blade. I take it carefully. *Hemoiesa Loi Cyion.* My fingers slider over the letters . . . so many goodbyes. I blink back tears. *lock it away Fraya. These people need a leader.*

"He is to remain with the rest," I say.

"Understood."

CHAPTER 62

The nights are the worst. The suffocating darkness of being alone keeps me awake and if I do manage to sleep, images of those lost plague my nightmares. Nothing but fragmented memories, filled with death and pain.

I sit up on the side of the bed, my feet grazing the floor. Without much thought, I pull my boots on and head out. The evening is muggy and the tents are quiet. The few guards bow as I walk by but other than that, the night is calming.

I wander until I am standing in front of Onyx, his raven-colored scales blending in with the evening. The night comes alive as a gentle breeze sways the tree tops, the leaves responding with a beautiful chorus. A million stars light up the night sky and the moon glows, casting shadows that dance along the forest floor. I take a deep breath, my lungs filling with the crisp refreshing scents of the surrounding trees.

"I was wondering when you would come find me." I hear him rustle around until he is beside me. His wings cover him like a blanket.

"I didn't know if I wanted to come or not," I admit. "It was you, who snatched me from a sandy grave, wasn't it?"

"It was my pleasure, little Alkazah," he says.

"Klaus is who needs you and his mother is who you loved." The giant creature lifts his head, his bright eyes surrounded by tiny horns. His chest is plated like armor while other parts look like aged leather.

"You make it seem like love is such a simple thing." He tilts his large head to the side. His beautiful eyes bright in the moonlight.

"Can I ask you a question?"

"I cannot stop you," he says simply.

"Did Ismene have the same marks as Klaus?"

"She did." He says without hesitation.

"What is it?"

"*I don't know, but . . .*" he pauses and looks back toward the camp. "*I know he fights against it. Ismene battled the darkness for years. I will not let the same fate befall her son, I promised.*"

"What happened to her?" I ask, my voice soft. Careful of the wound of losing someone so precious.

"*When the darkness consumed her, she almost killed Klaus. When she realized what she'd done, she couldn't live with herself.*" He closes his bright orange eyes, fighting his own painful memories.

A heaviness falls around us. "I am sorry."

"*Life is full of loss, Alkazah. And when you have been around as long as I have, you see a lot of it.*"

"What if I don't want to lose anyone else?" I admit.

"*Sacrifice is necessary to win a war. These soldiers know that and they are willing to lay their lives down in hopes of a better future,*" he says.

I nod but keep my lips closed, afraid I will betray my timid heart.

"*Fraya?*" His large head comes toward me and I reach up and place my hand against it, his hard scales warm to the touch. The intricate pattern of his scales weave under my hand. "*It should never become easy to watch people perish. Your heart makes you a good leader, but it can also make you stumble. Be careful.*"

The moon guides me back to my tent, my thoughts on Ismene and the mark that Klaus wears against his sun kissed skin. I push through the tent door and someone lingers by the wall. I clutch the dagger in my hand and press it to his throat. A trickle of blood slides down his skin and although the sight of it pangs my heart, I will not be fooled again.

"That's my girl," he chokes out.

The smell of freshly fallen rain wraps around me like a blanket and I want to dive into it. *How does he smell this good after traveling so far?* A sigh escapes my lips. "Litchska." His deep voice sends my stomach spinning. The pleasure of his fingertips grazing my skin sets me on fire.

My belly feels warm again but I ignore it. "What are you doing here?" I hiss.

"I need to speak with you," he says.

Questions swirl in my mind as I look into his stormy gray eyes, the same ones that threaten to pull me under and never let me go. "You couldn't have waited until the morning?"

"I have waited fifteen long days, I couldn't wait a moment more," he says. "I didn't know if . . ." he swallows. "I didn't know if you were okay." He has no walls up, nothing hidden in his words. I lower my weapon and stare at him for a moment more before stepping away.

"You mean after you pushed me to my death?" I all but yell.

"That's not fair and you know it," he says with hurt in his voice. "It was the only way I could get you off that island alive. Onyx was never going to let you hit the ground." He says it as if offended I could think otherwise.

I swallow hard. "I heard you in that cave."

"You heard what my father wanted to hear," he says. "What he needed to hear."

I clench my jaw, turning my back to him for a second as I gather my thoughts. "I am sorry about Momma T. I know you cared for her," I finally say.

"She raised me after my mother passed," he says. Torment and sorrow pour off him. "I am sorry about Astrid."

I say nothing . . . I can't. There are no words that will heal the loss of those we cherish. Instead, we sit in the heaviness of loss. Realizing no one's left unscathed from death's bony grip. *My father and mother, Astrid, Arik, the blue dragon, Maxine, Lucy, Momma T, and many more have been hurt or killed. . . because of me.*

"The men with me, they are good soldiers. Loyal. They will fight with you," Klaus whispers.

More innocent people marching to their deaths. The thought is so swift I have to sit down. How did my mother make these decisions?

"Your mother marched right beside them." Ciena's soothing words are like a cool drink of water on a hot summer day. *"She never asked them to do something she wouldn't do."*

I feel Klaus kneel in front of me. "Fraya?"

"How did she deal with the death? So many good people are going to die," I tell her.

"She never forgot them or their sacrifice. She carried that weight with her, so their sacrifice was never in vain." I sigh, pulling from her strength. *"You are a good leader Fraya, and you will be an even better queen. Your mother would have been proud."*

"Are you okay?" Klaus asks.

"No, I'm scared." I don't mean to say the words aloud but it is too late to take them back. The truth of it rattles me.

"If you weren't a little scared, I would be worried," Klaus says brushing the falling hair from my face.

He drops his head against mine, and I am unable to resist the way his touch heals me and grounds me. Unable to resist that his presence makes me feel safe. I take a deep breath, inhaling the fresh scent of him.

I look him over and see the mark on his skin has grown.

"We have a lot to discuss," I say with a sigh and pull away from him.

As the night bleeds into morning, Klaus spills his father's secrets. There are moments pain flickers across his face as he speaks about his brother. I sit beside him, my legs folded beneath me.

But a question plagues the back of my mind and I can't help but ask. "Were you trying to control me back in Rahkadyr?"

I had hoped he would deny it, say I shut down from fear, but the way he drops his head and runs his hands through his beard says otherwise. *I couldn't move because he didn't want me to.* The thought infuriates me.

"It's complicated," he says.

"You will never do that to me again," my voice trembles with rage. The idea that there was ever a time when my actions were not my own.

He reaches out, touching my leg. I jerk back and I watch the sting of my rejection set on his shoulders. "It doesn't work on you," he says. "Anytime I have done anything like that, the host cannot fight back. Let alone remember."

I grimace. "You realize how awful that sounds right?"

"The first time I used it, I was ten years old. My father was beating me especially hard and all I wanted him to do was stop, and then he just . . . did." His weary eyes tell a story of heartbreak and the helplessness of a child.

I could never imagine a father being so cruel. "I am so sorry," I say.

"The messed up thing is . . . a part of me still loves him. I hate him, but I love him. And Luca," his voice drops. "I tried for years to protect him from our father, half the scars littering my back were meant for him. I can't protect him anymore and it kills me inside." A darkness falls over him and I reach out, wanting to console him. My hand falls on his forearm, the black wispy marks on his skin seem to have darkened since I last saw them.

"Why are you not with him?" I know the question seems harsh, but he can't think I am going to let the King live after all he has done. I would understand his loyalty for his brother and the need to keep him safe.

For a moment, I think he isn't going to answer but when he does my insides twist in a knot. "From the moment I saw you fight for your life in Abahlum, there was no other option for me." The way he says the words makes my ears hot. "I tried to leave you, to stay away. Trust me," he says.

The strong, steadfast, rock of a man crumbles before me. "My life ended right there in those woods, and a new one began."

He turns, his hand settling on my thigh and air gets trapped in my lungs. The faint memory of his lips whispering against mine, makes me want to touch my lips. "I meant what I said, Fraya. I can carry your hate and I can live without your forgiveness, but I can't live without you."

Someone clears their throat and I jump back. Klaus emits a deep groan as my eyes flick up and lock with Arik. The devilish grin on his face makes me want to slap him. Like I have been caught doing something.

"What?" My voice is slightly more irritated than I would like.

"We have a meeting," he says with his eyebrows raised. "But I see you were already otherwise occupied."

I tie my hair up and stand with Klaus following behind me. His body touches mine causing my skin to flush. "I am coming. Have someone release the soldiers."

Arik leaves instantly and I turn to Klaus. "I need you to tell everyone what you told me."

CHAPTER 63

I walk into Sven's tent and a hush falls over the room. Arik goes to say something but I snap my eyes in his direction and he chooses to remain silent. Drawings of the castle have been replaced with the pictures of the valley. I don't see Sven's drawing of Arik, but I know it can't be far.

Klaus fills the group in and I watch him transform into a soldier. There is no emotion behind his words, and he has closed off the man I was speaking with well into the morning.

"Forty thousand men!" Sven exclaims. "We won't even have half that." He aggressively rubs his temple.

"Many of those men have never had dragon's blood, so it will kill them quickly," Klaus counters. "The first line of men will be the greenest recruits, easy to kill. The ones we want to aim for are the second wave." Klaus lays out his father's military strategy and the men listen. Rayne nods his head in agreement, chiming in every little bit. "If we have archers here, here, and here." Klaus points to the map. "We can weaken the second wave."

Klaus occasionally grazes my side or touches my hand. These whispers of touch makes me dizzy.

It won't last. The intrusive thought shakes my core.

"What's wrong?" a deep sultry voice asks.

I look up and all attention is on me. Klaus stares straight through me and I squirm under his gaze. He rubs his thumb between my brows, and for a moment we are not in a room full of people preparing to march to our deaths. We are just simply two people who fell into each other's lives. "Your brows crease and you chew your lips when you are worried, Litchska."

I feel naked under his attention. How can he see me so perfectly? I straighten my shoulders. "I am alright." I place my hands on his forearm, although I can tell he doesn't believe me.

I shake off the overwhelming grip of doom and focus on the task at hand. "If we stop them in the funnel here, they will be easier to pick off."

Rayne nods his head. "What about a fire?"

I smile. "Force them where we want them." I nod my head, our plan slowly coming together.

The clashing of swords and grunting of men has become almost comforting. "You aren't training with us today, Your Highness," Rayne says. No matter how many times I ask him to call me Fraya, he refuses.

"Why?" I ask.

"Because you are with me." I turn around and a shirtless Klaus stands before me. I catch others staring but I can't even be mad because he's built like a god, who could resist.

"My eyes are up here," he jokes.

I blush. "How do you expect me to train with you looking like that?"

"You are going to fight me with your abilities. We know your fire won't burn me and you need to practice using it in a battle setting." He throws me a long stick. "We will start with this as our weapon."

"I don't know if this is a good idea," I say as I watch him circle me like a predator.

"He is right, and if he isn't affected by your powers, he is the only one who can help you with this," Sven says.

"Can you at least put a shirt on?" I groan.

Arik comes up beside me. "Not a chance," he whispers. Sven glares at him as he ducks into the group of fighters. A sheepish grin graces Arik's face.

He spins the stick in his hand, occasionally tapping it on the ground. "I have learned how to keep from burning my clothes," I say as we begin to knock our sticks together.

"Bummer." His grin distracts me as the pole flies into my ribs, and although the leather protects me from the brunt of it, the sting takes my breath away.

I take him in, the hard lines on his stomach, the bulge of his biceps, and the twitch of his muscles as he maneuvers his weapon. "You are staring again, Litchska," he muses.

I dance around him. "I know." I smirk.

Then the assault is on, back and forth we battle, sweat dripping from my hair and down my back. "Use your abilities, Fraya," he demands.

I reach toward puddled water and wrap it around his feet, holding him in place. "Good." He fights against its hold while we battle with the sticks. "Now the fire," he says. Sweat slicks off his shoulders.

I kick up the puddle and land a kick in his side, but he easily catches it and sends me tumbling to the ground. The water melts away and he is on me, arms pinned above my head. "Fight me," he says. "Do you want to die?"

I struggle beneath his weight but he doesn't budge. "You are not even trying," he taunts.

His legs pin me to the earth. "Let me go," I hiss.

"Fight me as if your life depends on it," he growls.

"Klaus," I warn. Panic starts to slide down my spine as I thrash underneath him. I hear people approach but Klaus barks at them to stay back.

Klaus leans forward, hair falling into his face. "Break-" I smash my head into his nose, his hands instantly releasing me, then send water thudding against his body, knocking him back a couple feet.

I pick up my staff, setting it ablaze. Klaus staggers to his feet and wipes the blood dripping from his nose. "It's about time, Litchska."

He kicks up his weapon and advances. I throw a wall of fire up and wait. He parts the blaze with ease and starts his assault. Men gather around us, drawn by the spectacle. They begin to shout and whoop.

My mind clears as we battle, my only thoughts are my next attack. The rhythmic sound of the wood thwacking against each other focuses me. A smile plays across his lips, his tell. He thinks he has me. He brings his weapon up for the killing blow and I smother his head with water.

"Surrender," I yell. The men fall silent, waiting. I hold the water in place waiting for him to buckle. I am so distracted by my victory; I don't notice as his staff slips under my feet sending me flying onto my back. I lay there accepting my defeat, my chest heaving.

Klaus collapses beside me and the group roars around us. "We gave them quite a show," I say between labored breaths. My muscles twitch and jump, exhausted.

The crowd disperses and we're left lying in the mud.

"Klaus?" I turn to him.

"Mmm?" His chest vibrates. I stare into the sky, which is gray from the storm but a rainbow peeks through the clouds. The colors are so bright against the gloomy background, and thunder rolls in the distance as a chill bites into the air.

"Ready for round two?" I ask with a wild grin.

A wicked grin flashes across his lips that sends my stomach swirling. "Always."

CHAPTER 64

After my spar with Kamari, I'm riddled with fresh bruises, nicks, and puncture wounds. The worst part is I have a feeling she was going easy on me. I blot my bleeding eye with a cool rag.

"Why aren't you healing?" Klaus walks up behind me, his face creased with worry.

A cool evening breeze floats through the tent flap. "It will be gone by morning," I remind him.

"Fraya." The tenor of his voice vibrates my insides and when I turn and look into his smoky gray eyes, worry is trapped in them. I don't want him to see my broken mess. I need to be strong for these people, like my mother would have.

Run. My old instincts kick in. I attempt to step around him but with a gentleness he shouldn't possess, his hand wraps around my waist and places me back in front of him.

"Litchska." The word is so soft it is hardly a whisper. It threatens to destroy my perfectly placed walls surrounding my wounded heart. I won't allow it. A war rages inside me and a deep ache settles in my chest. He slides his hands down my arms, opening my palms. It is hard to swallow and when I go to step back, his hands remain locked in mine.

"So many people will die." I drop my gaze to the floor. "There is already too much blood on my hands."

"These people fight beside you because they believe in you," he says.

"They believe in who my mother was." As pitiful as it sounds, it's the truth. "They want my mother, not me."

His finger slides under my chin, lifting my face up to look at him. "Do you know what Litchska means?"

"No." I place my hands against his waist, the solid feel of him beneath my hands clouding my mind.

"It means light in the first language. My mother taught it to me."

"She must have been amazing," I say.

He smiles for just a moment before his face turns down in lament. "She was a lot of things." There is something hidden behind his words but I don't press.

"I have been trapped in darkness for a long time." His hands find their way into my hair and I am so full of him at this moment, I could burst. "You don't realize how amazing you are," he whispers.

"If I wanted to run?" My confession is a silent one but there is no judgment in his gaze. The candle flickers in the corner, causing shadows to dance upon my fabric walls.

"I will take you away right now," he says, his voice unwavering. He grips me tighter and I have no doubt he would whisk me away in a heartbeat. The look on his face tells me he may have already considered it.

"I can't," I say, slightly ashamed that part of me wants to. This was never in my plan. Kill the king and *if* I survived, run. Be free. He stares down at me with a fire that makes the deepest parts of me warm.

"I know." He drops his head to mine.

"Loving me could be the death of you," I whisper.

"So be it," he says. "I would walk through the gates of hell if you asked, Litchska."

My jaw clenches and I find myself leaning into him as his hands grip the back of my hair, pulling my head back firmly but gently. My breathing quickens and the only thing holding me together is his hands. He bites the side of his lip and a rumble comes from his chest.

He leans down, his lips a breath away from mine. I tremble as he pulls my hair farther back, my neck fully exposed. A slight moan escapes my throat and I try to hide my embarrassment.

His eyes darken and he presses my body closer to him.

"Come," he says with a sly grin. "Your friends are expecting us." Then releases his grip on me.

Seventeen thousand men, women, and children share our camp and although we are bursting at the seams, I feel more at home than I have in ages. Laughter floats to the heavens and music fills our souls.

Tonight is our last night before we head off to the valley and although what is before us hangs in the air, tonight is a night to celebrate. Deer, pig, and other wild game roast over open spits.

This is what we are fighting for, I tell myself.

Sigmond offers his hand. "Could you spare an old man a dance?"

"For you? Always." He takes me onto the dance floor, and I notice he looks happier here. His face no longer drawn and his eyes have a new life in them. My hair has grown down my shoulders and I wear a light cotton dress with a tight bodice.

"For an old man, you are light on your feet." I chuckle at the offensive gesture he makes. His eyebrows wiggle at me and I can't help but wonder how he hid in plain sight for decades. He must have been so lonely.

Rayne laughs deeply as he dances with Maxine. Her tiny frame fits perfectly against him. Lucy waves wildly with a large grin revealing one less tooth than before. All of it feels like a dream and I don't ever want to wake up.

Children squeal and run around the camp, their smiles bright and warm.

"Your parents would be proud of you and the woman you are growing into," Sigmond says. He stops and takes my hands. "You're incredibly brave." In the middle of a crowded dance floor, I'm overcome with emotion. His words catch me off guard causing tears to spring forth. I can't let the grief trickle in. If I do, it will become a flood and consume me.

I swallow and bite back tears, taking a moment to gather myself before I respond. "Thank you, Sigmond." His soft eyes smile back at me. "For everything."

"May I cut in?" Sigmond bows and Arik smiles before whisking me away.

I can't help but laugh as he spins me out and pulls me back in, the dramatic gesture so fitting. "Where did you learn to dance like this?"

"My mother. A man who can't dance is dull at a party, she would say." He chuckles and shakes his head.

"You might want to tell Sven that." I point over to the grumpy toad watching the party unfold before him.

A warm smile graces his face and he peeks over at Sven. "You should talk to him." The color drains from his rosy cheeks, his forehead creased in worry. "Tomorrow is not promised, my friend."

I spot Klaus watching me. He leans against a tree, his arms crossed over his chest and his eyes reflecting the moon. His hair falls loose around his shoulders, and although he is on the other side of the field I want to squirm. A warm trickle flows through my body as I remember his hands in my hair and his body pressed against mine.

A delicious smile graces his handsome face. "You have it bad," Arik says.

I scoff. "If that isn't the pot calling the kettle black." He dips me low and I see Klaus tense before Arik pulls me back up. Kamari bursts into a fit of laughter beside a few of Klaus' soldiers, her golden hair glowing in the moonlight.

"Fair," he says. The ground beneath my feet pulses from the music. "Thank you for always seeing me," he says, suddenly serious. Before I can say anything, he spins me out and I land in strong arms.

"If I didn't know any better, I would be jealous," Klaus' deep voice purrs in my ear.

"You don't know any better," I giggle. He spins me in his arms, his thumb grazing my skin. "What are you thinking about?" I ask.

His eyes turns hungry as he glances over my body. "Do you *really* want to know." I bite the inside of my cheek, warmth spreading in the depth of my stomach.

"Yes," I grin and slide my tongue over my lips.

He drops his head into my neck, his teeth nipping at my neck. My skin turns hot and I fall into him. He lifts his head, his breath heavy and his voice husky. "Go enjoy your party before I do something ungentlemanly, Litchska."

I could collapse in his arms right here but he pushes me back toward the party. We dance, eat, and enjoy our freedom.

When my eyes feel heavy, I turn and see Klaus speaking with some of the soldiers he came with. Although he speaks with them, his gaze is on me. I realize he has always watched me. Always close. My cheeks flush as he pats the man on the shoulder and walks toward me.

He looks at me with such intensity. A look that both destroys me and makes me feel whole all in the same breath.

He takes me away from the commotion of the party into the quiet of my tent. "Get some sleep." His thumb brushes against my cheek, so light it sends a shiver down my spine. Such a simple gesture, a featherlight touch sets my soul on fire.

"You don't have to leave," I say. The lantern burns low, just bright enough to see the curve of his smile.

"Are you asking me to stay?" he says.

"I am asking you not to go." I step closer, my chest pressing against his. I let my hand glide over each defined muscle of his stomach until my fingers slip between the open part of his shirt. His skin is warm and ridged from his many scars.

Our breathing turns heavy, and Klaus's touch becomes hesitant and unsure. His eyes plead with me, but I question whether they are begging me to have him stop or imploring me to say yes.

"I am not the good guy, Litchska. I would burn this world to the ground if you asked me to, and wouldn't even think twice about it."

My eyes drop to his lips and run my fingers through his hair. "I don't need you to be the good guy, DG. I just need you."

Before I can take another breath, his lips press against mine. Wrapping my arms around his neck, he takes my face in his hands while kissing down my jaw, causing me to melt. His shirt hits the floor and I relish at the sight of him.

His lips linger on the raised mark that claims me, that demands I be who it wants me to be. A moan escapes my lips and a deep primal growl vibrates his chest. His kisses demand more and his hands explore the curves of my body with hunger. The warmth of his body envelops me and I relish in it. He lifts me easily, my legs wrap around his bare waist as he walks to the bed, his hands pulling at my corset. My dress slides off my body and his hands roam my bare skin.

Everything is on fire as the deepest parts of me tremble at his touch.

He slows and pulls back, searching for any hesitance or regret but he won't find any here. I want this . . . I want him.

My heart threatens to beat out of my chest as I kiss him and I lose myself completely to him.

A perfect, hidden moment that I choose.

CHAPTER 65

A heavy arm drapes across my waist and I wiggle closer into its warmth. Klaus tightens his grip, pulling me closer.

"Your Highness?" a woman's voice says. My eyes flutter open and I see Kamari's long braided hair and relaxed shoulders as she waits for a response.

"Kamari?" I ask sleepily.

"I am sorry to disturb you, Commander Rayne sent me to fetch you," she says.

I feel Klaus' fingers tickle up my spine his teeth nipping at my skin. He has no shame.

"Of course. Tell him I will be right out," I say, gathering the blanket around me.

Arik pops his head into the tent as Kamari is leaving. "What is taking so –" His eyes widen like an owl as he fights conceals a wide grin with pressed lips. *Curse him.*

"We can wait!" he says as he wiggles his brows.

I groan. "Get out!" I say and throw a pillow that smacks the tent with a soft *thump.*

He ducks out, not containing his laughter. A hand grips my hips pulling me back into bed. "I am never going to hear the end of it." I turn toward him, tucking myself under his chin.

"Do you regret it?" I feel his heart rate increase and his thumbs circle my back.

"Which time?" I ask, smiling into his chest.

He pulls back and looks into my eyes. "I'm serious." He runs his fingers through my hair, his eyes soft and vulnerable.

I kiss his scars one by one. "I don't regret any part of you or this." I press my mouth to his smiling lips and a deep growl stirs in his chest making me shiver.

"We have to get to the meeting," I say with a groan, pulling away.

He pulls me close and kisses my forehead, trailing down to the tip of my nose, and finally lands on my lips. His kisses, sweet and soft at first turn demanding and urgent. When he pulls away, both of us are winded. His hand slips beneath the covers and a wicked grin plays across his swollen lips.

He leans over me, his hard body pressed against mine. "We're going to be late."

The camp is loud and full of people busy loading wagons and horses for our departure. Ophius will stay with the women and children until we return. *If we return.* My mind taunts. Loved ones cling to each other, afraid this will be the last time they hold one another. Unwanted tears spring up and I physically shake my body, trying to rid myself of the negative thoughts. We can't go into this already defeated.

Ophius sits across the camp. *"We need to talk, little Alkazah."*

I make my way to him and sit across from the ancient dragon, my legs folded beneath me. *"There are some things you should know before walking into this war."*

"I know about the Eternal killing your sister. I am so sorry." My head drops to my chest and I absently pick my fingers.

"Azius was a strong warrior when the world was new." There is sadness in his memory. *"Even then, humans fought and killed each other for power. When he lost his family, he seeked us out, begging for help. At first, we said no. As it would create unbalance in the world. I tried to soothe his grief but there was a war inside him and he was losing."* The turmoil that rolls off him makes me shudder. *"We were moved by his grief."* The sun peeks through the tree canopy and his scales glisten in response.

"We created a monster." He ruffles his wings, the memory tormenting him. *"When he murdered Azule, Moir was overcome with a ravenous rage. She hated how she now understood the depth of his wrath."*

"He murdered an Ancient, of course she would be furious," I say, defending her.

"Those are human emotions. We should have never gotten involved; it upset the balance," he says angrily. *"She could not bring herself to kill him, for he held the last thing she had of Azule, so she trapped him instead."*

"What are you saying?" I ask.

"This journal holds more than just how to become an Eternal it also reveals how to release the original. The earth groans in anticipation."

"The quakes?"

He nods.

"What happens if he is released?" A deep ache passes between us, the urge to lament until my body is dry of tears is overpowering. This is his pain, his regret.

"The end." For the first time I see real fear on Ophius' face.

CHAPTER 66

Nine thousand able-bodied men and women and seven hundred healers march slowly toward the Valley of Blood and Bone. Centuries ago, this very valley was the heart of the Eternal's ruthless massacre. Just two decades ago, the Dark King overpowered my mother's army, killing thousands. So much blood spilled here . . . and more will run before this is all over.

Twenty thousand men meet us at the outskirts of our destination. The night before, I pace until my soles are sore. Klaus watches me but remains quiet. Our journey was a long one and Onyx flew ahead of us to make sure our path was clear. The few soldiers we did stumble upon were dealt with quickly.

The closer we get, the more my heart trembles in fear. Our army stands on the outskirts of the valley when an ominous calm settles over the all of us. We know what comes next. *I* know what comes next.

"Your Highness," Rayne says as he trots up.

"You really do not need to keep calling me that," I say.

I peek a smile across his bearded face as he shakes his head. Then, he is serious as he kneels to the ground. I step back and realize others are falling to their knees, their heads bowed toward their weapons. Sven, Arik, and Sigmond have all taken a knee.

"We are yours to command, our blades yours to yield." He bows his head.

"I will stay by your side until my dying breath, Your Highness." When he meets my eyes, there is an unwavering commitment behind them.

The crowd ring in unison, "My loyalty and unwavering commitment are yours, until my dying breath."

Pride swells in my heart but close behind is crushing fear. The idea of leading people seems unimaginable to me, but I will not dishonor their commitment. "Thank you." A single tear falls from my eyes as I memorize each person's face.

Just when I think I can't take it anymore, Klaus kneels with his hand over his heart and bows. "Until my dying breath," he says.

I square my shoulders and hold my head up high. Drawing on the power that lives inside me, the leader my mother was, and the warrior my father taught me to be.

My heart hammers in my chest. "I stand beside you today, not as your princess but as your fellow soldier. We fight against a darkness that has plagued our land for too long. We fight not only for ourselves, but our families and those that come after us. I am in awe of your dedication, bravery, and unwavering sacrifice. Tomorrow, I will fight with you, bleed with you, until my dying breath."

Everyone is silent and just when I think my speech was dreadful, a roar erupts from my people. Everyone is on their feet chanting, ready to fight alongside me.

I motion for Sven, Arik, Rayne, and Klaus to follow me to my tent. I look over their faces and swallow my uncertainty, spilling out everything Ophius told me before we left.

"You are telling us . . . not only are we going to war with a crazy man to take back our land, but we are also trying to stop hell from being unleashed?" Sven scratches his beard in frustration. Arik walks over, placing his hand between his shoulder and I can't help but smile at the way Sven relaxes at his touch.

"It is no coincidence that he has been planning for the blood moon. If draining me didn't make him a god, appealing to an Eternal might."

"Why didn't you tell us until now," Arik asks.

"I have no excuses. I just didn't know how to tell you." Shame washes over me.

The color has drained from Klaus' face. I wait for him to chime in but he doesn't.

"We are on your side, Fraya. But we can't help if we don't know the full story." His rebuke is subtle.

"We need to stop him before he gets to the valley," Rayne chimes in, pulling a map out and slapping it on the desk.

We spend the rest of the day and well into the night planning our attack, until there is nothing left to discuss and tomorrow nears.

I lay atop Klaus' chest, my curves wider than his form. His grip tightens around me, while his other hand absently plays with my hair. "I have to tell you something," he says. The beat of his heart quickens and I look up into his tormented face.

"What is it?" I say, lifting my head on my hands. He smiles but it doesn't reach his eyes. Instead, he pulls me forward and kisses my lips. The crickets outside sing a symphony to the stars.

"When I was a boy, my mom used to put me to sleep with the same story. It never changed," he starts. "A man whose heart was so full of pain that it seeped into his skin."

I lift myself, draping the blanket around my body. He looks at the dark swirls on his arms. "Azius watched, unable to stop the massacre of his people. He begged the Ancients for help and when they refused, he wrestled with them until he changed."

I want to stop him. This is not the same story Ophius weaved, but the way he speaks with such conviction screams how haunted he is.

"He was cursed to walk alone for eternity." He sits up now, pulling himself away from me.

"Darkness consumed him and the same darkness overtook my mother." I reach out to touch his arm, but he moves away. "If he is released, what will I become?"

I pull him into my arms and he slides between my legs, wrapping his arms around my waist, his head resting against my stomach. "He won't be released," I tell him as I scratch his scalp and rub the tension from his shoulders.

"I could hurt you," he says into my stomach.

"You won't," I say, but my insides squeeze at the thought.

CHAPTER 67

The sun beats down on the valley as my men move the giant catapults into place. Large boulders rest atop cliffs and a thousand archers ready beside them. The air prickles with anticipation. We are as ready as we can be.

The atmosphere is heavy, as if holding its breath; like the earth is bracing for what is about to be unleashed.

I rub the smooth stone of Astrid's necklace in between my fingers, lost in thought as I let a familiar and deep rage settle in my belly.

Klaus tightening my vest brings me to the present. He readjusts the strap around my thigh, stands, and drops his head to mine. "Don't die," I tell him.

"Rather I than you, my love," he whispers.

The ground thunders, the stomping of thousands of feet beating the earth draws near. Kamari looks at me. "It's time," I say.

She nods. "Consider it done, Your Highness." She bows and takes off down the mountain.

I stop. "What does *Preima Ti'stin* mean?"

His smile is soft. "When we survive this, I will tell you." I squint at him in disbelief but say nothing. Last time we were at the valley we were also fighting for our lives.

He pulls me into him and kisses my forehead and too soon, he releases me. I sit on Onyx, like a spider in her web as she waits for her prey to fall into her deadly trap.

The valley sits behind us, we must keep the army out here. I rub the long solid neck of Onyx. "We can do this," I say mostly to calm myself.

"I am ever impressed by you, little Alkazah." The unexpected gentleness to his words pings my heart. *"Your bravery is to be admired,"* Onyx says.

"I am scared to death," I admit, my voice slightly wavering.

"But you stand firm despite it," Onyx says. *"When life decided to tear you down, you got stronger. Few people can do that."*

I am stunned into silence by his kind words.

Onyx spreads his wings and we lift into the air. My heart pounds as we climb to the sky. The dragon's muscles flexing beneath me. My hair whips around my face as we eye the King's Army.

We cast a shadow across the lush ground. A sea of men stand line after line, their armor glistening in the sunlight. The weight of an entire Kingdom falls on my shoulders. *I have to be strong, cunning, and wise, but most of all ruthless.* I tell myself.

The drums thunder in warning, a chant of arrival. My men stand ready, waiting. *I will not let fear cloud my judgment.* The tension is palpable as the wind ceases.

Bu-bum, bu-bum, bu-bum. We wait.

Bu-bum, bu-bum, bu-bum.

My hand raises to the air, all eyes on me. Waiting.

A deafening cry emerges from the enemy's side. Men charging toward us, their polished blades gleaming in the sun. My men don't move, not an inch.

Onyx dives, his mouth widening and a torrent of flames surge forth. I move the flame, blocking the entrance to the valley and crawling it out toward the approaching men. A wall of fire divides us. My hand remains fixed toward the sky.

Almost.

The eyes of the men are blackened. A few of the enemy's men drop, their mouths and eyes seeping blood. *Klaus was right.*

Their own men jump over the fallen, treading closer. Many run straight into the flames, they never even scream.

Bu-bum, bu-bum, bu-bum.

I drop my arm and a thousand whistles pierce the sky. Cries from injured men fill the grounds. I spot Klaus with the archers, his arrow flying true into the heart of our enemy.

"Again." I push Onyx forth, this time weaving deeper into enemy territory. He unleashes his fiery breath on the next line. It is not an uncontrolled blaze but a deliberate show of our strength. We will not back down.

I do not see the king as we weave through the mass of men. "Coward," I hiss. Arrows fly toward Onyx, but all fall short.

Another surge of men crashes toward the valley and Klaus commands more arrows. The sun disappears as they fill the sky, each one dropping from the sky and hitting their target.

I search for Rayne. The next wave roars to life and a deep war cry bursts forth from him as he and his men charge from the trees. The clash of swords bounces off the mountains. *We can do this.*

Onyx lands on the ground, the earth trembling under his weight. I slide off, my blade stabbing into an attacker's heart and moving on to my next victim. Hate, anger, grief, and frustration awakens something primal in me. My blade slices through the gut of another, his blood splattering across my leathers, its warmth spraying my face. Klaus appears beside me, snarling and ripping through the blood infused enemy.

Rayne slices his way through a group of men, who never stood a chance. His beard drips ruby red, beside him Sven battles. His lanky body a deadly weapon of grace.

"Fraya!" he yells before throwing his blade into the heart of a man behind me.

Our eyes meet and I nod in thanks before trudging farther into the battle.

Blood stains the earth, a heavy reminder of the price of war. I watch as my men fight and die as blood fueled monsters rip them apart. I slam my hand down, letting the fire creep over the earth, scorching everything in its path. One of my men is dragged into the flames by his enemy and I quickly extinguish the heat, his body burned but not dead.

A heavy rock flame is flung into the sky, crashing into the enemy's line. An arrow plunges into my back and I stumble forward from the force. I reach to pull it out, but I can't. Pain slices through me. "I need this out!" I cry in agony. More men pour over the horizon but then I see him, the Dark King, and beside him a gangly looking human.

Luca rides in front of the King, his father, his eyes fixed on the battle ahead.

"Fraya!" Rayne hollers, concern dripping from his lips. I don't have time to register how bad it must look if he is calling me by my name. "This is going to hurt," he says, gripping my shoulder. I throw a wall of flames around us and bite down. Without hesitation, he grips the arrow and with a swift yank, my vision blurs, the pain trying to overtake me. I let out a deep breath and command my body to heal.

"I don't know if I will ever get used to that," he says with a half laugh.

I look back at my friend, his eyes meeting mine with a nod before his axe plummets into a man brave enough to venture through the flames. Another flaming rock flings through the air, smashing a hole through their defenses. My men surge through.

I set my sword ablaze and fight through the crowds, toward the King. The echo of metal clashing together is a distant roar. Our men get pushed back, the valley edges so close.

We can't let them enter the valley.

Kamari fights beside me, her sword an extension of her. Small wisps of hair sling to her sweaty forehead and neck but other than that not a strand is out of place. She bleeds from many wounds but she pushes through, tearing a way for me.

We are soon surrounded; axes and swords swing violently through the air. My flame doesn't stop them, there are too many. I look around but find no one. We are alone.

"You will finish this," she says.

"We will finish this," I remind her. She smiles but it is short lived as she shakes her head and then I watch silver stained red emerge from her belly. She coughs and blood creeps from the side of her mouth.

"No," I whisper.

She drops her sword but clutches a dagger in her hand. I fight to keep our enemy off her. She twists sending the small blade into her attacker's throat before stumbling forward.

Another ball of flame lands beside us clearing the way. I try to drag her but she pushes me off. "Go!" She hollers, pushing me toward the clearing, over the sea of bodies.

"Until we meet again," I say as she falls to her knees. I bite back tears as I run. There are so many men, too many dying. Sven disappears into a hoard of soldiers.

"No!" I cry trying to fight my way to him, but it is useless. He is too far away. The last thing I see is the gleam of his steel before he is overrun. A new anger burns inside me as I watch those I love fight and die around me.

I let out a whistle that breaks through the sound of war. A dark shadow appears, lifting me above the chaos. From up here, the battlefield is a body of corpses. The sun starts to set and a new crimson bleeds through the sky. An eerie silence follows. "We are too late." I swallow the lump in my throat.

"Take me to him," I tell Onyx.

I drop from the sky, the King's eyes meet mine, a vile grin spreads across his face. His scar seems more gangly than normal and he feels more cloaked in darkness. I stand between him and the valley, and I will hold this space until the sun rises or I take my last breath, whichever comes first.

"There you are!" he bellows. "I have to admit, I didn't think you would put up such a fight." He pulls a person beside him. Gripping her hair and shoving her forward, her hands tied in front of her. She winces and he grips her tighter but when she opens her eyes, I know her immediately. The emerald eyes staring back at me are my mother's.

CHAPTER 68

I am in a trance as I look at the woman who stands before me. Her body is thin and frail. Her long gray-streaked hair falls past her shoulders, and her mouth gasps open when she sees me.

The Dark King whispers something in her ear and she jerks away in protest. "It seems like we have a family reunion happening." His laugh makes my stomach turn. I don't see when a large form tumbles into me. All I see are my mother's eyes growing large in warning.

I struggle beneath the man; his fist raining blows at my head. I search for my dagger as he wraps his meaty paws around my throat. In the distance, I hear my mother screaming but her words are drowned out by the pressing forming in my skull. This man is no longer human, the eyes staring back at me are lifeless black voids.

The rocks in the ground bite into my skin as my fingers grip the handle of my blade. It feels like an old friend. I stick it one, two, three times into my attacker's side. Warm liquid pools around me but his fingers remain tight around my neck.

A deep growl comes from close by then the massive man is knocked off me as I gasp for air. Klaus is over me in a second, his hands scouring my body, patting my bloodied clothes.

"It's not mine," I scratch out. My voice is hoarse and my throat burns. Relief floods over him and by the time I am on my feet, my body has healed and my dizziness has faded. Luca stalks forward, his eyes blacker than night.

"Oh no," I gasp. Klaus turns to his brother and I watch so many emotions pass over his face. Anger, remorse, brokenness. He turns toward me, his face drawn in grief. "I have to stop him," he says.

The fighting has spilled into the valley and the earth trembles. Fear grips me deep in my belly. Klaus holds my hand and I nod as the moon slips over the horizon. Everything is washed red as the full moon fills the sky. The blood moon is breathtakingly haunting, like it was plucked from the blood that has been spilled here.

Klaus holds me for a moment and time slows down. A small smile plays on his lips, completely transforming his face. The creases between his brow fade, and the heaviness lifts from his shoulders. His lips meet mine, a too brief moment. It is a beautiful, soul shattering, heartbreaking goodbye.

My lips still tingle as he slashes through men, something animalistic in his movements. The smell of fresh blood coats the air, metallic and hot.

"You ruined him, you know that?" The King hisses. "He was a killing machine, meant to rule by my side before you." My eyes tear away from Klaus.

My attention darts to my mother, who works quietly on the restraints around her wrist. "How does it feel to know you will die today?" I ask.

He bursts into laughter, a deep mocking sound. Sweat pours from my brows and I try not to look at the bloody marks on my mother's wrists as she edges free. Luca and Klaus battle together. Swords clashing and punches thrown.

I feel Ciena before I see her. Her anger and worry all colliding into me like an angry ocean. Wave after wave of panic. "Ciena." I watch as her fury ignites the ground, a blue blaze devouring everything in its path. Soldiers scream before being silenced by the Ancients' anger.

"Move aside," I warn the men who stand before me. I pull the water from the ground and the men stare in disbelief as the ground floods underneath them. I hold the water over their heads. "If you run now, I will spare you," I bite between gritted teeth. Only three heed my warning, but I watch as arrows fly into the backs of those who chose to flee.

I lock eyes with the King, a new urgency pushing me forward. I need to stop this. I meet his blade; the sound is deafening. "I knew you had it in you. You just needed a little . . . encouragement." He pulls his head back from my fiery blade. "That murderous look in your eye is no different than mine."

I swing my blade, tirelessly waiting for any opening. "You will die today for what you have done."

"We will see." He throws me off but I come back quickly. This time, I let my fire drip down onto his hands. He hisses in pain.

A large crash shakes the ground under my feet. I turn to see Ciena diving in. "Capture that dragon!" the King yells through the chaos, greed burning in his eyes. The war rages around us. Onyx drops a man from the sky, his silence sudden. "Ready the spear!" the King roars.

I watch in horror as a large contraption rolls up with an arrow the size of two men locked and ready. I can feel the blood drain from my face as the king relishes in his killing machine. It takes five men to maneuver the weapon around and steady it on the dragons.

"Fire!" he yells.

"Onyx! Ciena!" I yell, my feet flying over the battlefield, but it is too late. Onyx flies in front of his god. The spear lodges into his big heart and his wings falter as he plummets. "No!" Tears sting my eyes as the beautiful dragon tries to lift his head from the ground.

I spot Klaus in the chaos, no longer locked in battle with his brother. Instead, he looks toward his fallen friend. The wave of rage and pain swirling through his features is devastating.

"Keep him from his darkness, little Alkazah." Onyx whispers to my mind as I choke on a sob.

Klaus watches as his dragon, his friend, his connection to his mother passes. I don't know what exchanges between the two but I watch as he dies inside.

Klaus' eyes find me and his pain is quickly replaced by horror as he stumbles toward me. His legs pump faster, "Fraya!" he shouts. Turmoil creeps over his features and I find myself moving toward him, tripping over fallen bodies.

My heart aches for him. He reaches me and in one swoop I am cradled in his arms, my hands around his neck and my face buried in his chest. "I am so–" my words are cut short as the air is knocked from my lungs.

I look between us and the tip of an arrow nicks my skin. The blood in my veins pumps too quickly and my head swims when I spot the arrow protruding out of Klaus' chest. Frantically, I look up but there is no fear as he pushes wild strands of hair from my face.

I glance past him, his father stands like stone with Klaus' bow at his side.

He turned me. He knew the arrow was coming. My stomach rolls.

"No. Not again." *Ophius can heal him*, I tell myself.

"It's going to be okay," I tell him, trying to keep him upright.

"You have never been a good liar," he chokes out.

"Please," I beg. My voice catches as he takes my hands in his. "I need you." I look down at his wrist, wrapped around it is the mermaid glass I gave him when we were last here. *He kept it.*

"You never needed me," he says as my soul shatters. "It's one of the many things I love about you."

His knees buckle and we are crumbling to the ground. When I look around, we are just inside the Valley of Blood and Bone.

Sacrifice and rebirth.

I glance over at Luca, his face red and puffy, his scarred face twisted in agony. His eyes have returned to the color of the ocean.

Sacrifice and rebirth. Dread sweeps over me.

Panic rises in my throat. "You cannot die!" I order him.

"Rather I, than you remember?" He tries to smile but the color has already drained from his face.

"Ciena!" I cry. My heart pounds in my chest making it hard to focus.

"Preima Ti'stin," he says. "It means–" He coughs, blood splattering across his face.

"No." I place my hands against his lips. "After all this is over, remember."

He smiles weakly. "I would do it all again," he chokes. His hands squeeze mine one last time as my soul shatters.

"Ciena!" My insides scream.

With hot tears streaking down my face, I look up to see the King stalking toward me. The roar of the battle that rages around us seems to clear as he passes. "See, Fraya. I always get what I want." He laughs and grazes his blade against my flesh, a tiny line of crimson escaping from within my body. "You are weak, just like your mother." His eyes are soulless, blacker than night as the dragon's blood courses through his body.

I clench my jaw tight and force a small smile. He stops and stares at me. "What do you have to smile about?"

I wipe the tears that fall from my eyes, staining my cheeks. "I told you. You will die today." His face flashes between confusion and fear.

The Queen stands behind the King, her sword level with his neck. She is frighteningly fierce. The King pales then turns to face her. She stares into his dark eyes, neither wavering, her sword like an extension of her arm.

Her voice is menacing as she asks, "Are you scared to die, Zekiah?" *Death has called his name today.* I hear the King swallow and as he starts to speak her blade slices through the air without hesitation. His head falls to the ground, creating a sickening *"thunk"*, then his body quickly follows.

CHAPTER 69

I feel a feather light hand on my shoulder and when I look up, my mother is staring down at me. Her eyes mirror my pain with an understanding that only comes from suffering deep loss.

I will heal him. The thought comes quickly. The raging around us has ceased. News of the Dark King's death passes quickly through the battlefield. Few blood enraged soldiers are quickly slaughtered and then for a brief moment there is a painful silence.

I am part god. The plan begins to knit itself together in my mind. *I can save him.* I don't feel the blade as it slices my palm, my blood pouring down my hand and dripping from my elbow.

Ciena slams into my mind, landing before me with an earth rumbling shake. *"Fraya, don't!"* she orders. I shut her out.

I carefully raise his head. I look down at his chest and realize the cursed mark now covers his whole body. I plead with him to stay as I coax my blood into his mouth. But he doesn't stir.

I look up to see Rayne supporting Sven and for a moment my heart feels less heavy. Ciena's anger pumps through me and only intensifies when she spots his exposed skin. I'm thrown back against the ground, a blade sticking up from the ground knicks my side.

"Do you know what he is, child!" she screeches, the pressure crushing my head.

I get to my feet and stomp toward the old dragon. "I know that he has been here while you have been hiding in your cave!" I hiss.

The ground grumbles, shifting us all around. People try to run from the quake but stumble instead.

"He murdered Azule." The pain that circles through her is thick but I don't care.

"No," I spit. "Your failure killed her." Now the earth is silent, and I rush to Klaus' side while Ciena is left stunned by my hurtful words.

He is gone. I stand, wiping my tear-streaked face. Placing my dagger in its sheath and I straighten my shoulders. *Lock it away, Fraya.* Luca leans over his brother, his hands searching his skin.

"What are you doing? Don't you think you have done enough?" Klaus fought to protect his brother so I will leave him breathing, for now.

"His mark," he says.

An explosion pierces my ears and I watch the ground split in two and the earth peel itself back, revealing its insides.

I try to stay standing but my legs do not win against the great earth. Screaming comes from all around us as men shuffle away from the gaping hole that grows against the ground's surface. Some succeed while others fail, their cries lost to the earth.

Sacrifice and rebirth.

Arik lifts Sven and runs toward the trees but I am stuck here, my feet planted firmly in the ground. Ciena lifts from the ground, scooping my mother up easily. She comes for me but I run from her.

"This is not the time, child!"

"Fraya! No." My mother's shrill cry tears at my heart. She fights against the Ancient, but her cries fall on deaf ears. I see Luca running for his life and when I glance back toward Klaus, horrified to be leaving his body like I left my father's, he is gone.

Everyone I love dies. I never wanted to be a hero. Heroes never get the happy ending, not really.

I stumble, falling into a warm red liquid. So much bloodshed and it stopped nothing.

I rub my hands against my pants as I try to stand. Darkness falls over the sky, and looming over me is a creature unlike anything I have ever seen before, both man and beast.

A gruesome grin curls at the edges of its lips. "Hello."

ACKNOWLEDGEMENTS

Mark of Ancients has taken me two years to complete but if I am honest it has been fifteen plus years in the making. I have started and stopped so many stories over the years. Writing the final page was emotional and surreal, but I did it! I completed my first book, but I could not have done it alone.

First, I want to thank my husband. He would stay up until the early morning while I wrote and bounced ideas off him. He also stopped me from trashing the whole book on more than one occasion. You are my rock and my biggest supporter, I love you tremendously.

To my kiddos, who constantly asked for updates on my book and never once doubted I could do it, even when I doubted myself. Thank you for your understanding while I spent hours hunched over my keyboard. I love you guys.

I also want my wonderful friend Nikki to know that I wouldn't have started this book without her support. She also read the very first rough draft and I know that must have been tough! The hours we spent pouring over our books helped me tremendously.

Thanks to everyone was apart of this process. To my editor and cover artist, this book would not be complete without you.

Lastly, thank you to my readers. Thank you for spending time in the world I created. This labor of love is a dream come true and I am so grateful that I get to share it with you.

Reach out to the Author on all social media platforms.

Tiktok: @kricewrites

Instagram: @kricewrites

Youtube: @kricewrites